# HIVE
# SPECIES INTERVENTION #6609
## Book 4

J.K. Accinni

E. K. Publishing
Lakewood Ranch, Florida

www.SpeciesIntervention.com

This is a work of fiction. Names, characters, places and incidents
either are the product of the author's imagination or are used
fictitiously and any resemblance to actual persons, living or dead,
business establishments, events, or locales is entirely coincidental.

HIVE
SPECIES INTERVENTION #6609
J.K. Accinni

ISBN: 978-0-9899769-4-7

An E. K. Publishing book published in arrangement with the author,
Lakewood Ranch, Florida.
Copyright © J.K. Accinni
All rights reserved.

# Books by J.K. Accinni:

Baby (Species Intervention #6609, Book 1)

Echo (Species Intervention #6609, Book 2)

Armageddon Cometh (Species Intervention #6609, Book 3)

Hive (Species Intervention #6609 Book 4)

Evil Among Us (Species Intervention #6609, Book 5)

The One (Species Intervention #6609, Book 6)

Alien Species Intervention Books 1-3

# Dedication

I would like to dedicate this book to my sweet baby, Echo, who never stood a chance in her short little life. I sadly lost her as I finished this book. She only lived a few days after her first birthday. I wanted to be able to concentrate on just my little one for a while but the congenital illness she was born with stole her from me and my family. I am having a difficult time with our loss and berate myself daily for not having done more to overcome the illness. (Gosh, the tears come even as I write this.)

I want to send a special thanks to Jill DeOpsomer and Amanda Misco for bringing her into my life. Amanda, you and I will always share a special bond over our baby. I know you loved her just as much as I did. Thank you both.

# Chapter 1
# 2057 AD

Abby and Captain Cobby stood shoulder to shoulder at the helm of the luxury yacht as it swayed with the waves, staring down the approach into Tampa Bay. Abby's heart thudded, the timbre of its pace increasing as she scanned the bay, noting the positions of other nearby craft. She knew, sooner or later, another boat would spot the unusual nature of the occupants spread around the deck of the *Lucky Lady*. She hoped to avoid that as long as possible.

"Cob, I'm getting scared. How in the world are we going to pull this off?" She trembled as Cobby gripped her shoulders, turning her to face him. He removed her sunglasses, braving the mesmerizing effects of her shining golden eyes to look deeper into her soul. His deeply tanned, overtly handsome masculinity blended well with all of Abby's golden fragile beauty, the contrast of their ages belying any assumption they might be lovers.

"My dear, you've gotten us this far. You can't fall apart now. Too many rely on you. We have a child and a pregnant woman onboard. They need protection and confidence from you. They can't see you waver. The rest of us know we can depend on you. I might not understand why we must do this, but I have no doubts whatsoever that this is the right thing to do. I know it's our only hope." He pulled her close, his lips brushing the golden hairs at the bridge of her noble forehead. "I'm here for you, we'll get through this. As soon as you give me the word, I'll cross the bay to the industrial docks. The trucks are all in order?"

"Yeah, they're just waiting for us." She removed her sunglasses from Cobby's hands, sliding them back into place as they heard the clatter of water buckets from the deck below.

Leaning out from under their protection from the sun, they observed poor Peter attempting to distribute water to the wildlife.

Sweat dripped copiously down his red face and neck, saturating his once fresh Oxford shirt. His glasses sat askew on his red nose as his body shook from fright, warring with his implant's directions and his own fight or flight response to the threat perceived from the wild beasts.

"He sure looks pathetic. How's he holding up?" Cobby turned to Abby, assessing the strain in her hands as they beat slowly against her thighs. Personally, he thought Peter hovered on the very edge of madness. The fact that his lady love had turned out to be a calculating prostitute attached to a psychotic murderer had already pushed him to the precipice of sanity. And Cobby thought the guy might be strung a bit too tight to begin with. The implant Abby had used to keep him calm and do her bidding might just be enough to push him off the ledge to insanity.

"I'm not really sure about him." Abby's voice faltered. "I need him to hold up. I trust him. If something goes wrong before we get back home, I can rely on him. If I remove the implant now, I know he'll freak. I think Ginger Mae might be the first girl he's ever had sex with. Once we're safe and I remove the implant, he'll still have to deal with her betrayal." Turning to Cobby, she placed a hand on his chest, her face tilted admiringly to the captain. "You're the one I thank God for."

Cobby's large callused hand enveloped her own. "Abby, I—oh, hi." He calmly dropped his hand from Abby's as Jose's head, then his body, appeared on the stairs from the deck below. His thick tawny tail flicked in a sultry fashion as if to deliberately draw attention, apparently indifferent to the sensibilities of those in the salon still reeling from the shock over the big disclosure Abby had made regarding Echo and the changes to their bodies.

"Captain, do you mind? I'd like some privacy please."

Cobby felt the soft pressure of Abby's restraining hand on his arm. Backing up slowly, he returned to the helm, making himself comfortable in the captain's chair. If there was going to be fireworks, he didn't want to be in the line of fire. He enjoyed Jose's company, but was well aware of the sidelong glances he had been sending toward Abby and him since he returned from his trip. Given half a chance, he thought Abby might consider him as a lover, but for now they needed to be fully engaged in their tasks at hand. Another emotionally fragile jilted young man in their entourage could spell catastrophe. He didn't yet know the complete story of Scotty and his traumatized girlfriend, Chloe. Maybe Kane could clue him in. The kids all seemed to be thick as thieves. *Guess that beats their readiness to rip out each other's throats a month ago.*

"Abby, do you mind telling me what the fuck is going on? I think I've been patient enough, and now you've got me scared shitless. And who are those people downstairs? And why is that poor disfigured women with the screaming child with Peter? When did he find time to get a girlfriend?"

Cobby could sense Jose working up to an explosion, but he refused to be drawn in. It was Abby's baby now. He watched as Abby made shushing sounds at Jose, wrapping her arms around him and murmuring in his ear.

"Babe, you have to trust me. There's just no time. I'm doing this because Netty and Echo have asked me too."

"Netty? Who's Netty? Does this involve Echo's mission?"

"Yeah, it does have something to do with his mission. And with saving our lives. We must bring these animals, and the ones from the zoo, to Echo's hive. They claim we'll be safe there. But they insist these animals be saved. You'll meet Netty soon enough."

"What zoo? What zoo are you talking about?"

"There's a large zoo not far from Newark Airport. I have trucks meeting us there. I'll send everyone on to Sussex County, except Scotty and Echo. They need to help me. If you could direct everyone else to the place you met Echo, you can wait for me there."

"But what about all of these animals? How the hell am I going to make them go with me into the woods?" Jose's tone of voice gave away the skepticism he felt toward Abby's plan. "Wait just a gosh darn minute. Are you talking about the Bronx Zoo? Is *that* the zoo?"

"Yes, that's the zoo."

"Are you out of your ever-loving mind? Do you know how many animals are there?"

"Please, Jose. Everything is all set to go. Just take everyone to the Hive," Abby beseeched him, glancing at her watch. "I need you to let everyone know we're headed into the bay and will be docking within an hour. That about right, Cobby?"

"Yes. We need to be ready to roll. The cops will be called as soon as the harbor master is informed by a snoop about our cargo. I think we have a window of about forty five minutes before we get hassled. If the trucks have their doors open and the ramps in place, we can get the cats and bears loaded before trouble starts. The rest should be a cinch."

"*Okay.*" Abby's bright voice suggested the subject was closed. She leaned out over the bridge and hollered down to Peter, waving him to join them. Turning back to Jose, she begged him again, "Can you please just do this for me? We have our whole lives to sort this out. First, we just need to survive." Her voice softened. Wordlessly, Jose turned to the stairs, ignoring Peter as he stepped aside to let him pass.

"Abby, you wanted to see me?"

Cobby eyed the man confronting Abby. His round moon face dripped with sweat. His clothes appeared to have been slept in for the last week, yet Cobby knew Peter to be a fastidious dresser. His eyes stared at Abby, unblinking, his face slack-jawed. Cobby's head snapped back as he got a whiff of the odor rolling off Peter: acrid, sweet, organic and foul. It couldn't all be the result of his exposure to the animals. Was it the smell of fear? He glanced at Abby for her reaction, but she apparently didn't notice. Her hand rested on Peter's arm.

"Are you alright, Peter?"

"*No, Abby, I'm not alright.* My girlfriend is a professional whore. I abetted the murder of a psycho who held a gun on me for two days. I just finished watering some cats that weigh three times what I do, and they know it. A camel spit in my face, then shat on my feet. My boss, who I cared for, just turned out to be some kind of alien freak, and we seem to be running for our lives with a boatful of hungry, dangerous, smelly creatures. And it's hot." He spoke calmly and precisely, his face expressionless, belying the drama of his words.

"You think I'm an alien freak?"

"I don't know what you are." He stared at Abby, his eyes unblinking and unwavering, his face subjugated and beaten. As Abby gently took him into her arms, Cobby watched carefully. He knew a close eye on this character would be a necessity. He appeared ready to go postal and, as captain, he needed to get this vessel to shore. Maybe Abby would let him dump Peter in the rush to load the animals. He planned to vote long and hard on leaving this guy behind.

"Abby, I'm ready to cross the bay. Why don't you take Peter below and make sure everyone is packed up and ready to disembark? Push those monkeys and the birds up on deck."

"Aye, aye, Captain. Come on, Peter, why don't we go down together? I still need your help with Ginger Mae and Daisy."

As she guided Peter back to the stairs, she turned to meet Cobby's steely gaze and his imperceptible nod in Peter's direction. She slipped him a quick thumb's up, then disappeared down the stairs.

# Chapter 2

Scotty sat with Chloe in the once elegant salon of the family yacht, the air conditioning failing to suppress the cacophony of animal odors mixing with the smells of human sweat.

They sat watching Kenya try to convince Kane and Ginger Mae to bolt from the yacht as soon as it hit the dock in Tampa. She paced madly, one hand on her big belly and the other gesticulating wildly as she tried to sell the idea to an indifferent Kane and a numb Ginger Mae, her swollen face and grotesquely stitched lip refusing to allow her a moment's peace.

Chloe sat unmoving and silent, unless Scotty happened to shift his weight. She then clutched at him convulsively, refusing to relinquish her anchor to sanity.

As Kenya continued to rant, she failed to notice Abby and Peter as they descended into the salon from above. Peter selected an upholstered chair nearest the stairs and collapsed like a deflated blow-up doll, smelly and wrinkled with a wicked sunburn. Abby quietly stood behind Kenya as she railed at Kane, reaching hysterical proportions and refusing to concede a losing battle.

Abby's hand suddenly shot out, grabbing Kenya by the arm, swinging her around and slapping her across the face.

"I want you to go sit down and for Pete's sake, shut up. This is not good for the baby."

"How dare you? You're not my mother!" Kenya held her hand up to her reddened cheek as she nonetheless took a seat. "You can bet I'm gonna report you when we get back to town, chicky, you wait and see."

Abby stood in front of Kenya and whipped off her sunglasses, exposing her flashing golden eyes, anger and impatience surging at high tide.

"Don't you get it, young lady? We're not going back to town. How much clearer can I be? You can stay here and die with everyone else or you can come with us and live. Your baby will live. But you must stop. No one wants to hear it. And I don't need any more problems. I have enough to worry about as it is. Got it? Now what will it be?"

Kenya appeared genuinely frightened, but everyone knew Abby meant business. Scotty watched as Kenya scanned the room for support, finding no one to meet her eyes. With a sob, she nodded her head at Abby and leaned back against her seat, finally acquiescing.

"Peter, I need you and Scotty to keep everyone together. *Peter*, are you listening to me?"

Peter sat with his chin on his chest, his eyes shut. They flew open as Abby made her way toward him. "I hear you. Consider it done. Animals first, then we make a dash for the limos."

"Yes, okay. Scotty, you two good?"

"Yeah, Sis, we're okay. We'll be ready."

"Good boy. Be prepared to make a wild dash. Just make sure all the animals make it off the boat first." She turned back to Kenya and leaned down to gently brush her wild tresses back from her face. "It'll be okay, hon, this is the worst part. Once we head for the airport we're gold." Glancing at Jose who stood with the monkeys in the galley, she gave a brave smile. "I'll be up top if you need me."

Scotty watched his sister mount the stairs and disappear. He could feel the boat pick up speed. It wouldn't be long before they had to run for it. He wanted to make an effort to stay out of the way of the tigers. He didn't want any repeat of the previous confrontation with Caesar.

"Hey, Scotty." Kane rose to squat in front of Scotty and Chloe. "You ready for this?"

"Yeah, just do what you can for Kenya. I'll take Chloe. Jose and Peter will handle Ginger Mae and Daisy."

Scotty felt a tug on his shirt from under the sofa. He glanced down to see the posse creep out from underneath, urged on by Echo, her long, slender leather-like fingers patting Mimi as she happily joined the rest of the dogs, which sat like sentinels clustered around

Echo, Barney at the helm. An aura assailed Scotty, spastic with agitation.

"It is time, Brother Scotty. I will stay with My Barney."

"No, Echo, I think you need to let me carry you. I can't run the risk that you'll get knocked around if you're underfoot or with Barney."

"No, Brother, I need to be with My Barney no matter what. I need."

"*You need*? Don't be silly, Echo." Scotty reached down to lift the furry creature to his lap. Chloe reached over to softly stroke her head. "You need to stick close to me, girl, Abby might need us."

"No, no, no. I cannot. I must be with My Barney." Echo wiggled out of Scotty's grasp, then slid down his lap to quickly wobble over to Barney. The two stood cuddled up to one another, and Scotty cocked his eyebrow at Echo.

"Something you want to tell me, Echo?"

"No, my Brother. I should not bother you. We will stick close, do not worry."

Dismissing Echo's odd behavior, Scotty readied himself for the next leg of their escape.

The *Lucky Lady* picked up speed as she made her way across the sun-glared water of Tampa Bay, throwing out huge waves of wake from both sides of the craft. Captain Cobby's eyes searched for the buoys marked on his map which would steer him into the private dock of a long abandoned industrial park where an old buddy from his young yacht jock days worked as a security guard. A green flag would mark the dock slated for their use. He should be able to spot Abby's caravan of trucks, lined up and ready to accept their unusual cargo.

"Hey, Dad, I see we're almost there. I'm going down to put the gangplank in place. Scotty will pass it out to me after we dock. I'm not looking forward to this part. I keep waiting for one of the cats to jump one of us." Kane nervously paced around his father.

"Don't worry, Kane, as long as we stay calm we'll be safe. I believe in Abby and this is our only chance to save ourselves. I'm not going to blow this chance for you, Son." Cobby wrapped his arms around his handsome boy, grateful for the intimate moment. With a swat on the butt, he sent Kane down to the deck to get in position.

They were a few minutes from docking, Cobby having spotted the green flag. He could see the trucks lined up on the other side of a chain-link fence about two hundred feet from the dock. *Damn*—he had counted on them parking closer. The idea of crossing two hundred feet of wide-open space with a bunch of apex predators in unfamiliar territory made his stomach churn. Steadying his hand on the wheel, he throttled back to ease the big boat slowly into the dock with a soft grumble from the twin diesel engines. Kane dropped down to the dock to secure the ropes, tying them tautly.

From below, Scotty appeared, shoving the heavy gangplank out for Kane to position for the animals.

Cobby could hear the restlessness in his four-legged charges as they became aware of the docking and reacted to instructions from their implants.

"Yo . . . you there. I'm looking for Abby. Oh boy, here we go again." One of the truckers approached at the same time that the bears decided they would be the first to depart. Six hundred pounds of muscular fur and clacking claws would make anyone shit their pants when they were close enough to feel the hot breath of a chuffing ursine on their colorless lips. Rooted to the spot, the trucker let the bear pass before he hightailed it back to the safety of his truck. The truckers knew what to do. Sit tight, say nothing, do nothing. Abby would tell them when to close the backs of the trucks. They knew the drill. Then they would follow the limos to the airport, about a twenty-minute ride in normal traffic.

Cobby wiped his sweaty brow with a well-used rag, observing his wilted and odorous human passengers huddled on the starboard side of the boat, dogs and luggage milling at their reluctant feet, the relentless heat adding to their discomfort. Christ, it sure was hotter than a naked babe on the back of a motorcycle.

Cobby stood up, waving to the small crowd down on the deck below.

"Kane, check the boat, top to bottom. Make sure all the animals are off. Where are Abby and Scotty?"

"They're bringing up the turtles."

Cobby watched as Abby emerged with her brother, a huge tortoise held between them.

"We've got it, Cobby. Two more to go." Abby tilted her chin in his direction. "You might as well abandon ship. Go with Jose and the rest to the limos. Get the women settled. Peter and the boys will help me with the other turtles. Meet you at the limo."

One look at Peter and Cobby could understand why Abby wanted him with her. He stood uselessly apart from the knot of women, a walking zombie. Maybe he would respond more effectively if he hadn't been forced to help Ginger Mae and little Daisy. Sliding off the captain's chair, he shut down the engines, slapped his hand on his chair and said a final goodbye to the beautiful craft he had piloted for over ten years. She didn't deserve the piles of animal crap and pools of urine left to decorate her proud decks, but they planned to leave her at the dock to whatever her fate may be, knowing she may have helped save their lives.

Quickly descending the stairs to the deck, he swept Chloe and Teddy, Ginger Mae, Daisy, Kenya, and Echo and her dog pack down the gangplank to the waiting limos with most of the luggage. So far, the animals and people had found the dash to the chain-link fence uneventful. Casting his gaze around, Cobby glimpsed Scotty and Kane delivering the last tortoise to a truck.

"Okay, Dad. That's it. Let's get out of here." Kane ran past his father, slapping him on the back as he slipped into one of the limos with Kenya, Scotty, Chloe, and Echo and the dogs. The other limo would carry the rest of them. Not a happy bunch. Cobby shrugged, feeling the weight of responsibility as the oldest of the group, stretching his strong arms as he made his way out of the hot sun into the air-conditioned limo.

Abby ran to catch up as the trucks revved their motors and eased the convoy away from the last forlorn glimpse of Tampa Bay that any of them would ever see.

*

Abby sat between Jose and Captain Cobby, her hand resting on Jose's lean leg. Occasionally her hand would spasm, her exhaustion and adrenaline warring with themselves to control her body, the implant placed by Netty guiding her mind. She tried to relax her body as her curiosity focused on the mystery that was Netty. She felt a clean uncomplicated honesty emanate from the regal woman. An overwhelming sense of gentle confidence which contrasted with the strangeness and urgency of the tasks she had entrusted Abby with. Everything was such an enigma. But Abby knew one thing for sure. One frightening, cataclysmic, irrefutable fact: hundreds of millions now lived their last days, and she fully intended to survive. If she could save a few others in the process—great.

She actually understood that humans as a species didn't deserve this planet, but her heart bled with the thought of the uncorrupted babies and children who would perish. Tears escaped from under her sunglasses as she thought of the creatures that really deserved to live; the exquisite and the mighty, the docile and the fierce. All part of God's garden, all tragic victims. Abby hadn't been raised as a particularly pious devotee of religion, but she, along with most, believed in God. But where were the answers to God's eternal indifference to the pain and brutality inflicted by Homo sapiens on all life since the dawn of early man? Where were *those* answers? Abby's fist contracted painfully on Jose's leg. He glanced at her with a raised eyebrow.

"Babe, you good?"

She picked up his hand, raising it to her lips to reassure him. "I'm fine, just nerves. Maybe we should call Mama Diaz and give her an ETA? Jose, I don't know what you've told her, but could you ask her to pack all the tools we left at the house? And make sure they're ready to move everything to the woods. I'll have extra hands to move the heavy boxes when we get there. I'm going to ask some of the truckers from the second caravan if they want to join us. That's why we tried to hire nonviolent drivers with no family connections. I want them to be able to make a fast decision. And it's why I asked them to bring their pets with them. I thought it would help. I would never get over leaving Barney and the gang behind if the situation were reversed. It should be a big help."

"Oh, yeah, that's a big help." Peter's bitterness intruded from across the seat. As Abby opened her mouth to respond, she thought better of it. Sighing audibly, she closed her mouth, determined to say no more.

The caravan entered the approach to the commercial cargo ramp for air freight. This next phase would include Echo. One by one the vehicles and trucks passed through the gigantic metal security device which read the presence of all explosive and metal objects. Their progress continued as slowly as a snail on vacation, Abby's impatience ready to ignite.

Finally most of the trucks made it through, pulling up to join the limos on the tarmac. *Now, here comes the dicey part.* Abby climbed out of the limo quickly, pulling open the door to the other car.

"Come on guys, hurry, hurry . . . Find a seat onboard. Sorry, but you have to cram in there. It's going to be a little cramped. It's not a luxury airliner, but it'll get us where we need to go. The important thing is the animals." Abby looked over her shoulder as the inspectors approached, looking for her permits.

"Echo, come on girl, you're on!" Echo scrambled out of the limo, Barney sticking to her like glue.

"Scotty, take Barney with the rest of the dogs. Get them secured on the transport."

A violently fluctuating aura assailed her mind, forcing her hand to her head in shock. The whispers screamed. "*No,* Sister. Barney *must* stay with me. I need."

"Okay, okay, whatever. Bring Barney if you must." Turning to Barney, Abby gave a quizzical look at his loyal mug, eyes bright, shining with love and unquestionable trust. Her heart melted at the thought that someone had once thrown this joyful personality away as a pup like a piece of disposable garbage. Shaking her head, she realized what an arbitrary lady Fate could be. Look at Barney's life now: loved so well, and loved far, far beyond anyone's wildest dream by the most enigmatic creature on the planet, part of his adoring family. Abby knelt down to place a kiss on Barney's tender muzzle, happy to have him remind her of the smallest of the fragile lives that would be saved by her efforts.

The airport officials approached. Abby turned to Scotty, whispering directions under cover of the airport noises. Pointing out their transport, she directed him, "Get the trucks to start unloading. I won't be long." Turning to the airport officials, she nudged Echo forward. "Gentleman, I believe you are looking for me."

"If you are in charge of the contents of this transport, miss, may I have your permits please?"

Echo stood with her arm wrapped around Barney's neck as her antlers split, releasing just the correct amount of implant creatures, which flew to the ears of the officials who could destroy all hope of leaving the airport with her precious charges. Naturally, Abby had been unable to obtain all the complex permits and vaccination records needed to transport wildlife of this kind. CITES, the Convention on International Trade in Endangered Species of Wild Fauna and Flora, required reams of paperwork and certifications to protect the transportation of wildlife. Abby was shooting from the hip here. Echo's facilitation made everything so much easier.

The implants did their work as Abby waited for the signs that the inspectors were under control. Shaking their heads and pulling on their ears then grinning like simpletons, they assured her she could proceed safely.

"I want you both to return to your desks. Everything is in order here, correct?"

"Yes, ma'am. You have a nice flight now. Nice doggies you have there." With a quick pat on Echo's head, they turned smartly on their heels and walked away. One down, just the pilots to go. Cobby should be briefing them at the moment. She hoped to avoid grief from them regarding the lack of proper cages for the animals. She had selected Pet Air because the cargo bay came equipped with built-in cages that would help secure most of the smaller animals and some of the cats. The rest would be forced to settle down on the moving blankets and make their own nests. Turning, she heard Cobby shout her name and saw him running toward her.

"You were right, I need Echo to handle the pilots. The loading is going smoothly, just very slowly. I'm going to take Echo with me, okay?"

"Yeah, take Barney with you too, please, Cobby. Don't let Echo implant them unless you're forced. And keep Echo hidden until you need her. I'll join you as soon as I can."

Cobby ruffled her long golden hair. "You holding up, kiddo?" His smile reflected nothing but worry and admiration for her.

She smiled back, her lips threatening to collapse on her. *Suck it up girl*, she thought. *This is not the time to cry in Cobby's arms.*

"I'm fine, Cob. I'll see you later." She watched as Cobby marshaled the furry pair off to the animal transport for a sit-down with the pilots. Looking over the receding shoulder of Captain Cobby, she noticed another transport pulling in toward their parking area. It featured the insignia of the British Royal Air Force on the side of the transport. *Why the heck is the Royal Air Force here?* Mentally slapping herself across the face, she pulled her mind back to what she needed to focus on.

Fifteen minutes later, as Abby watched her animals offload from the trucks and settle into the belly of their transport with much complaining and shuffling of space mates, she found her ears assailed with the strange sounds of trumpeting and rumbles which gripped her deep into the very marrow of her bones. Following the frantic sounds, she found herself led to the very transport that had caught her eye a few minutes ago.

The belly of the transport lay open with milling activity focused on some black men dressed in blue-green coats signifying some kind of uniform. Creeping closer, she noticed agitation and helpless sorrow permeated their demeanors. The trumpets sounded more frantic the closer she got. As her presence alerted the attention of the men, she nodded politely, getting a nod from one of the taller men, his world-weary chocolate eyes dripping with disconsolate acceptance.

"Jambo, miss." Abby nodded respectfully, understanding a friendly greeting if not the Swahili language. Peering into the belly of the transport, she got the surprise of her life. In the rear of the plane stood an unhappy group of elephants. Yes, elephants, practically extinct after the horrendous slaughter of the 2015–2019 ivory wars and the subsequent decision to slaughter the largest and wisest for meat to feed the refugees in Sudan, Uganda, Libya and South Africa.

Abby noticed grave differences in the elephants. The largest and oldest, almost elderly; two smaller juveniles; one adult tusker and three tiny babies, one of which lay prostrate on the floor of the plane, a few feet from the men, who she now realized must be their keepers. The tiny baby looked to be only a few weeks old with the tip of its delicate tiny trunk missing. It appeared to have been bitten off and now lay lifeless, swollen and infected. The poor thing's breathing sounded labored, obviously on the doorstep of death.

"Oh no, the poor thing." Tears trickled unnoticed from under her shades. *Who are these people?* She addressed the tall man who appeared to be in charge. "Hello, I'm Abby Preston."

The man gave a quick bow. "I'm Johno. It is my pleasure to meet you, Miss Abby." His grin reached from ear to ear, but his heart clearly neglected to join in.

"Where did you come from? And what's wrong with the little one?"

"She has pneumonia. She is dying." He hung his head. "There is little we can do now."

"What in the world are you doing here, in Tampa?"

"We are from Nairobi, Africa. The radical Islamic leaders ordered all non-native landowners to turn over their land to the government. They were given forty eight hours to vacate the country. We could not leave these precious few elephants behind. They would have been eaten, just like this poor little one's mother. The babe was found stuck in a shallow well. She must have run in her panic after her mother was slain and fallen in. We were notified by a kind Masai. Her trunk was savaged, probably by a hyena. It is common. We set down here from the Miami airport because if she dies, the others will be upset and they need calmness. It is not a good time to be in an airplane for them."

"I don't understand why you have them, elephants are almost extinct. It's against the law to bring an elephant out of Africa."

"Yes, Miss Abby. I work for the Elizabeth Siggins Wildlife Foundation. I have worked for them for over forty years. Ms. Elizabeth's husband started the Kenya Wildlife Protection Corp. so many years ago. Ms. Elizabeth was a very famous woman, loved by many all over the world for her spirit and dedication. She created miracles for her beloved elephants. When the government threatened the land that belonged to the foundation, the family enlisted the help of Her Majesty's Royal Air Force to secrete the elephants away to safety in the United States. They have always been important supporters of Ms. Elizabeth's efforts. Everything happened so quickly. Unfortunately, we were only able to save these few before the soldiers came. We were lucky to get away. Many more were left behind." Johno's voice broke and he raked his arm across his eyes, wiping away his tears. "My babies . . . so much trauma and terror in their short lives." He broke down, sobbing uncontrollably. "We could not save them all. I am sorry, I cannot speak further. Please excuse me." He turned back to the pitiful creature sprawled on the floor surrounded by the other keepers, tears in the eyes of the anguished men.

Abby slowly approached the circle of men. She reached out to rest her hand on Johno's shoulder. "Johno, I can help you. I can help the baby."

Johno's head snapped back to her with uncontrolled hope. "You can help our baby, Miss Abby? Please, please. How can you help? Do you have a miracle medicine?"

"No, Johno, I have something better. Please, stand back." She moved Johno to the side, waving away the attentions of the other keepers. Johno's face fell as he realized she would not be forthcoming with medicine.

Seemingly from out of thin air, Abby's tail flexed and snapped high into the air, extruding its healing membrane, sending pressure felt by all and the accompanying odor of sulfur. The keepers didn't understand the significance of her tail or where the path of pressure emanated from, and reacted by throwing themselves flat on the ground, screaming.

As the excited screams slowed to frightened mutters, the men finally absorbed the complete quiet settling around their shoulders, no more sound coming from the belly of the transport, the elephants' silence ominous. Then a squeak. And a squeal, coming from none other than the dying baby, who struggled to stand under her own power as a cacophony of excited trumpets emanated from the back of the transport, happy elephants eager to caress the newly healthy baby.

The keepers rose slowly, frightened and unbelieving, their hands making the sign of the cross. Abby watched Johno, his face impassive and calm, a cypher. He turned to her, holding out his hand. "Miss Abby, the Lord has sent you to us."

Abby stepped up to grasp his hand in hers. "Where are you traveling with these elephants, my friend?"

"We have been offered sanctuary in the most wondrous place. It is called the Bronx Zoo."

Abby smiled wide. "Yes, I have heard of it. I think we will meet again, my friend. I'm going in that direction myself. Will you be leaving soon?"

"Yes, miss, we will leave as soon as possible." Johno's eyes searched hers, his voice giving out and reverence overwhelming his impassive nature.

As Abby turned to take her leave she glanced back. "You may want to have a look at the big elderly girl in there. She is one happy ele." With a nod, she returned to her own transport.

*

Johno stood rooted to the spot. He thought he had seen everything in his sixty two years. He had never considered himself a superstitious man as so many Africans were wont to be. He prided himself as one of the lucky few with parents who were able to afford a uniform that enabled him to attend school as a youngster. Fate stepped into his young life when he met the first extraordinary woman of his life, Ms. Elizabeth Siggins. She had recognized his deep capacity to love her little orphan charges as the adults fell under the onslaught of ivory poachers, poison arrows, droughts, angry cattle herders and the fences which had appeared across their traditional migratory routes, displacing them. No one could have foreseen the political shift in Kenya from staunch ally of the United States to the radical Islamic stronghold which had turned to the wildlife to feed the hordes of refugees they displaced in other African countries, causing chaos and turmoil to all English landowners, instituting a land grab, evicting them from their land and confiscating all their personal property, including their creatures.

For rescue centers, rehabilitation stations and wildlife biologists with decades-old study groups, the outcome was catastrophic as they struggled to fight the confiscation of their creatures for the slaughterhouses. Many noble men and women lost their lives to the merciless onslaught, refusing to desert the creatures they had long loved. Those that stayed behind with Johno to salvage what they could had heard rumors of the tragedy at The Dian Fossey Research Center at Karisoke in neighboring Rwanda. A habituated family of thirty gorillas had disappeared with no trace, thought to have been vanquished by poachers who had probably slaughtered them for bush meat.

Six months later, the staunchly loyal personnel had been murdered as they tried desperately to protect the remaining families of the fragile yet magnificent mountain gorillas who remained in their charge. The reports of copious quantities of blood and stiffening gorilla carcasses displayed high on the back of triumphant Islamic trucks quickly reached the ears of all in the conservation community in Nairobi. Heavy hearts at the Siggins Wildlife Foundation quickly formulated plans to evacuate.

Johno and the other keepers escaped with a very small amount of elephants, two young rhinos, and a pair of kudu through the efforts of the Royal Air Force and the daughters of the long-deceased Ms. Elizabeth. Johno's heart bled at the thought of how his benefactress gratefully resided in heaven with her beloved husband. He knew they were surrounded by all the baby eles who had never recovered from the trauma and shock of their brief introduction to this brutal world. He glanced to the heavens to thank the Lord she did not have to know of this bitter catastrophe.

Johno's thoughts returned to Miss Abby's parting remark about his elderly elephant. She had no way of knowing how he had insisted this special wise creature accompany them to salvation in the United States. He just could not have lived if he'd been forced to leave Tobi behind. She remained one of the pride and joys of the Wildlife Foundation, a success story beyond their wildest dreams, and a personal favorite of Ms. Elizabeth and Johno. A wild elephant who had never forgotten her love of her keepers, and had returned endlessly to check on new babies and preen as the keepers lavished adoration and affection on her.

Poor tiny Tobi had been found near death's doorstep in September of 2002 near a waterhole in the Imenti Forest in Meru. Her mother was thought to have been a victim of poaching, their small herd having been cut off from their traditional migration route to the Mount Kenya forests by the fencing that followed the expansion of human settlements.

They had estimated Tobi's age to be only days old. The only measure that had kept the poor newborn alive was the discovery by Ms. Elizabeth that when a newborn did not have the opportunity to draw on its mother's first milk, they missed out on the critical colostrum needed to trigger the infant's natural immune system. When a colostrum-deficient infant was discovered, they had to ascertain whether severe enteritis was present, producing bleeding from the rectum and the onslaught of deadly pneumonia. Ms.

Elizabeth had discovered that a transfusion of blood extracted from another newborn could be distilled to plasma and injected through a vein in the ear of the stricken orphan, saving its life. Such had been the case with Tobi. After the successful transfusion, they had given her hope for a new chance at life. In the Meru dialect, Tobi means life.

Johno's decision to bring her in from her life in the wild had given her hope again. She would now escape the ruthless slaughterhouses along with the three young orphans; the two four-year-old juveniles; the young bull, Medoc; and their two young rhino, the youngest completely blind.

Johno heard a trumpet from inside the plane. A trumpet of glee and happiness—but loud, very loud. The big ones must be overjoyed about the recovery of the little nameless one. Hefting himself up onto the cargo deck of the transport he could not believe his eyes. Tobi looked ten years younger. The nasty rip in her right ear was gone, the long gnarly scar near the tip of her delicate trunk, nonexistent. She shifted happily from side to side, lifting her feet as if her swollen arthritic joints no longer pained her. The bull and two juveniles excitedly ran their trunks all over her legs.

*My Lord*, thought Johno, stunned to the core. *I think I have just met the second most important person in my life.*

# Chapter 3

Abby ran from truck to truck ensuring all were empty. To her consternation, she inadvertently attracted the attentions of one of the truckers.

"Come on, babe, slow down. I just want to say a proper how do."

Abby ignored him and continued to check the trucks. She wanted to shove off and get the transport in the air. In the back of her mind she began to worry about the manpower it might take to properly care for all the animals she planned to save. She wanted to ask members of the Bronx Zoo trucking convoy to voluntarily join them, yet she couldn't be certain that would give her enough manpower.

"Babe, come on. I just want a little time to chat ya up seeins I might be back in these parts again, ya never know. Sure would be nice and neighborly if ya let me look ya up." The unfortunate lothario was none other than the skinny, weasel-faced, cigarette-smoking trucker who had pissed his pants back at the Big Cat Sanctuary when he had unexpectedly confronted a bear and a lion as they calmly padded to his truck. It seemed he had finally recovered his dignity and located his missing balls. She stopped in her tracks to face him.

"Look, *babe*. I don't have time for this. I appreciate the job you did for me, but it's time to move on now." *Or is it?* Abby's head shot straight up with an idea. Turning to the shit-kicker, she plastered on her best smile.

"Whoa—Dezi likes." His face lit up like a kitten that had just discovered the keys to a sardine truck.

"Dezi. May I call you Dez?" Abby flinched to herself at the sound of her cheesy come-on, even though Dezi's had been far worse.

"Babe, you can call me anything you want as long as you call me." He snickered and preened, tugging semi-discreetly at his crotch, the area experiencing an unmistakable swelling. Rolling her eyes, she sensed that the pathetic guy spouted his annoying repartee to make up for his unfortunate mug and unimposing stature, yet she also sensed something broken and hurt in this impudent guy. Freezing the smile on her face, she tried again.

"Dez, if you're available, I would like you to accompany us to Newark to help with the offload of the animals. I'll pay you well. The job will take about twelve hours, including flying time. I need additional help at a zoo and could really use you. I'll fly you back to Tampa first class and cover the cost of leaving your truck here." She bit the bullet and placed her hand seductively on his arm. He jumped a foot in the air with surprise at the unexpected touch.

"I'd be doin' you a solid?" He looked as anxious as a puppy trying hard to hold its urine.

"Yeah, Dez. You'd be doing me a solid."

"So you and me might find some time in the future to do the dirty?"

Abby recoiled. "For Pete's sake, Dez, let's take things a bit slower. We'll talk about that when the job's done. Do we have a deal?"

Dezi narrowed his eyes suspiciously. Abby identified his transparent emotions as they flickered across his homely face, clearly wondering how far he could go with her, hoping she wasn't putting him on. He broke out in a smile.

"Yeah, babe, let's go for it." He held out his hand for a shake. Abby clasped his hand only to be pulled off balance toward him and rewarded with a sloppy attempt at a kiss.

"Damn, Dez, I said, slow. S-l-o-w. Got it?" His shit-eating grin made her wonder about the wisdom of her offer.

"Yeah, babe, I got it." He pursed his lips and made kissing sounds.

*Oh, please deliver me*, she thought. "Why don't you head to the transport after you park your truck someplace safe? Introduce yourself around and find a seat like a good boy, okay?"

"Okay. See you later, babe." He turned toward his truck with a slap and a caress on his own butt, turning once to wink before disappearing from sight.

*Puke.* Abby shook her head, her long golden hair swaying as she wondered how in the world she would explain this to Jose.

Coming upon the last truck, she recognized the driver. "Hello, Mr. Calloway. You must be in a hurry to get on with your next gig."

Clyde straightened up respectfully from his lounging position alongside his truck, his portly belly still hanging well below his belt. "Miss Preston, happy to see you. This sure has been a first for me and my rig. You have a mighty magic touch with the beasts." His clear hazel eyes bore into hers. Abby recognized a man not easily fooled but practical enough not to ask questions. "I'm in no hurry. I'm not running to the next job. My wife and the grandkids are in Tampa for a couple of weeks. I'm going to join them, kick back a beer and let the kids have their way with me." Clyde's lined but still relatively attractive face shined with pure bliss. And of course, that gave Abby an idea.

"Mr. Calloway—"

"Call me Clyde."

"Clyde. And I'm Abby. As I was saying, would you be interested in lending me a hand for another twelve hours? It means going to Newark with us on the transport and help with the logistics of another load of animals at a local zoo. The pay is rich."

"How rich?"

"Rich enough to make it impossible to turn me down."

"Well, now you're talkin'. But just twelve hours. I need to get back to my grandkids."

"No problem, Clyde. Why don't you pull your truck over there and find a seat on the transport? If you could sit with Dezi and keep an eye on him, I would be most grateful."

"Dezi?" His eyebrow rose.

Abby laughed knowingly. "Yeah, I know. But the guy's harmless, he just needs a firm hand."

She waved as Clyde nodded and climbed into his truck with a smile. "Twelve hours, not one minute more."

*

Jose eyed the passenger seats on the transport. The door separating them from the cargo hold didn't appear strong enough to resist the efforts of Barney, let alone the Bengal tiger Scotty and Echo called Caesar. Abby may have them under control with Echo's implants but she was a novice at this. *Christ, anything can go wrong.* He thumped down in a seat near the middle, wondering when Abby would join them. His list of questions now reached from Tampa back to Sarasota. He steamed quietly as he caught a glimpse of Captain Cobby picking a seat near Kane.

Sizing up the transport, he wondered how much this jaunt would cost, not that money was an issue. The cabin appeared capable of holding them all. The seats sported an undistinguished brown vinyl, hard but serviceable. The backs of the seats were designed to allow a line of sight around the whole cabin. *All the better to spot the carnivore planning to eat you.*

Jose heard the cabin door bang. Turning around, he spotted a ferret-faced skinny dude coming down the aisle, followed by a big man with an enormous beer belly dragging him down.

"Hey, call me Dez. This here is Clyde." Dez gave a two-finger salute from his brow and kept moving, nodding and saying hello.

Clyde stopped at Jose's seat, extending his hand. "Nice to meet you. And you are?"

"Jose. Nice to meet you, Clyde."

"Oh, you must be Miss Preston's brother. You look so much alike." Jose flushed.

"No, her brother's further up. I'm her boyfriend."

Now Clyde flushed. "Sorry. It must be the shades." Nodding amiably, Clyde moved on to introduce himself to the others. Jose overheard him explain to Captain Cobby that they had joined the expedition as extra hands to help wrangle animals at a zoo. *For heaven's sakes, is she still going through with this?*

Jose sat back in his seat and glanced out the window. From out of nowhere, two sets of tiny wizened hands shot out to grab Jose's pants, hauling themselves up to make themselves comfortable on the seat next to him. Two white-faced monkeys had somehow slipped through the door and managed to locate Jose where they decided to seek refuge. Wouldn't he love to watch Senior Brooks' face if he could see this? Yeah, he would watch him in Hell where he belonged. Thanks to Echo, he'd been dispatched by the mysterious creatures that resided in her antlers, melting him down to less than the crud on the bottom of Jose's shoes.

He absently stroked the monkeys that had once played a short, happy act in his childhood. Taking stock, Jose realized his shock over the discovery of who had murdered his parents and the unveiling of Chloe as his kidnapped sister, was finally starting to dissipate. *But where's all this anger coming from?* He realized he sounded like a petulant angry child. Jealousy? *Boy, no wonder Abby's distancing herself from me.* Her plate runneth over and his anger, while understandable, was of no help to her. He made a note to himself not to overreact to anything while he was still digesting the brutal events and discoveries at Chloe's—no, not Chloe's—the despicable slime ball, Omar Nasir's, mansion. Chloe had *never* been his daughter.

Making an effort, Jose turned to the elderly monkeys to find solace in their warmth and the distant memories of the joy he had shared with them so long ago in Costa Rica.

# Chapter 4

Abby entered the cabin of the transport, gently closing the flimsy door after peering in at the wildlife who all sat quietly impassive as if waiting for a streetcar. All heads turned toward her as she entered the passenger compartment.

"Okay everyone, buckle up. The pilots want to take off." Seeing Jose occupied by his rescued primates, she slipped into the seat behind him, buckling up and sliding her hand between the seats to find his shoulder. She felt a gentle slap on her arm. Peering over the top of the low seat back, she met the suspicious eyes of one of the elderly white-faced monkeys. "I can see you have some new companions. I think you need to introduce me, let them know I'm your girlfriend so they won't get jealous."

"Oh, really? Could have fooled me."

Abby gritted her teeth, not prepared to deal with Jose's churlishness. "Sorry you feel that way." She sat back in her seat, closing down on Jose in frustration.

As the plane pulled out toward the runway, she peered out the window, spotting another commercial transport on an adjoining runway waiting its turn. Searching the craft's skin, she located the emblem of the RAF. Little did they know how their life would change . . . again. She thought the oddity of having the same destination more than a coincidence. She wondered if she would need to implant the elephants. The keepers were well experienced in their handling; she would play that by ear. First she must convince Johno and his keepers to follow her.

After the plane taxied and rose into the air, Abby released her belt and prepared to check on the wildlife.

Cracking the door to the cargo bay, she marveled at their still placid demeanor. So far, no cats seemed to be licking their chops. Even the tortoises were still. Looking closer, she noticed most of the creatures appeared to be asleep. *Great, let them rest up. They'll need their strength for the two-hour long ride in the trucks to Lily Pond Road.*

Gently closing the door, she gazed up the aisle. A quite tension permeated the cabin, causing her stomach to tighten painfully. She took a slow deep breath to calm her jitters, holding out her hands to examine their tremor. Unable to make it stop, she rolled them into fists and determined to ignore it.

*Time to check on how everyone is holding up, especially Echo.* Now she could afford the time to address matters she had put aside in their rush this morning. *Gosh, so much has happened since this morning.* She checked her watch, calculating the time before they land. *Good. It will be dinnertime when we arrive, say another hour and a half before they start for the Bronx Zoo. It should be getting dark and the zoo will be near closing time. That will make our task so much easier.*

"Hi Sis . . . how we doing?" Abby knelt in the aisle to talk to Scotty, who sat with his arm resting around Chloe's shoulders. As usual, Teddy lay curled up on her lap; sharp peanut eyes missing nothing.

"Hi, kiddo. We're good with time. So far we haven't encountered any big problems, *yet*. Be careful what you talk about, we have two of the truckers on board to help us load at the zoo. I thought it made sense to bring them. They know what to expect from the animals and won't freak out. It might help keep the other truckers calm after they see what we're up to."

Abby perched on the edge of Chloe's seat. "Hon . . . you doing okay?" She gazed into Chloe's eyes, recognizing the insecurity and confusion. Hardly a surprise when a sheltered young girl discovers she isn't who she thought she was and watches her uncle and her father die before her eyes.

Abby wondered if Jose had been able to spend much time with Chloe. She wearily rubbed the side of her face as she realized he must feel just as lost as Chloe did. It's not often that an infant sibling is assumed dead, then pops up in your life as your girlfriend's brother's girlfriend, very much alive.

Abby made a mental note to go easy on Jose and try to spend an hour with him to reconnect and bring him up to speed. If she could just get him to understand, maybe he could rally himself to take some of this pressure off her. She felt like she would fall apart if someone challenged her hard enough. Where this internal strength and determination to save the animals came from mystified her.

A sudden flash hit her. *Oh, Mama, this is exactly what you did for us.* Her mama relied on no one to help them escape the dangerous tenements of Short Hills when they were children. She had expedited everything alone. She had sucked it up. She had pulled strength from deep within herself and never complained. She hadn't stopped when she was tired; she had stopped when she was done. Abby's heart wrenched with pity for her mother. She ached for her mother's arms, regretting the missed opportunities to thank her for the love and support that had imbued her with the same depth of strength and pragmatism. Again, she couldn't help remembering her mama's death that had occurred less than a year ago; the pain and loss still so fresh.

Moving on down the aisle, she nodded at Peter who sat with Ginger Mae; hostile postures advertising their shattered relationship. She sighed; another problem to work on when they reached their destination.

Smiling to herself, she spotted Kenya and Daisy holding Mimi on their lap, enjoying her sweetness. Nothing like a little doggie to help enchant a traumatized child. She noticed the bruise on Daisy's face from Armoni's fist beginning to lighten to a yellowish purple. *Good to see* some *things are healing.* Kenya caught her eye and quickly erased the smile she bestowed on Daisy, needing to continue directing her frosty hostility toward Abby who she refused to forgive for the slap across the face. Clearly Abby would have her hands full after they settled down. She guessed she'd be forced to hold off on that emotional breakdown she planned to pencil in.

"Miss Preston? A word?" Behind her, Clyde Calloway crooked his finger, beckoning her toward him. He leaned over into the aisle to whisper. "I know it's none of my damn business, but I feel compelled to inquire into the pedigree of that odd little animal sitting up front with the white dog. He doesn't look quite right and he seems to be in some kind of distress." *Echo? How could I forget to check on her?*

"Thanks Clyde, and that's Echo, she's a girl. I'll check on her immediately."

"But what kind . . .?"

She absently patted his shoulder, dismissing him, all thoughts focused on Echo. Making her way to the front of the aisle, she noticed Echo sitting with Barney's head on her lap. She watched as Echo, unaware of her presence, stroked Barney's head lovingly yet with a frenetic energy. The creature bent down to grasp Barney around the neck as if he might try to escape, then bent further to rub her face on Barney's fur. Abby could feel reverberations of an unstable aura, desperate undertones but no word whispers. As Abby knelt down in the aisle, she detected an unusual quality to Echo's motions; she appeared intense, her stroking verging on obsessive.

"Echo? Is everything okay with you and Barney?" Echo appeared not to hear her.

Abby reached out, placing her hand on Echo's shoulder, slowing her down and getting her attention. "Echo, I know something's going on. For heaven's sake, what is it?"

Echo just stared. A moment passed then a clean aura whispered a question. "What is heaven's sake, Sister Abby?"

"It's just an expression."

"But what is heaven?"

Exasperated, Abby decided to answer the question to appease Echo and get back to the problems at hand.

"Heaven is where you go when you die. If you have lived your life as a good person, God will welcome you with open arms. If you have lived your life without honor, you will go to Hell where the devil lives."

Echo's aura fluctuated. "Has My Barney lived his life with honor?"

Abby felt taken aback by the question. She placed her face close to Barney's head, getting a sloppy tongue wash for her efforts. Laughing and wiping her face with her sleeve, she answered Echo. "*All* dogs live their lives with honor, Echo, *especially* our good old Barney."

"Is My Barney old, sister? You said he is old."

"Echo, relax, Barney's not going anywhere." Abby wrapped her arms around the two buddies, kissing them as she rubbed her face on theirs. "I'm going back to Jose. If you need me, just send me a message, okay, Echo?" She stood, turning back down the aisle as Echo resumed her obsessive affection with Barney who, despite Abby's concern, obviously reveled in it.

As Abby made her way back down the aisle, she looked away from Clyde, not wanting to give him an opportunity to reopen his questions about Echo.

Glancing at her watch, she was surprised to see how much time had passed since they had taken off. They should be landing in Newark in an hour or so. Her breast swelled with relief as she congratulated herself for getting this far without mishap. A feeling of confidence and euphoria engulfed her, stimulating the urge to shake out her wings and tail that remained firmly constrained underneath her clothes. Maybe now she could take the time to rest her eyes and clear her mind for a quick twenty. With a smile, she slid into the seat behind Jose and his monkeys, leaning over to report.

"Things look pretty good, Jose. I'm going to try to take a nap. Why don't you try too? You and I can discuss the logistics of the next leg later while we wait for the plane to land."

"Yeah, I can use a nap." Jose yawned.

Abby settled down, her eyes closing against the gentle murmur of occasional conversation from the other passengers and the droning vibrations of the engines on the transport.

\*

As Abby closed her eyes, full of confidence, she dozed, unaware of the creature that sat at attention on the other side of the rickety door separating the passengers from the cargo area.

Caesar's unblinking watchful eyes scanned the cargo area, inventorying his fellow refugees from the Big Cat Sanctuary, wondering where the elderly primates had come from. He knew they had not lived at the sanctuary. They seemed to get along fine with the sanctuary's primates, although he could see the young chimpanzee might be a little too much for them. He turned back to the door that he had observed closing on Scotty and his companions over two hours ago as they disappeared down the aisle to take their seats, Echo clinging to Scotty's arms. He must not lose sight of their whereabouts. Very slowly he inched his powerful, magnificent body down onto the smooth metal floor of the plane, forgoing the comfort of the moving blankets enjoyed by the rest of the wildlife. Fastening his eyes to the door, he waited patiently.

# Chapter 5

Ten minutes before Captain Marc Segal and his co-captain, Karen James, were to start their approach to Newark that usually took approximately twenty minutes, the captain found himself consoling his partner about her lackluster love life.

"Karen, if you'd consider moving to Vegas where I live, you could get away from all the hillbillies you date in that Podunk town you hang your hat in."

"Come on, Marc, you don't care about who I date. You just want a free sitter for all those kids of yours." Captain Segal stretched his Nevada-tanned and muscled arms as he cracked up over Karen's comment.

"I know the company would love to have you at home base instead of that backwater you live in. Even though we don't have the mountains and wildlife you love so much, I can promise you, Vegas men know how to treat a girl. They also know what a dentist is. No missing teeth or hinky marriage connections to their cousins."

Karen reached over and gave him a hard punch on his sculpted shoulder. He reached over and flipped the cap off the short, dark hair that made her look like a gamin pixie. Not an easy feat for such a big girl.

"Pet Air 1952, this is ground control. You are ordered to immediately change course and put down at JFK. Repeat, change course for JFK for immediate landing. This is a federal emergency. Repeat—this is a federal emergency. All aircraft being diverted to their nearest airports." Marc grabbed the mic, glancing at Karen's white face, all traces of horseplay vanished.

"Ground control, this is Pet Air 1952. Diverting to JFK. Any heads up on the problem?"

"No information at this time, Pet Air. Order issued from National Security Council with the consent of the White House. Radar jammed here, it's a mad house."

"Ten-four, ground control. Out." Karen busied herself plotting their new course. Marc ran his hand over his thatch of caramel hair in frustration, tension creeping into his voice.

"Karen, what the hell could be up? You got your XiPhone here?"

"Yeah, take it, I need to finish this. We don't want to run into any other craft being rerouted this way."

Marc snatched up the phone and called his wife in Harrison, a large residential community directly outside Vegas. Most residents lived there to quickly commute to their jobs in the casinos that had all but closed their gaming halls. Who had money to gamble? The giant structures had been converted to housing, service businesses and support industries for the millions of people who resided in this most unusual city that still retained the architecture and outward glitter of a bygone decade. A few of the hotels still held tightly to the business of conventions and corporate meetings that managed to funnel precious dollars into the economy of the tarnished city.

Marc drummed his fingers impatiently as his wife did not pick up the phone. He suddenly drew his breath sharply as he listened on his end. Karen watched as he disconnected and set the phone down, hesitant puzzlement coloring his voice as he reported to Karen. "All service is out in Harrison. Why would that be?"

"I don't know, Marc. Check the wires, the media will know by now." She watched as he flicked his finger over the screen, stopping to read. He sat frozen as Karen quietly noticed the lines of silent tears coursing from his unblinking eyes.

"Marc? Marc, what is it?" Panic sputtered like a child's lit sparkler, deep in the pit of her stomach.

He raised his eyes to her. "Vegas . . . hit. Some kind of bomb. No one knows yet. Harrison . . . oh, God, my babies, my wife." Marc looked gut shot, the impact not yet registering with Karen. "Oh God, oh God, they've done it now."

"Who, Marc, what's happening?" She grabbed the device from his hands to read for herself as Marc continued to cry and moan into his trembling hands.

"Oh no. God." She read the dreadful report, knowing their very lives rested in the hands of cowardly politicos and what was left of their gutted armed forces. Reading on, she could sense the panic in the chaotic writing of the media outlet.

*"Losses in the millions . . . experts to the scene . . . barricades . . . radiation . . . denials . . . from Iran . . . Russia being eyed . . . China defensive and outraged. The President to speak within the hour. Retaliation assumed . . . all aircraft ordered grounded . . . questions being asked . . . are there more?"*

Shell-shocked, Karen took a moment to think. First, they must inform the passengers. If they suspect the pilots had changed the flight path, they'd be angry and belligerent. Better to start with the truth. *Then I need to get this puppy to JFK.*

"Marc, who's going to tell the passengers?"

Marc stared at her like a zombie; his eyes unfocused, his face slack.

"Okay, I'll do it. You need to pull yourself together. We need to be strong. I don't need to tell you those passengers back there all have families too." She rested her hand on his shoulder, squeezing gently and, with a white face, pulled herself out of her seat and stumbled to the door of the passenger compartment.

# Chapter 6

Abby's eyes popped open as she realized the background noise in her nap had changed. She looked around the compartment, observing all eyes resting on a standing figure at the front of the plane.

*The co-captain, what's her name . . . Karen something?* Abby assessed the demeanor of the tall, robust young woman, instantly alert. *Something's wrong.* The co-captain's tight smile struck Abby as unnaturally grim. She reached between the seats to poke Jose.

"Jose, wake up."

The pilot moved down the aisle, clearing her throat. She started to speak, the words catching in her throat.

"Um . . . hello, I'm Karen James, your copilot. All aircraft have been ordered to land ASAP at the closest airport available, by order of the White House and the National Security Council. I am sorry to announce . . . a . . . that a bomb of some type has wiped out the city of Las Vegas."

A chorus of audible gasps emanated from the stunned passengers. As demands for the facts overwhelmed them, the passenger's voices erupted, peppering Karen with questions as she stood in the aisle holding her hands up against the onslaught. She managed haltingly to convey the facts as she knew them.

Abby's mind operated at full speed, trying to calculate the effect this news would have on her plans. Before long, all eyes turned toward her for guidance. Karen took this moment to inform them of the change to their destination.

"*No. Absolutely not.* We'll continue to Newark as planned." Abby stood tall, brooking no argument. "I need to have a conversation with the pilot if you don't mind."

Karen dejectedly turned to enter the cockpit. As Abby marched down the aisle, hands and plaintive voices flailed at her, hindering her progress. She turned to make an announcement.

"Please, please. I know this is quite a shock. Let me speak to the pilot and I'll get back to you. Just give me a moment." As she turned to enter the cockpit, she reached down to scoop up Echo so quickly no one noticed.

"Whoa, what the heck is that?" Captain Segal's voice cracked, his worry and heartbreak leaking a quiet bitterness as he stared at Echo.

Abby ignored him to ask a question. "What will happen if we try to continue on our original route?"

"Well, we *are* still headed toward Newark. Ground control has been calling, questioning why we haven't rerouted. Karen, you about ready?"

"Ready."

Abby bit her lip. She didn't want to implant them for fear of impairing their coordination. But she would allow Echo to do it if it became her only option.

"Name your price. I want you to put us down at Newark. It's critical for everyone on this plane. And the animals. My trucks are in Newark. I can't house them anywhere if we put down in JFK. You have to make them understand."

Captain Segal's eyes narrowed. "Miss Preston, there is no amount of money you can offer to me to do what I don't want to do. My family lives in Las Vegas."

"Oh, God, I'm so sorry." Abby's hand flew up to her mouth in dismay, tears surfacing behind her shades to dribble down her chin. They all stared at one another, the cockpit thrumming with tension. Captain Segal's tone softened as he reluctantly picked up the radio transmitter.

"I'll see what I can do. I'm sure I can come up with an emergency of my own. Didn't you just say a male lion broke out of his cage?" Nodding gratefully, Abby held out her hand. He held it briefly and waved her out of the cockpit. Karen silently nodded as Abby left to return to the passengers.

*

"You didn't tell her, Marc."

"What difference would it make? It's pure speculation that another bomb is headed to New York City. The authorities don't have any proof yet. Check your XiPhone for an update. I'll call ground control and break the news to them." Captain Segal and his copilot reverted to type: trained professionals doing a job that entrusted them with other people's lives. The job took precedence no matter what was happening to them personally.

"Ground control, this is Pet Air 1952, come in, please." Marc steeled himself, drying the last vestige of bitter tears from his eyes with the back of his hand as ground control came in.

Abby stood in the aisle as everyone shouted questions. She dropped Echo back in her seat with Barney, who looked anxious until Echo curled up next to him.

Echo's aura swirled in her mind. "Sister Abby, there is no time. We need to go quickly."

Abby held up her hand against the voices peppering her with questions; Clyde's and Dezi's the loudest. "What do you mean, Echo?" Abby looked up as Clyde's lumbering figure approached. "Echo, let me calm these people down first. I'll be back as soon as I can. We'll talk then." Smoothing down a tuft of curly white hair over Barney's eyes, she rose to face the coming onslaught.

"Miss Preston, can you please spare me a few minutes?" Clyde's mature handsome countenance showed dregs of weariness, his eyes aching with suffering. Dezi stood behind him, fidgety and wired.

"Hey, babe, ya know I didn't sign up for no trouble. We need to turn this plane around and get back to Florida. I'm no way gunna get stuck in New York or New Jersey."

"Dezi, can you please take your seat. Let me handle a few things with Clyde and then I'll get to you."

Dezi's face fell like a pimply faced skinny geek rejected by the prom queen. His whining softened to a pitiful squeak. "You won't forget Dezi now, will you, babe?"

"Shhh, go sit." She patted him encouragingly as Clyde stood quietly, clearly in grave distress. She turned her attention to him.

"Miss Preston, I'm not liking the sound of all this. If there's one bomb, there'll be others. Our damn fool President might even decide to retaliate, bringing on a shitstorm. My wife is alone in an unfamiliar town with my grandbabies. If planes are grounded, how will I get back to Tampa?"

"Clyde, I do have a plan with a safe place for us all to wait this out. I'll make an announcement as soon as we land and are joined by the other truckers. I'm concerned about the safety of us all. I have a mission to complete with other animals but I'll put our safety first. Can you reach your wife on your cell?"

"Yes. I've spoken to her and the girls. She said the news is shaky but the authorities say they think there's another bomb."

Abby's face blanched. "Does your wife have access to a vehicle?"

"Yes, why?" Clyde's brow furrowed.

"Tell her to get to the grocery store and load up on containers of gasoline for the car, water and food that won't need to be cooked. Tell her to stand by after the shopping. We'll have a resolution within about an hour. She must get the supplies right away. There'll be a run at the stores if it hasn't already begun."

Clyde smacked his head. "Damn, I should have thought of that."

Abby guided him to his seat. "We're going to land any minute now. Why don't you buckle up?" Abby continued to work her way toward her seat. Arriving next to Cobby, she knew she could count on him. Reaching out, he grasped her hand.

"Is this it, Abby? Is this what you were expecting?" His voice grated; his tone fatalistic.

"I don't know, Cobby." Her voice faltered. "It might be. There are reports from the media that another bomb might go off. Clyde seems to think the U.S. may try to strike back at another government. The situation doesn't sound good."

"What do you plan to do when we land?"

"Can you help me load everyone into the trucks and head for Sussex? Scotty and I will still head to the Bronx. I need Echo with me. Jose will go with you too. Clyde and Dezi were supposed to help me at the zoo but Clyde is useless now. His wife and grandkids are on his mind. I need to prevent him from trying to return to Florida. It's no longer safe there."

"How do you know that, Abby?" Cobby's face furrowed, his voice laced with skepticism. He glanced over at Kane who sat tensely with Kenya, her hand resting on the bulge of her belly. Abby followed his glance.

"I know you're worried, Cob. Please trust me. The best thing you can do is get everyone to Sussex as soon as possible. Jose will lead you to safety. I'll join you as soon as I can."

"Okay, kid. I'm behind you." She gave him a grateful hug.

"Abby, one more thing. What about Peter? That dude is wound too tight as it is. I think we're asking for trouble if we take him with us."

Abby reacted with shock, not believing her ears. "Cobby, I'm not comfortable with what you seem to be suggesting. Don't worry about him. He won't cause a problem. I know he appears a bit unstable but it's just the betrayal talking. He needs time to get over what happened with Ginger Mae and Armoni. Keep your eye on him if you must, but I have him under control." *Well, at least the implants do*, she thought.

As she moved away, she could tell from the intractable expression on Cobby's face that his opinion remained unchanged.

Abby slipped back into her seat behind Jose, his anxious face waiting for an explanation. Taking a moment to catch her breath, she shut her eyes to marshal strength.

"You okay, Abby? How bad is it?"

"Bad. I think this is it. This must be what I was compelled to prepare for. Both Netty and Echo said it would happen quickly, I guess I just didn't fully understand how quick it would be. I thought we had more time to get situated." She dropped her head down to her hands to indulge in a brief thought of just running away when they landed; the panicked desire swiftly banished as she raised her head, clear eyed and resolute.

"What's taking so long? We should have landed by now." As she spoke, the captain announced they would be landing in ten minutes, please take your seats . . .

"Okay, this is it. Jose, I need everyone to get the animals on the trucks and head for Route 80 to Sussex County. Scotty's coming with me. So is Echo. Will you be okay? Can you show everyone where to go?" Jose squeezed her hand through the seat.

"I don't like the idea of us splitting up. We've been apart long enough. And what about the bombs, what if one goes off in New York? It's not safe. Abby, they'll probably shut down the bridges and tunnels anyway. And if they're open, I don't think they're going to let a convoy of trucks through." Abby's lips pressed together tightly. She felt thwarted at every turn as she tried to work out her plan to get to the zoo.

"I'll be fine. I have Echo if I reach a roadblock."

A turbulent aura engulfed her, sending her mind reeling. "Sister, Sister we must hurry. The bomb comes. There is no time. It is not far off."

"I hear you, girl." Abby's heart tripped with anxiety as the transport landed and taxied to a stop in the north terminal. She scanned the tarmac for the truck caravan, spotting six or seven clumped together. *Where are the rest of them?* She had requested forty five trucks. Advances had been extended, contracts signed. In the distance, she could identify the RAF transport. No trucks for the elephants in sight.

Abby stood, waving her arm over her head. "Okay, everyone, let's get these animals loaded."

The belly of the transport opened and Abby ran to greet the truckers. As she approached, a lean, muscled pepper-haired woman in her late forties stepped down from her rig with a potbelly pig on a leash. The woman wore a plaid flannel shirt and a pair of jeans; the pig wore a white sequined tutu with a bandana that matched her owner's shirt. Attractive, it was not.

"Miss Abby Preston?" The woman bent down to fluff her pig's costume and walked toward Abby, the pig trotting along, happy as can be.

"I'm Crystal and this here's my pig, Tulip. You said to bring pets, right? Though I don't rightly think of Tulip as a pet, she's more like my muse."

"Where are the other trucks, Crystal? I made arrangements for over forty drivers."

"Well now, Miss Preston, I guess you all got the news 'bout the dee-zaster in Vegas? The other truckers got it, too, and most of them lily livers hightailed it outta here. Now how bout we get to work? I plan on gettin' home sometime today."

Abby tried to cover her shock, holding back the tears: *All those innocent glorious animals.* Her stomach clenched as she finally admitted to herself there would be no rescue for the zoo.

"Pull right up to the transport. Open the back of your trucks and please stay inside your cabs. Not all of the cats are in cages. We can handle them just fine but I like to take precautions. Any questions, look for Jose, Scotty or Cobby. Pass the word to the other drivers and let's get going."

Crystal nodded her head smartly and headed for the other drivers to pass the word, the pig in the tutu trotting demurely alongside.

# Chapter 7

Abby headed at a run to the RAF transport spotted in the distance. All around her sat the evidence of planes brought down in a hurry, disarray everywhere. And this terminal serviced freight. She could imagine what the main terminals looked like.

The smell scorched her lungs as she breathed in the hot exhaust, and the gruff sounds of engines roaring and excited panic in people's voices assaulted her. Wheezing and out of breath, she spotted Johno and the other keepers sitting on the edge of the transport bay, the babies pushing at their backs to get their attention. Johno himself sat with a large bottle of what appeared to be formula, feeding an infant who sucked greedily on the upraised nipple.

"Forgive me for not rising, Miss Abby." The other keepers scrambled to their feet, black faces gleaming in the late afternoon light, expressions reverent as they bowed to her.

"Hello, gentlemen. I'm pleased to see you again even under these difficult circumstances. I'm here to see if I can be of assistance. I assume you find yourselves stranded with no way to get to the zoo?" She scanned the surrounding area unsuccessfully, not locating any sign of a truck for the elephants.

"This is true, Miss Preston. We are concerned about the lack of a truck to remove our charges to safety. We have been waiting for some time. I am afraid our transportation is absent due to the emergency."

"Well, Johno, I have a solution for you. I can move the elephants with one of my trucks. We will have to double up because I'm short myself. Can the elephants stand to have other animals ride with them? Just goats, horses and camels. The infants should come with us in the truck with my people—our cars didn't show either."

"Yes, but I must have two of my keepers ride with the elephants to keep order with the other animals. It should be workable." He handed the bottle to one of his men to finish and jumped off the ledge to join Abby, his face joyful beyond all hope.

"But, Miss Abby, what is our destination? The zoo is expecting us." Johno's face fell as he realized the impossibility of his own statement. Abby stifled a sob as she herself recognized the fate of all the lives that no longer stood a chance of rescue. Placing a hand on Johno's arm, she pointed to where her transport sat, trucks lined up to load the animals.

"I'm going to run back to the trucks to make sure we save space for your elephants. Can you walk them over?" She scanned the hustle and bustle of the north terminal with its loud industrial sounds and strange smells, totally inappropriate for gentle creatures from the African plains.

"Never mind, stupid question. I'll send a truck over to you. You can relax about your safety. We will have a two-hour drive, northwest. We will all be completely safe no matter how many bombs are dropped. We must hurry though. This area is not safe."

"Thank you so much, we are very grateful, Miss Abby. We will unload right now."

"I'll be right back with the truck." Abby took off at a sprint, waving down the truck furthest from the transport, thankfully still empty. Opening the side door, she hopped in and directed the driver to pull up to Johno's RAF transport.

As they approached, she realized John's herd was bigger than she had anticipated. Her heart rejoiced at the sight of two baby rhinos and what looked like an unidentifiable species of African deer. As she approached the little herd, she noticed one of the rhinos needed special attention from its keeper. There must be a problem. She would attend to that when they arrived at the Hive. Unfortunately, unless it threatened the life of the creature, all healing must wait until they were safe.

She jumped out of the huge truck, instructing the driver to assist with the loading.

"Johno, we're ready for you. Do you have supplies for the babies?"

Johno hurried over, an inventory list in his hand. "Yes, Miss Abby, we have many pallets with formula and browse."

"Johno, there's no room for all of that. Split open a pallet, take enough for two weeks only. Have the animals been watered?"

"Oh yes, Miss Abby. But the formula is critical. It was especially developed by Ms. Elizabeth decades ago. They cannot survive without it." Johno's expression brooked no argument. Abby realized a tiny lie would have to do for now.

"Yes, I know. Don't worry, I have that under control. All the supplies we need are at our safe haven. Two weeks' worth should help get them over the hump of acclimation." She felt secure about what they would find to eat and drink. Netty had surely planned ahead for this necessity.

"As soon as you're loaded, pull over to the caravan and join me. Leave the other keepers with the animals. I want you to ride with us and the three babies. I'll have a truck ready to transfer the babies. There'll be a few elderly primates with us and a bird. That shouldn't present any problems for the babies, will it?"

Johno laughed. "No problem, except for the people maybe. The babies love lots of attention. Perhaps it will be a welcome distraction for everyone." Abby laughed with Johno, welcoming his irrepressible spirit. She thought he would be a valuable addition to the Hive. Once he adjusted to the shock of the realities, of course.

Abby ran back to her transport, dodging airport vehicles, hand trucks and frightened personnel; the cacophonies of exhaust smell and strident sounds threatening to overpower her. Panting and tired, she arrived in time to observe Clyde as he said goodbye to Dezi.

"Hey, hey, where do you think you're going? Clyde, do you think it'll be safer somewhere else? You *must* come with us for your own good." She tried to restrain his arm, turning him to face her. Her stomach fell as she assessed the sharp pain in his eyes, his rugged face haggard with worry.

"Miss Preston, I'm worthless to you if I'm worried about my wife and grandkids. I need to be with them."

"If you can't make it back to Tampa or if you're killed on the way there, how will that help them? I have a better idea. Let's get them up here where we can give them a real safe harbor to ride this out. Come stay with us. We have enough supplies and shelter for everyone. She can drive the kids here, avoiding the east coast cities. Get her on the phone. Tell her to load the car with all her supplies. I'll help you give her directions. Now call her before the cell towers go down. What do you say, Clyde?" She tried to interpret his indecision as it rippled across his face. Clyde glanced at Dezi to grasp at straws.

"Don't look at me, dude, I'm going with doll face. I'm no fool."

Clyde stared at Abby.

"Come on, Clyde. We don't have much time. We need to get out of here. You need to call her and get her on the road as soon as possible if we stand a chance of getting her to safety."

# Chapter 8

Lorna Calloway left the local gas station after topping off the tank of the rental car and placing the five plastic gas containers in the trunk. That gave her an extra thirty gallons of gas. She didn't know if she would actually need the extra fuel, but when Clyde said to do something, she did it. She had learned thirty nine years ago when she married him that he possessed an uncanny knack for always knowing the correct path to take when presented with a problem.

Easing her still trim figure behind the wheel, she turned to her two granddaughters, aged five and twelve, who sat belted in the back seat getting restless. She had promised to take them to the beach late in the afternoon to avoid the harmful rays of the sun, but had had to interrupt their plans when Clyde had called with these instructions. She had known nothing of the disaster in Las Vegas until Clyde had informed her, shocking her to the core.

When they arrived at the hardware store, people were pulling into the parking lot, obviously with similar thoughts. Confusion reigned, the girls getting rudely jostled as people elbowed one another, grabbing at items on the shelves. Clearly, no one knew what might be needed if the whole country faced an emergency.

"Gram, are we going to the beach now?" Her granddaughters resembled their mom: red hair, freckles and creamy skin that tanned well without burning as long as they stayed well protected. They overflowed with enthusiasm and affection but, like most children, possessed the attention spans of a gnat.

"Not yet, baby, we still have to stop at the grocery store. Then we'll wait for Grandpa to call again."

"Don't be a nitwit, Suzy. It'll be way too late to go to the beach, anyway." Suzy's big sister Jen, although she preferred to be called Jennifer, happily used Suzy as her verbal whipping post as she honed her little preteen identification with her mother. Lorna grimaced as she acknowledged just how much Jen was starting to sound like her bossy mother.

Forcing her attention back to the matter at hand, she took a deep breath at how lucky they were to have had only a half-hour's wait at the gas station. People must still be in shock over the attack. She finally admitted that it really was an attack. If she could just zip in and out of the grocery store they might make it home in time to watch the President speak.

Turning the corner that would put them one block from their vacation home, she prepared to pull into the Publix grocery store parking lot. To her surprise, she judged the line of cars must number over fifty. And that was just to get in the parking lot.

Police cars flanked the entrance to the store, shotguns brandished as angry crowds threatened to overwhelm them. Shocked, Lorna bypassed the scene, regretting her decision to stop at the gas station first. She assumed all the other grocery stores would be experiencing similar mobs. Even if she could manage to get inside this one, she would likely face empty shelves. Hurrying to their rental, she thanked God the refrigerator and pantry overflowed with items she had purchased with Clyde, as they had stocked up for the week before he left for Sarasota to complete his new contract. They would just have to make the food on hand last.

Lorna pulled in to the driveway of their rental, noticing teenagers run from the house across the street with a TV in their arms and a sack of other stuff over their shoulders. *Good grief, looting already?* She decided not to leave the car in the driveway and pressed the button to open the garage door. As the door rose, she glimpsed a pair of legs, then the full sight of two young men slamming an ax on the doorknob to the door that led directly into the house.

Locking the car door behind her, she jumped out screaming, "Hey, what the hell do you think you're doing? *Get the hell out of there.*"

As Lorna made a move for the garage one of the men ran forward, punching her in the gut and knocking her to the ground. Watching the men run off, she heard the locks on the car door pop and the girls scramble out, Jen hollering, "Gram, Gram, you all right?"

Suzy threw herself down on Lorna, the little girl crying uncontrollably. Lorna tried to comfort them as she held her stomach, trying not to vomit. Struggling as she pulled herself together, Lorna managed to usher the girls into the house.

After locking the doors and checking all the windows, Lorna gathered with her grandchildren in front of the television, catching the end of the President's speech. She sat stunned; the girls slow to comprehend the ramifications of the President's words.

Lorna's head reeled, her mind on overload. She needed to get the girls out of this city and now. According to the President, major cities would be targeted first. She couldn't take the chance of Tampa being on the top of any enemies' lists.

"Girls, please go pack. Jen, can you pull your suitcases out of the closet and help Suzy pack? I'm going to pack Grandpa's clothes then work on the pantry and fridge. Meet me in the kitchen when you're done. Just throw everything together, we need to be out of here in thirty minutes." Lorna began to worry about what the roads would look like with everyone trying to escape the cities. Rummaging through a drawer in the kitchen, she located a map. Scanning the routes out of the city, she decided to drive north, away from the city, avoiding the routes along the east or the west coast, sure to be targets where they passed through the major metro areas. Her heart hammered loudly as her cell phone rang. *Oh, my God, please be Clyde.*

Abby watched Clyde turn off his cell after having a long conversation with Lorna, who had apparently cried through most of it. He looked up at her, wiping his traces of tears away.

"I think she got most of it. She knew enough not to try to go up the coastal highway. She'll go north until she hits Sandusky, Ohio, then head east on Route 80 until she hits Sussex County. I gave her the directions to Lily Pond Road. I sure hope she can find the rock in the woods."

"Are you kidding, Clyde? All she needs to do is follow the trail of elephant, lion, tiger and bear dung. She'll find it okay." Abby patted his arm reassuringly. "How long do you expect her drive to take?" Clyde pursed his lips.

"On a normal drive, I can do it in twenty four hours. In a truck with a load, two and a half days. Law only allows drivers to be on the road for a prescribed time. Lorna reported chaos at the stores, looters already taking advantage of the situation. Traffic'll get bad real soon as people try to flee the cities. I think it might take them a good week, worse case."

"You going to be okay?" Abby searched his face, finding him difficult to read.

"Yeah. We better get a move on now. Hard to say what the parkway is going to look like." He turned and headed toward a tractor trailer, wanting to give it a last eyeball before they set out.

Abby ran to the back of their small caravan. Spotting Crystal standing by the last truck, she realized they would have to ride together with Crystal doing the driving. Johno stood respectfully waiting for Abby, having loaded the infant elephants. Abby walked around to the side peering in. *Oh, boy.* She knew the trip would not be as comfortable as she had hoped.

Feeling a tap on her shoulder, she turned with surprise to be confronted by Karen, the copilot of their transport.

"Miss Preston, I happened to overhear your conversation with the gentleman regarding his wife in Florida. I didn't mean to eavesdrop but I heard you offer him a safe place to stay." Karen's smile slipped, the desperate hope in her eyes getting the best of her. "Do you perhaps have room for one more? I'm very good with animals and I'm willing to do most any kind of work to pull my weight."

Abby smiled at her direct and earnest manner. "I think you'll fit in just fine. You realize the siege might last longer than you think?"

"It is what it is. I'm mighty grateful, Miss Preston."

"Abby, please call me Abby." With the decision made, she gave Karen a hand up into the back of the truck where she found a seat near Kenya, who welcomed her with a stingy smile.

Scotty, Kane, Dezi and Cobby wrestled affectionately with the three babies. Jose sat in a corner surrounded with the six elderly monkeys. Ginger Mae and Daisy leaned against a wall, as comfortable as possible on the moving blankets. Kenya watched the elephants' antics from a distance, her hand cupping her expanding midriff and the macaw trying to compete with the baby bump for a spot on her lap.

Chloe sat nearby with the posse, trying to entice Teddy off her lap. Echo and Barney huddled together like forlorn lovers destined to be separated by the vulgarities of fate. Almost everyone appeared settled—except Peter. He sat alone, his pasty face and owl eyes inviting all to stay away.

The interior of the truck felt pleasantly cool as Clyde joined them, giving Johno and Abby a hand up. She could smell the sweet aroma of sweat coming off Johno as he found a seat between her and the baby ele horseplay. Taking a subtle sniff, she detected other odors; animal and human, feces and fear. Light streamed in from opposing window slides that allowed observation from outside. She thanked her forethought for requesting temperature-controlled trailers. At least that would help keep the smells to a reasonable level.

From the corner of her eye, she watched Teddy rise from Chloe's lap and trot over to Peter, lifting his leg on Peter's trousers, his stream not much more than a dribble. Even this indignity failed to elicit a reaction from Peter.

Crystal stuck her head in the door opening. "Okay folks. This is it. See you on the other end. Abby, if you need to talk to me, you have my cell." With that she shut the door, locking them in.

Abby asked for everyone's attention to introduce Johno. The response was mixed with tentative smiles. Kenya picked up the slack with a friendly wave.

"Hey, chicky, why don't you come over and sit by me? I can use some company."

Johno turned to Abby, his expression hopeful.

"You don't need my permission, Johno, go relax for a while. A pretty girl is always good medicine for stress."

As Johno made his way carefully across the truck to sit in front of Kenya, they felt the truck start to move. Abby's heart quickly jumped to her throat as she wondered how much time they had left before the next bomb fell. She suddenly felt an aura strike her mind.

"We must hurry, Sister. We are not safe. My Barney is not safe." She looked across the truck to meet Echo's eyes.

Squatting down next to Clyde, who couldn't pull his attention from his XiPhone, she asked for an update.

"The news is bad, very bad. Israel is in shambles. *The Times* claims it was Iran. They couldn't resist with all the confusion diverting our attention here." His voice sounded flat and hollow, bereft of all hope.

"Clyde, tell me. Did Israel strike back?" She saw no change in his expression. "Clyde, what happened?"

"It's all over, Abby. We're done. Israel dropped the bomb in Iran and Pakistan. Russia announced plans to strike Israel, not that much can be left. The President has declared war on Russia. The Chinese have threatened to back up Russia. What difference does it make now? We're toast. I'll never see my wife again."

"Can we keep this between us right now? I don't want a panic. This is our only chance to get to safety."

Clyde nodded blankly. Abby knew that promise wouldn't last long.

"Sister, we must hurry."

Without speaking, she sent back her own aura to Echo for the first time. "We'll make it, Echo, I can feel it. Tell Netty to pray for us. It's in God's hands now."

# Chapter 9

Chloe dozed off and on as the caravan of trucks inched along the parkway headed for Route 24 that would take them to Route 287 and then Route 80. Scotty said they would be in good shape when they hit Route 80. She straightened up, yawning, and readjusted her position as the dogs crowded in on her, each one trying to compete, striving to be the closest to Chloe's body for comfort, Teddy triumphantly refusing to be outdone.

She sniffed her shirt as a happy snort from one of the baby eles woke her for good. She noticed the ripe smell in the truck, discovering it came from all of them, not just her.

Catching Jose watching her, she acknowledged his interest with a stingy wave, wondering how long it would take her to adjust to the fact that she now had a big brother. She remembered how often as a child she would pester her mother for a brother. Guess that never stood a chance now that she knew her father—rather Omar—the man who had kidnapped her, actually hated her mother. Sighing, she realized Jane really wasn't her mother either. *What a bunch of screwed up psychotic nut jobs.* Uncle Brooks too—not her uncle. It became more and more difficult to wrap her mind around the reality of her new life. How could she have thought those people loved her when they had turned out to be such sickos? And what did life hold for her now? Seemed she might have gone from the frying pan to the fire.

At least she still had Scotty and Teddy. She scanned the truck, giving everyone a quick assessment.

Kenya looked interesting, although she didn't have the faintest idea who the black man with the big wide smile and green scrub coat could be. Noticing the gorgeous black girl cup her belly, she wondered where the baby's father was. Poor thing, she knew that infant was in for a tough road.

She watched as the poor lady with the knife wound on her face whispered to her little girl, who seemed to be snapping out of her funk, exhibiting a smattering of interest in the baby elephants.

A skinny weird-looking man suddenly slid down to rest next to her. His breath wheezed as his exertion with the eles made him breathless.

"I could sure use a smoke right now." Breathing heavily, he turned to her and the dogs. "These guys all belong to you?"

"No, Teddy is mine."

"Teddy? He looks like a ratty pain in the ass. You got a smoke?"

She picked up Teddy, holding him defensively in her arms. "You can't smoke in here, can't you see that?" She eyed him contemptuously. "You'd be able to breathe if you didn't smoke those disgusting things." He didn't appear to be listening.

"Gee, those elephants sure can wear you out. We shoulda left them behind. They're gunna be a real pain in the ass, I can sure see that right now."

"Why did you agree to help out if you don't like them?"

He nodded suggestively, his weasel face and pisshole eyes directed at Abby, who crouched next to Jose. "The babe made me an offer I couldn't refuse. She's got it bad for me."

Chloe burst out laughing, causing Scotty to look over in surprise, a happy smile on his lips. Sobering, Chloe snorted at him. "You better take your skinny butt out of here. Abby is my boyfriend's sister and that's her boyfriend she's talking to. Looks to me you are shit out of luck, bud. And if you don't like animals you sure are in the wrong place."

Dezi shrugged, her words sliding off his back like Crisco on a roasted ham hock. "What do you know, kid? The Dez begs to differ." He slid over to the wall of the truck.

"Okay, you smelly mutts. I'm gunna get myself some shuteye. Now back off." In a second, he began to snore, chasing Mimi to the other side of Chloe, oblivious to all.

*

After their progress inched slowly over a drive of more than six hours, Abby felt the truck slow, coming to a complete halt. Under normal conditions the drive took two hours. She looked out the window, calculating they were far along Route 80 near the exit for Route 15, about a normal thirty-minute drive from Lily Pond Road.

Jose, Cobby and Clyde joined her at the window.

"Holy Mother, look at all those people." Clyde's demeanor had failed to improve during the drive, the crowds clogging the highway causing his face to fall further.

"Don't worry, Clyde, she'll make it."

"How's she going to make it here if *we* can't even get through?"

Abby pulled out her cell phone, the signal still available. "This is Abby, I want you to inch right through the crowds. They'll move. Easy on the horn, the animals are already agitated from the long ride. The crowds should break up once we're on Route 15." Within minutes, she felt the truck move forward.

They watched as they passed the crowds filled with poor people; families without vehicles lugging children, blankets and bags of food and water. The sides of the road were littered with discarded family valuables and possessions. Strength drained, their most valuable possessions now their lives.

Abby spotted two children trudging along the road, a girl of about ten holding hands with a boy of about three; tears falling from the toddlers eyes as his mouth cried soundlessly for his mama.

"Jose, look, can't we stop for them?" Abby's hopeful voice tapered off after a bitter laugh from Cobby.

"If we stop, we'll be overrun by the horde fleeing into the hills. They'll toss these baby elephants off this truck so fast you won't know what hit you. What do you think they'll do to Echo? God forbid they find out about your ehm . . . changes."

They heard a poorly suppressed sob and Clyde turned from the window to sit in a corner away from everyone.

A stone suddenly hit the window, then a rock. The rocks from the crowd pelted them heavily as the slow-moving tractor trailers became the focus of the crowd's anger. The sliding window shattered, sending Abby to the driver's side of the truck. To her horror, she observed men with long poles trying to pry open Crystal's door. As it caved in from the onslaught, she felt Crystal rev the engines, blowing a bone-shattering warning to the crowd.

As a man jumped up to Crystal's window wielding his pole, she tramped on the gas. The huge truck bucked, threatening to stall, then caught, springing forward into the crowd. The man with the pole fell from his perch along with those standing inside the truck. Abby fell to the floor, landing on Scotty and Kane. She felt the truck pick up speed, tires riding over bumps in the road, thumps vibrating through the truck, the horn still spewing its threatening salvo.

Peter, Johno, Cobby and even Chloe tried desperately to calm the babies, the unfamiliar sound setting them to panic.

Dezi clung to the rim of the window, managing to stay upright.

"*Holy shit* . . . oh my God." He hung his head, the palm of his hand rubbing tears that threatened his macho pose. Abby screamed from the floor, rising to run to the window. Dezi caught her, holding her back in his skinny arms.

"You don't want to see this, babe, I promise you." His voiced cracked with emotion.

"Let it go, Abby." Jose's voice rang loudly. He stood motioning for her to join him. Dezi released her and she flew to Jose's arms to sink down on the floor of the truck, trying to forget the feeling of the bumps that weren't road under the wheels of the truck.

"It was them or us." Jose's voice sounded with the bitterness of deathly reality, the trucks finally making time on the road.

The moon gleamed happily high in the sky, indifferent to the misery of the occupants of the truck caravan as it pulled into Lily Pond Road. Abby scrambled out of the truck, avoiding the blood splattered on the bumpers of Crystal's big truck.

She flew to the front door to be met by Mama Diaz with open arms.

"Oh, my child, it's so good to see you."

Abby cried as Mama stroked her hair, making her feel like a youth again, wanting to disappear into her capable arms and never emerge.

"Oh, Lord, what do we have here?" Mama Diaz faced the trucks to see a stunning Siberian tiger standing on the lawn, his head swaying from side to side as he scanned the people emerging from the last truck in line, eyes glowing as he spotted Scotty.

"Mama, you must follow Scotty. Take the girls into the woods. He'll show you where to go. We must hurry. There is little time. I'll be there shortly. I need to get the rest of the animals headed to the woods. They won't hurt you. It's okay." Mama hesitated.

Abby called to Dezi. "Dez, I'm putting you in charge of getting Mama and the girls to the woods with their stuff. Don't leave their side. Clear?"

Dezi winked. "Sounds like a chance to do you another solid there, babe."

She rolled her eyes. "Yeah, Dez, I'll owe you." And she ran off.

The unloading progressed nicely. Abby ran from trucker to trucker, reminding them not to forget their personal pets, counting a pregnant tabby cat, a pair of bunnies, a male German shepherd, an aquarium of mice (rescued no less) and a female poodle. Her fear of trying to persuade the truckers to join their refuge no longer worried her as they all expressed their gratefulness over the shelter. She secretly shuddered at what their reactions would be when they realized what they were *really* in for.

She loaded Karen, their ex-copilot, with suitcases from Mama Diaz. Loaded down heavily, Karen caught up with Dezi to climb the hill that led into the woods.

Echo and the dogs stood to the side, waiting to bring up the rear with Abby.

"Go, go, go." She moved everyone on as they tried to encourage her to join them.

Abby scanned the dark houses in the neighborhood wondering why they failed to attract any curious eyes. *Must all be hunkered down in their basements.* No sooner did the thought cross her mind when she spotted a small figure running down the hill towards her, nothing less than a turtle in his small hands. *Kimir. Oh, no.*

"What are you doing outside at this hour, Kimir?"

The young boy stopped in front of Abby, breathless. "I watched every day for Scotty to come back. I want the monster in his shirt to fix my turtle again. Something's wrong with his shell. It's all soft. And he won't eat anymore." Kimir started to cry. "He won't eat his favorite donuts."

"Donuts? That's not what a turtle should eat."

"Where's Scotty? I need him."

Abby made a quick decision. She knelt down and pointed to the trail of animals disappearing over the hill. Glancing toward the last truck, she spotted Crystal hooking her pig up to its halter and leash. Kimir's tear-stained face and dark beseeching eyes pleaded with her for help; a simple request from a little boy who counted the biggest thing in his life to be the health of his turtle.

"See that nice lady over there? She's taking her pig to Scotty. Crystal. Over here." Crystal trotted her pig over to Abby. "Can you take Kimir up the hill with you? Help him find Scotty."

"Sure. Come on, doll, we have to hustle." She took Kimir's hand and started for the hill leading into the woods. Kimir glanced back at Abby, lost and pitiful.

"It's okay, Kimir, I'll be right behind you in five minutes." She smiled encouragingly. As she reviewed the remaining trucks, she felt a strong aura probe her mind.

"It is time, Sister Abby. There is no time left. We must go now." Abby noticed that Mimi, Penny, Barney and Echo remained behind waiting for her.

"Abby, come on." Jose ran down the hill, waving for her to come. She scooped up Echo and Mimi, heading for the hill.

"Come on, Penny, Barney. You big guys can walk."

Penny whined softly then stood, waiting for Barney. The aura gyrated. "My Barney is different, Sister Abby. He is sick. I need to cure him, put me down."

"Not now, Echo. Barney's fine." She glanced back to check on their progress as Barney stood, walking forward slowly, with Penny at his side. Jose met her at the base of the hill.

"Here, let me take Echo. Let's go . . . double time." They scaled the hill, plunging into the woods, following the well-marked trail, animal droppings marking the way in the moonlight. As they approached the huge granite rock, Penny ran ahead to follow Jose into the Hive. Abby paused to steal a last quick peek at the ever-present moon, wondering how long it would be before she enjoyed the pleasure of standing under it again. Hurrying on, she followed Jose into the Hive.

The iconic moon sent its silvery beams down to the quiet neighborhood on Lily Pond Road, illuminating the silent homes; the abandoned tractor trailers motionless, no movement anywhere. Cool air settled to the ground as wisps of fog floated over the backyards where the laughter of children sounded, just a fragment of elusive memory mocking the moon. Crickets sent their nightly message to the gleaming globe, grateful for its magnetic presence. A red fox skimmed the edge of the forest, startled by the unfamiliar smell of cooling elephant dung, shivering at the image of the beast that had left its calling card on the edge of its territory. The fox picked up the trail of other canines, following the scent that led toward a huge boulder he knew well. A sound perked his ears. Cautiously, the fox crept through the underbrush where he came to a stop.

Three yards from the brush lay a medium-sized white dog with curly hair. The dog whined, its body shaking with tremors and seizures. The body stilled; then the dog's head rose. Struggling to its feet, the disorientated dog walked in a circle, its legs trembling. Its body seized again, falling to the ground. The fox moved, causing the underbrush to rustle. The dog glanced at the spot where the fox hid, his tail thumping a lonely message of hope, then fading and still.

The moon cast a beam on the clearing, the fox trembling as he watched the light in the white curly-haired dog's eyes dim and fade.

The fox stood rooted to his spot in the underbrush. After a time, he crept slowly up to the body of the white dog, sniffing . . . sensing the warmth of the body saying goodbye. Suddenly the fox raised its head to the air, his nose to the east and, in a blink, disappeared into the woods, leaving the forgotten white curly-haired dog named Barney alone under a moon that mourned.

# Chapter 10

Abby and Jose marched down the corridors of the cavern; what Echo called the Hive. Jose was the only one other than Echo who had explored the depths of the Hive.

Appraising the walls, she noticed they appeared coated with a thick, viscous, vaguely undulating layer of glop, almost as if it lived. *Well, that can't be possible.* She felt pleasantly cool, breathing in an overtly organic odor, suddenly feeling a sense of déjà vu. Abby scanned the walls, trying to locate the source of light that enabled them to traverse the corridor so nimbly.

Suddenly Echo bucked in Jose's arms. Her aura flashed painfully, forcing Abby to drop Mimi, sinking to the hard floor to hold her temples, the aura nasty and black.

"*Help . . . I need, I need.* Let me go, Brother Jose. My Barney is still outside. Let me down." Echo squirmed out of Jose's arms and headed back to the cavern opening. Without warning, they were tossed up in the air as the ground shook.

*The next bomb has arrived.*

"*Echo, come back, girl!* Echo." Jose picked himself up and ran toward the cavern opening. Abby screamed.

"No, Jose . . . Echo, stop! *Please don't go out there.*" She grabbed Mimi and Penny, who tried desperately to follow. If indeed the bomb had exploded in Manhattan, they would feel the devastating aftershock this far away. She didn't know enough about radioactivity to guess how far it could reach. She didn't even know what kind of bomb had destroyed Las Vegas.

As she lay sprawled on the floor of the cavern, Cobby and Kane appeared, taking the dogs from her and pulling her to her feet. She adjusted her shirt, smoothing it back down over her wings.

"Jose and Echo," she sobbed. "They went back for Barney after the shock." Kane turned to his father.

"Dad? Want me to go after them?"

*"Absolutely not.* We don't know what's out there. Come on, Abby. We need to get deeper. Everyone else is in a huge cathedral further up. They're scared shitless and ready to bolt. Most of the animals are oddly calm but we need you to take charge. It might be time to clue us all in to what this is really all about. Jose can take care of himself."

Cobby's stern voice snapped her out of her panic. She hiccupped, admitting to herself that she better get a grip. *Fast.*

"I don't know how you and Echo managed to leave Barney behind." Kane sounded peeved. "For Christ's sake, they were glued to the hip."

Abby's face burned as she remembered Echo's entreaties as they ran into the woods. *Oh, my God. It's my fault. Echo knew and I didn't listen.*

Very shortly they spilled into a large cathedral-style room. The dark rock ceiling rose almost three stories; people huddled on one side, animals on the other. Johno and the keepers huddled apart from everyone else; the larger elephants restless. Tobi kept a strong matriarchal position between her small herd and the big cats, sending an occasional warning trumpet their way.

As Abby made her way to the crowd huddled with their pets, Scotty's voice rang out. "Where's Jose and Echo? Where's Barney? Abby, what's happening?" A chorus of voices followed, everyone shooting questions at her, the truckers the worst.

Crystal stepped up, yelling at everyone to *"Shut the hell up for a minute."* Sitting back down, she said, "Now, one at a time."

No one spoke; the silence was awkward and reeking of belligerent fear. Out of the void, a watchful damaged voice demanded answers. Ginger Mae stood up to challenge Abby.

"You promised us. You said we would be safe. We can't stay here. It's a cave, for heaven's sake. We have no food or water. And how long do you think it will be before these cats decide we look good to them?"

The swelling around her mouth had improved enough to allow her bitter tone to project loud and clear. The truckers started shouting again, calling Abby a fool and worse. Her head whipped around as someone called her a stupid bitch.

"Why don't you shut the fuck up?" Scotty jumped to his feet, quick to defend his sister.

Mama Diaz sat stoically, her arms around Bonnie and Emma, trying to cover their ears. Kimir and his turtle found Clyde to latch on to, bucking each other up. Abby prayed Clyde's grandfatherly maturity would be a strong influence on Kimir when he freaked out about not being allowed to go home.

"All right, all right."

All heads turned as Jose entered the room with Echo trailing behind, her wobbling gait stumbling and chaotic. Jose stopped in the middle of the room and dropped to his knees on the floor. He gently set down the bundle in his arms, removing his jacket from Barney's lifeless body. Echo caught up and waddled over, throwing herself across the dog.

Abby snapped out of her shock as Scotty and Chloe knelt down, tears dripping quietly to anoint the cold body of the sweet grateful dog that never stopped begging for love.

Abby watched as everyone stared in wonder, observing the tableau that included a very strange-looking golden creature that they recognized did not belong to this world.

Echo suddenly sat up, detaching from Barney's cold body to wobble over to the side, then collapsed on the floor next to Penny and Mimi. Everyone watched as Abby talked to the creature.

"Echo, I'm so sorry, I didn't realize." Her voice sounded beaten and low, tentative and pleading. She sat next to Echo on the floor. As she tried to pick Echo up, the creature wiggled out of her arms. Abby sent an aura to Echo that remained rebuffed.

"Please don't freeze me out, girl. You know we all loved Barney too." Silence. Everyone watched; the truckers frozen in shared incredulousness. Abby's tears dropped freely, yet Echo did not relent.

"Well now, if you're all finished crying over the funky thing there, maybe you could tell us where the supplies are that you mentioned. I could sure use a little something to wet my whistle on. How 'bout you all?" one of the truckers said. Another struggled to his feet, a scrawny middle-aged guy with the German shepherd, his hands on his dog's leash visibly trembling.

"Look, I'm a little shook up, so you have to excuse me." He pointed to Abby's group of huddled refugees. "Do you mind telling us who these people are? This is just a gig I got filling in for a buddy. He didn't say anything about trucking people from the airport. I know the bombs aren't your fault but I have a sneaking feeling something else is going on here."

"Yeah."

"Yeah—what the fuck . . ."

"How 'bout some answers?"

"What the hell is that creature thing over there?"

"What's with the dead dog?"

Angry voices and suspicious questions aimed their ruthless poison at Abby. She slipped her fingers under her glasses to remove lingering tears.

Jose crossed to her side, his arm wrapped protectively around her against the angry onslaught. Abby opened her mouth to speak when she fell awkwardly on her butt, Jose landing painfully on top of her, the cavern shaking from what they horrifyingly supposed could only signify another bomb.

The elephants trumpeted in consternation as the babies fell over, unsteady on their feet. A lion snarled and the dogs whined, clinging tightly to the closest warm body.

In the melee, Abby's glasses fell off, radiating golden swirls around the cavern.

"Holy fuckin' shit."

"Oh, my God."

"What's wrong with her?"

The truckers shrank away from Abby as she stood to face them. The odor of fear and fright mixed with the organic smells from the animals, causing her stomach to roll.

Abby glanced over at the wildlife, strengthened by the improbable sight of a magnificent Tobi standing her ground against an assortment of twenty five awesome predators and a twenty-five-pound male turtle that was determined to sort through a pile of elephant dung, happy as a pig in . . .

"There is nothing wrong with me."

Abby turned her head to find Scotty and Jose at her side. Behind them stood Cobby and Kane. She gazed into Cobby's eyes, recognizing the quiet support she fervently needed to lean on. She placed a hand on Jose's arm, raising her eyebrows, seeking assent.

Scotty spoke out to the crowd. "You want answers? You got it."

As the truckers gasped in astonishment, the three removed their shirts and remaining glasses. Shaking out their wings amid astounded exclamations, Abby realized they would never again be forced to disguise who they were. She felt poking fingers on her legs.

Gazing down, she discovered Echo holding open her arms to be picked up, recriminations forgotten. Abby bent over to pick up the creature, setting her on her hip to proudly stand before the survivors, the golden glowing commonality between the creature and the three humans perfectly clear as four sets of luminous eyes faced, quite likely, the last of the human race that would be assured of surviving Armageddon.

# Chapter 11

"Mommy, Abby's beautiful." The child's voice rang out in the stunned silence, the atmosphere changing from belligerence to reverence. And fear, always the fear.

"Well, I guess I was right about you after all. I knew you were more than you pretended to be." Ginger Mae rubbed the side of her face, her pronouncement reeking with resentment.

"I don't know what this attitude is about. You must realize Abby just saved your life again. Would you rather we'd left you back in Sarasota with what we left behind of Armoni? Is that what you wanted for Daisy?" Scotty defended his sister's actions, shutting Ginger Mae up.

"Peter, you've been awfully quiet the whole trip. Are you okay?" Peter raised his head displaying a sickly, resentful grin, his owl eyes unblinking, glasses askew and unnoticed. "What do you want me to say, Abby? My life already got shot to shit the day ole Ginger Mae walked into it." Ginger Mae turned on him like a starving vampire at a blood buffet.

"You were all over me, couldn't wait to have me to yourself, so don't get all sanctimonious on me. You aren't the one left with this." She pointed to her face and turned away to let her bitter resentment smolder in private.

"Excuse me, eh, Abby, if you don't mind, I need to know what is going on here? Who are you? What do you want with us?" Crystal knelt on the floor, her arms around her pig, who tried mightily to stretch as far as he—or she—could on its leash, just dying to root in the elephant dung with the turtle.

Abby prepared to speak, flexing her wings and her tail doing the stretch it had long waited for. She watched the faces of the people before her. There were no signs of fear on the faces she knew well. Just acceptance and was that respect on some?

The truckers presented a problem, though. If they didn't accept the situation and fought to leave, she couldn't allow that. She didn't know how she would stop them, but she couldn't have them on the loose, talking about the cavern. They would be swamped by humanity as word spread about a safe place to wait out the catastrophe. Little did anyone know the wait would be a mighty long one.

"Hey, babe." Dezi's impudent voice shook her from her reverie. She watched as Jose took a step toward him.

"Hey, hey, now. I don't mean no disrespect." Abby placed her hand on Jose's arm, restraining him.

"You better watch your tongue, buddy. You don't know who you're talking to." Jose's clenched fist relaxed as Abby's intervention calmed him down. Crystal opened her mouth to speak again but found herself silent as one of the other female truckers stood up, the one with the rescued mice.

"My name's Gloria. We haven't met formally. My contact has been through Peter. I would like to know one thing." Gloria teetered on her tiny feet, her two-hundred-and-fifty-pound frame threatening to topple her over.

"What is it, Gloria?" Abby asked. Gloria cleared her throat nervously, her plump black face shiny with nervousness.

"Are you all angels?" Abby glanced quickly at her brother and her boyfriend, a suggestion of a smile tugging at her lips. She wrapped her arms around them both.

"Believe me, my brother is no angel, but yes, I often think of Jose as an angel." She reached out to give Jose a hug and Scotty a punch on the arm. Her levity helped to relax them a bit. Gloria cleared her throat again, her tone suggesting she failed to recognize the humor in her question.

"I'm not comfortable with your answer, so if you don't mind . . ." Her voice cracked and started to shake. "Ummm, I think it would be best if me and my mice just let ourselves out the back door. Anyone else want to come?"

Gloria started to edge away, picking up her diminutive aquarium with its plastic wheel and huddle of wild mice.

"I'm sorry to tell you this, but . . ." Before Abby could complete her pronouncement, the cavern filled with an ethereal glow emanating from a corridor that disappeared deeper into the Hive.

The group of truckers recoiled. Gloria shuddered and cowered over her mice, preparing to run.

Abby broke away from Jose, taking tentative steps toward the light as she remembered why the cavern felt familiar, hoping . . . All eyes focused on the golden swirls encased in the light, transcending anything their minds could conjure. And then they appeared.

Netty, Wil and Baby stepped into the cavern to be greeted by a stupefying silence. Baby stepped forward, a young tabby kitten trailing comfortably under his arm. They watched as Echo scrambled out of Abby's arms to wobble over to Baby.

The two creatures stood silent, glowing eyes reflecting wildly, faces stoic. Baby reached up with one long leathery finger to trace patterns on Echo's face. Echo reached out to stroke Baby's kitten.

Gloria opened her mouth to speak, but was soundly hushed by Dezi. They watched as Echo touched Baby's face with her slender finger then placed a hand on his shoulder, guiding them both to where the dead dog lay on the hard floor of the cavern.

Baby squatted down, releasing her kitten to pat Barney's cold body reassuringly. Echo turned to Scotty then bent over to awkwardly scoop Barney's body up in their arms as Scotty rushed over to help them lift.

Together they maneuvered Barney's body to a wall of the cavern where they held him high, kissing his head lovingly. They pushed him toward the wall where he was sucked into the organic membrane lining the walls of the cavern and disappeared.

"Oh, shit." The soft exclamation came from someone in the crowd on the floor. Abby heard the restless anxiety pass through the crowd, breath held as everyone turned back to the two mesmerizing adults still standing at the back of the cavern.

Abby hurried over to Netty, suddenly shy. Ignoring the people in the cavern, Netty took Abby into her arms, encircling her with her wings. She held her hand up to Abby's ear as a drop of brilliance fell into her hand.

"You no longer need this assistance, my dear. I will always be available to you now to answer any of your questions and to help you through the next chapter of your life with us in the Hive."

Netty released Abby, glancing softly at Wil. Her voice filled with the same loving pride heard in the voices of women in love for millennia all over the world.

"Allow me to introduce you to my husband, Wil. We are the Elders." She drew Abby and Wil toward the others. Wil's smile swept the room, including them all in his powerful gaze. His muscled arms stood out in bulging relief as he gently flexed his fine down-covered wings. His lion-like tail hovered in the air, occasionally reaching out to brush subtly against Netty.

"We are happy to finally meet you. Netty and I have waited for your arrival for a very long time. The Womb, along with both of us, is here to help your transition from your old world to the new one that awaits you after the planet heals from the destructive forces wrought by humans. You might say you are the lucky few."

"Are you shitting me?" The voice emerged from within the group of truckers, a large red-faced, red-headed man, his arm wrapped around the neck of a black standard poodle.

"And you are?"

"My name is Billy Susseman. I'm from Atlanta."

"Billy, do you have a problem I can help you with?" When Wil focused all his attention on Billy, he backed down, losing some of his steam. His voice faltered as he inquired, "Transition . . . Womb . . . new world? I think someone made a mistake. I don't know what you're talking about. Somehow, I got mixed up with you people." His hand made a sweeping gesture to include everyone. "I think the best thing would be for me to go. You want to go with me, Gloria?"

Gloria stood, mice in hand, ready to support Billy.

Wil raised his hand. "I am sorry, sir, but I do not think you want to go back out there. Millions have already died. There will be more bombs. This is just the beginning. The famines will start next, civilization will break down completely. No electricity, no machines. No gasoline, no air conditioning, little drinking water, no laws. Savagery." His voice slowed to a knowing hiss. "Every savage capability of man will become magnified. Is that what you want to go back to? How long do you think your dog will last after the grocery stores are empty?"

Billy leaned away reflexively, glancing down at his poodle. Gloria slowly let her big butt flop back down on the hard cavern floor with a splattering thud as Billy searched wildly into frightened faces. Not recognizing any support, Billy sat down with a lonely whimper as Netty began to speak, her voice confident and earnest.

"Excuse me, darling, I must get back to my duties. Come along, Baby . . . you will visit with Echo later. We must prepare the little surprise."

Netty coaxed the other creature to her side. After kissing Wil goodbye, she waved to everyone, sent a special smile to Abby, picked up Baby and swept out of the room, her golden beauty disappearing into the corridor.

Jose stepped forward, his hands held in a consolatory fashion. "I'm with you guys. I might resemble the Elders, but I'm in the dark just as much as you are." He joined the rest of the crowd, sitting down next to Chloe for comfort.

Wil nodded his head. "Well then, please make yourselves comfortable and I will begin."

# Chapter 12

Whining softly, he fought to understand why his paws lacked traction on what he supposed was the floor. He whimpered, his insecurity heightened as he realized Echo was not with him to allay his fears.

Slowly, he realized the crushing pain that had forced him to fall behind no longer deviled him. His breathing felt eased and comfortable. His heart beat normally, no longer threatening to explode inside his aging rib cage.

He gazed up at the sky, absent of the friendly moon that had always reliably guided him. His dry nose explored the air, searching for the scents of his masters and his mistress, sending a silent woof of apology for not being able to keep up.

A sickening feeling of disorientation made him dizzy. A piercing light focused directly on his eyes, pain forcing him to squint and leak a tear.

He suddenly picked up a scent. A scent he remembered from far back in his puppy memories. His oldest and most treasured memories of his mama and his squirmy littermates before he had been cruelly yanked away to face the ugly world that had slapped him down until found by Papa Diaz so long ago.

The scent reminded him of himself when he was a puppy; the warm, clean, slightly poopie smell that belonged to newborns. He thought he heard voices, a lilting mistress voice. And the welcoming pressure of the golden aura that his beloved Echo used to talk to him . . . yet he failed to understand any words.

He began to tire, longing for a nipple to suckle and a nap. As his mouth opened to yawn, he felt hands holding him to insert a warm rubber nipple into his seeking mouth and he began to suckle, finally drifting into the sleep that brought happy dreams to a tiny newborn puppy that remarkably bore the memories of a life already lived.

# Chapter 13

Wil scanned the faces sitting on the floor, all gazing up at him with an assortment of expressions. He could sense strong emotions: fear, bitterness and wonder. The cavern roiled with the odors of musky wildlife and unwashed bodies. All very natural, all expected. He knew they would have no trouble adjusting to their new way of life physically, but the mental toll might be too much for many of them.

His eyes strayed over to Scotty, taking his measure. He appeared to be a strong lad, sensitive and hopefully courageous. He would need to be if he truly meant to be the salvation of his species. If he was *The One*, time would tell, for they would have much more than their share of time.

"I understand your confusion . . . and your fear." He waved his hand over his own figure. "I went through something similar myself, a long time ago. Perhaps someday I will tell you the story of how Netty and I met Baby and were saved by the Womb."

Wil resisted mocking their incredulous faces, knowing soon enough the bravado and disbelief would fade when faced with the unremitting boredom that awaited them as the world above settled down and cleared to make way for the new life that would come.

Scotty spoke up boldly. "Are you going to tell us why we were transformed into Elders?"

Wil nodded his head, pacing slowly in front of the gathering, his bare feet soundless on the hard rock floor. *Where to start?*

"I'm sorry to say, Scotty . . . the fact that you all are Elders truly was a simple mistake. It is forbidden to heal a human with the powers of a minion."

To the rest of the crowd, he explained, "Echo and Baby, our creatures that we love as much as our own lives, are minions. They serve at the pleasure of the Womb. They are like little scientists combing the planets from galaxy to galaxy monitoring the life placed by the Womb, including here on Earth. That is how we met. We each clashed with misfortune, needing to be healed, which is what started our changes. Baby was damaged when he finished his journey to earth. He could not remember the laws or his mission, allowing us to heal and convert to Elders. The healing unleashed a dormant enzyme that sped up our evolution or, should I say, devolution."

"But, dude, you look a lot like the little creatures." Dezi's observations were met with universal nods and agreement from the gathering as they contemplated the resemblance between the shimmering wings they shared with the creature called Baby, not to mention their mesmerizing eyes and the golden glows from the same fine fur.

"Well, it is only natural, since our original ancestors were created by them from one of their own cells." His statement was met with silence, faces uncomprehending.

"Yes, you did not know? The minions went against the law of the Womb and created life in their own image. As punishment, the Womb stripped them of their immortality. The Womb allowed the new life to evolve here on earth where it could be watched as it evolved. We were given chance after chance to redeem ourselves but failed in the eyes of the Womb. Too aggressively bloodthirsty it appears. The minions were sent to begin the process of eliminating our species. It is what they refer to as an intervention, Intervention 6609 to be exact. That is exactly how many times they have intervened on one planet or another. And it is not the first time it has been done on this planet.

"Do you recall the dinosaurs, another species that was ruining the planet? There were just not enough resources to maintain them in the long run. A simple meteor strike combined with extreme volcanic activity started the chain of evolution over again. Of course, the Womb supplied the raw material for new life after the glaciers wiped the plate clean.

"Baby was sent to Earth to begin the process again while saving most other life forms this time. Unfortunately, Baby was pregnant with Echo. He gave birth to Echo upon landing. I am sorry to say that Baby has never fully recovered from the effects of the journey and his rebirth, he is still damaged. His poor brain failed to fully recover. But we love and are delighted by him just the same. He is like a child to us."

"What the *fuck* are you talking about?" Billy shouted at Wil, clearly unwilling to accept what he was hearing.

"Echo and Baby were pre-empted by our own miserable leaders in their atomic war games. I do not know how this started, but when the Womb realized what was in store for the planet, it ordered Netty to persuade Abby to rescue these animals. The Womb is fond of the rest of the creatures of this planet, always has been. They are the innocent. I am so, so disappointed you were unable to rescue the rest from the other zoo." Abby hung her head in shame.

"We understand, my dear. You did your best. The fact that you and the other people have managed to survive is meaningless to the Womb, but we have made provisions for your survival. We will take you on a tour as soon as Netty returns."

Cobby stood up facing Wil, his expression puzzled. "This story you're telling us. It sounds like you're trying to say there's no God. How can that be?"

"My dear good man, you do not understand, do you?"

"Understand what. . . . exactly?" Cobby's perplexed voice evinced a slow dawning horror. "No . . . you can't mean?"

"Yes, of course . . . that is exactly what I mean. The Womb *is* God."

The stunned silence reverberated through the cavern, open mouths sagging with confusion as the crowd tried to absorb the truth that contradicted everything man knew about his past and all that so many relied on to give hope to futile lives.

Johno's melodic African voice spoke first. "Sir, you truly look like an angel to me. Are you saying there are no chosen ones? That we are all the same?"

Wil stopped his pacing. "I am sorry to say this, but not only are you all the same, but the only chosen ones are the *other* creatures on this planet. The Womb has no affection for our species. We have evolved with so much, yet we continue to subjugate all species on this planet as we anoint ourselves rulers of all. The Womb has had enough. If our species were allowed to continue, we would eventually extinguish all other life, to the detriment of the planet. The Womb loves this planet. The decision was made for intervention, hence Baby's mission. You might want to call him an intervention specialist. As I said before, this is not the first time. It has been necessary only six thousand, six hundred and nine times, in all of space and time—an almost unnoticeable drop in the bucket. Unfortunately, as you know, it appears that the intervention did not come soon enough. Your politicians seem to be doing Baby and Echo's job for them."

From the corridor at the back of the cavern came a yip, sounding like the high energy bark from a puppy. The golden light brightened and Netty entered the cavern with Baby and his kitten on her hip and a tiny puppy with curly white hair tripping at her bare feet.

She stopped, allowing the puppy to advance into the room. The puppy's nose rose to sniff the air. It froze as Echo shuffled and bobbed as fast as she could toward the puppy. A switch turned on in the puppy's eyes, his tail a metronome of pleasure. He began to whine, high pitched and painful as he rushed toward Echo to be embraced.

"Gee, the creature sure likes dogs," Bonnie said, her sister cooing, trying to coax them to her side. Netty strode further into the cavern.

"Young lady, this is no ordinary puppy, this is Barney . . . Echo's Barney." Scotty stood, turning to Netty, yet keeping his eyes glued to the curly-haired white puppy now sitting in Echo's lap.

"That isn't possible." Scotty whistled. The puppy's head popped up, and he stared at the crowd of people spread around the floor. Without missing a beat, the puppy tripped over his own chubby belly in his excitement to welcome Scotty, then ran unprompted to Jose and Abby. The three of them felt an aura of lightness engulf them.

"My Barney is back, Brother. I knew he would be. Sister Netty and Brother Baby promised. I am happy. My Barney is happy. He is the same, only better. His heart is brand new. Everything is wonderful now."

Scotty suddenly remembered back to Bird Key, to the night Echo plucked hairs out of the coats of Barney and Mimi, depositing them in tiny bottles that she carried around in her fanny pack.

"Echo, where are those bottles you carried in your fanny pack?"

"They are no longer in my possession, Brother Scotty."

Their thoughts were interrupted by the voice of Netty. "I have the containers of Barney's hair. The other dog too. We planned this some time ago. Animals can be cured but do not possess the minion enzymes that will enable them to achieve immortality like humans do, at least not without assistance. So as an accommodation to Echo, we agreed to save Barney. We knew the time would soon come."

"An accommodation? You saved him? How can that possibly be? Barney was dead, for Pete's sake."

Netty worked her way over to where Echo and Barney frolicked. Kneeling down she ran her fingers over the hard ground so Barney could chase them. She laughed with delight, enjoying his antics, then glanced up.

"Fear not, young Scotty. There is much you do not know. I am sure you recognize the existence of the theoretical soul? Well, the soul, which is in actuality the mind, the energy of the brain, can be rescued from the body as long as some of the brain matter can be retrieved and not much time has elapsed. We need but one brain cell. It was a simple matter to clone a new puppy from the follicle of one of the hairs Echo plucked from Barney. I merely had to collect them and grow the cells into a new Barney as the time grew near. The Womb made the mind transfer and here we all are."

Scotty thought he had her. "And how did you collect the hairs from here? We lived in Sarasota."

"Well, I simply came to Sarasota, silly. Do you not see I have the same wings you do?"

Jose interrupted, his face flushing with blood, his heart visibly pumping madly. "Does that mean we can fly?"

"Of course, my dear, we have many forms of flight."

With that, Netty snapped her wings, enfolding them around her body to disappear. Her voice came from the front corridor that opened into the cavern. She appeared, entering the room, not a golden hair out of place.

"Just a demonstration, I could just have easily flown. We have plenty of time for more questions. And endless time to teach you the things you will need to know."

"Wait a minute now, lady. Did you forget about us?" Voices from the crowd rose.

"Yeah, what are *we* going to do?" The din of frightened and indignant voices grew.

Wil joined Netty to stand at her side, a wide smile on his face. "I think you will be pleased with the arrangements the Womb has made for you. If you can be just a bit more patient, I am going to collect all the animals and escort them to their separate living spaces."

He eyed Tobi and her herd. "Johno? I understand you and your men can control the elephants without the need for implants?"

"Implants? I do not understand. What are implants?" Johno's face reflected anxiety, his arms strapped protectively around the neck of the recovered infant. "We would be most appreciative if we could just bed down with our elephants. The babies need us. The juveniles, even Tobi, would be disturbed if we were separated."

Wil nodded his head.

"I understand. Please remain behind while I remove the rest of the wildlife. The elephants will remain with people. Any other animals need to remain behind?"

Jose raised a finger. "I need the primates and the dogs with us. The primates have implants."

"Okay, in time some of the other animals will become habituated and you might wish to make new arrangements. Netty will show you around as soon as I am gone. I will join you tomorrow to discuss the new laws."

An undercurrent of murmuring charged the atmosphere as the crowd watched Wil signal to the animals to follow him to the back of the cavern.

Quiet voices whispered anxiously among the group as the procession departed. It became clear as everyone discussed Wil's pronouncement and awaited the tour of their new home that everything they were taught as children about their faiths and the world was wrong. The difficulty of processing the new truth overwhelmed them as they attempted to absorb their incredible situation. A deep feeling of insecurity insidiously infected them as their heads reeled with the announcement of the discussion of 'new laws'.

Soon the cavern emptied of all the wildlife except the elephants, the dogs, the primates, the turtles they decided could go wherever they pleased, and one quiet and glorious Siberian tiger named Caesar.

"Oh, no." Scotty sighed as he realized the big cat's magnetic jeweled eyes bore into his own. Chloe traced Scotty's line of sight to the tiger.

"Is he the one that pissed all over you on the boat? Why's he looking at you like that?" Chloe didn't appear concerned, just curious.

"Okay, ladies and gentleman, if you'll just follow me?"

Scotty and Chloe scrambled to their feet with a backwards glance to Caesar. They gathered the dogs and fell in line to follow the crowd that clustered around Netty. As they disappeared into the back corridor of the cavern, Scotty cast another glance to the rear, not surprised to find Caesar padding softly toward them, eyes like lasers, only for him.

# Chapter 14

Lorna and the girls drove down the highway at about thirty five miles an hour. Lorna's time behind the wheel counted about eight or nine hours now. They had made good time when they left Tampa. The highways were jammed but the traffic moved at a good clip.

They drove about four hours north of Tampa before the freeway slowed to a crawl. Four hours later, Lorna noticed they were getting low on gas. In the last three hours they had averaged fifteen miles an hour with all the stops and starts in the flow of traffic. She decided they had better pull off the freeway and attempt to find a gas station without a huge line. The last thing she wanted to do was tap into her precious supply of gas stored in the trunk.

She thought perhaps she should find a motel for her and the girls to rest. Eight hours of driving in heavy traffic under extreme stress would take a toll on the best of drivers and she was waging a constant battle with her eyelids as it was.

Lorna pulled off the freeway ramp to find herself in a rural town without a main street. She drove along deserted streets, most houses boarded up, lumber strapped to windows, shades drawn. She found it difficult to ascertain if people were hiding inside to protect against possible bombing or if they had fled down the freeway, hoping they would have a life and a homestead to return to after the madness.

Within a few blocks, she came upon a gas station, the attendants sporting guns strapped to their hips like old-time western gunslingers. Grim expressions told her they were in no mood to suffer fools. Getting in line, she and the girls faced a long wait. She prayed the station would still have gas to sell by the time her turn came.

As she watched the cars leave the station and head toward the ramp for the expressway, she realized the station's customers all came from out of town.

"Girls, see the stars coming out? How would you like to stop and rest? We can take a nap and have a bite to eat before we get back on the road." Suzy sat in the front seat between her grandmother and her big sister. She sat curling her short legs up so her feet reached her mouth where she tried to suck on her toes, cramming them in as she mumbled softly.

"Gram, I have to go potty."

Lorna glanced down at her doll baby. Suzy's grin stretched from cheek to cheek as her sister, Jennifer rolled her eyes. "Can you wait a while longer, sweetie? There's only six more cars in front of us. Then we'll find a motel."

"Okay, Gram." Her slobber-covered toes reclaimed their spot.

"Do you think the TV will work, Gram? My show comes on in an hour." Jennifer sounded perturbed and annoyed. Her demeanor had screamed *bored to death* since they had left Tampa. Lorna's efforts to engage her in games fell on affronted ears.

They finally reached the pumps and had the tank filled. Lorna breathed a sigh of relief, comforted with the shot of confidence a full tank of gas can give a girl. The attendant directed her to a motel along the road with the warning that they had better lock up their car real tight.

"Marauders and gangs love to prey on a car full of pretty women." He threw a wink Jen's way, getting a reluctant smile for his effort.

As they pulled into the crowded gravel parking lot of the two-story nondescript motel, Lorna prayed they would find an available room. Instructing the girls to keep the car locked, she pushed her way through the heavy lobby door to be met with screams.

The shabby lobby held a rough Naugahyde plaid sofa containing a chubby young teen with short black hair. A cheap plastic lamp on the floor appeared to have fallen off a small table next to the sofa, and the girl was fending off the attack of an older woman with a name tag pined to her nylon shirt that failed to completely cover her bloated stomach. The young girl's legs fought with the woman's fingers as she tried to wrench an apple out of the young girl's hands.

"If you don't give me that apple back, you little brat, I'm calling the cops. They'll make sure you have a nice place to sleep tonight, though you won't like the food, I can assure you." She stopped struggling with the young girl as she spotted Lorna standing at the reception desk. She yanked the apple from the girl's hands, smoothed down her shirt and scampered behind the desk to put on her bright welcoming smile.

"Can I help you, madam?" Lorna's gaze shifted from the desk clerk back to the young girl on the sofa, who now sobbed into her elbow, hopelessness oozing from her defeated posture.

"Don't mind her, madam. She's just a transient, begging for food and a place to sleep." She leaned over the desk to holler at the girl.

"Move on now, you hear . . . before I decide to kick your ass again."

The chubby young girl picked up a knapsack at her feet and limped out the heavy door, briefly making eye contact with Lorna. In that split second, Lorna saw pain and panic.

Quickly checking into the motel, Lorna gathered her room key and purse to exit the reception door, scanning the parking lot for the young girl. Sitting on the lumpy gravel, the girl leaned up against the wall of the motel, her eyes focused skyward as if searching for the star that would wish a solution down into her lap.

"Hon, are you okay? Do you need some help?" Lorna waved to her grandchildren in the car as she knelt along the concrete wall of the motel. The young girl's eyes closed up like a trapdoor and a hand reached up to wipe away the evidence of tears.

"My name's Lorna. Where are your parents?"

The girl sighed, her eyes downward as she begrudgingly gave her name. "I'm Maryann. My parents are in Pennsylvania." She swallowed heavily, turning big sad cornflower eyes to Lorna.

"What in the world are you doing here, Maryann? Do you know about the bombs? Come on, come with me. Let's get you something to eat. You can stay with us for tonight." Maryann protested as Lorna forced her to her feet, directing her to the car. She motioned to Jen to unlock the car door as she shooed them over to squeeze Maryann into the back seat. Maryann stopped resisting as Lorna introduced her to the girls.

"We can talk more after we get settled into our room. We have two beds so we can double up. All set?" Lorna started the car without waiting for a response, driving the car to the rear of the motel. They quickly unloaded the few things they would need, including just enough food to make sandwiches and some water bottles.

"Jen, please grab me those empties on the floor in the back seat. I think it would be wise to refill them from the tap."

"Oh, Gram, is that really necessary?" Lorna swallowed, counting to ten.

Settling inside their room as best they could, Lorna pushed herself to make the sandwiches even as she longingly eyed the ramshackle beds. They girls took turns in the tiny bathroom without complaint.

"Gram, can I turn on the TV to watch my show?" Jen stood munching her sandwich, switching on the big clunky television, at least a decade old.

"I don't think your show will be on, hon. I'm sure everything has been pre-empted. We want to hear some news, anyway." Lorna reached into her bag for her hand lotion, inspecting her manicure. "Try one of the New York stations if you can get it, that's where we're headed. Grandpa is going to meet us in that area. He has a place that will keep us safe. It sounds like a huge bomb shelter."

"Gram . . . you better listen to this." Tears dripped from Jen's eyes as she ran to her grandmother. The other two girls glanced up from their eating, alarm in their eyes.

"Fox News sadly reports that our broadcast headquarters and that of NBC, CBS, and ABC have been hit. We are coming to you from our satellite office in Atlanta with the tragic news that at 11:25 p.m. Eastern Standard Time, the once iconic center of the financial world, New York City, was the target of the second bomb . . . President of the United States . . . to Canada . . . twenty five million . . . unaccountable suburbs . . . highest alert . . . shelters limited.

"In further news, reports are streaming in about the catastrophe in Israel. The United Nations Security Council urges calm as the

President decides how to respond to Iran's nuclear attack. Russia issues a stern warning against any U.S. interference. Officials regretting prior administration's capitulation to Russia of U.S. missile defense systems. North Korea on high alert."

Lorna snapped off the TV, her heart hammering painfully as she paced, raking her fingers through her frosted hair in cold horror.

Suzy sensed her frenzy, clutching her grandmother's legs to make her hold still. "Pick me up, Gram, pick me up."

She bent down to embrace the little girl, turning to Maryann. "Maryann, I'm sure you realize I can't just leave you here. Why don't you tell me how you got here and we'll try to figure out what to do."

Maryann quickly told Lorna the story of her parents in Port Jervis, Pennsylvania. When a wealthy couple from Connecticut advertised for a summer sitter for their two children she had jumped at the chance to get out of their poverty-stricken town for the summer. The couple planned to visit family in Naples, Florida, taking her along. They decided they no longer needed her services after other relatives showed up and, paying her a bonus, put her on a plane home that had a stop in Houston, Texas. Of course, the plane never made it out of Houston because of the grounding. So she had been hitching ever since. She had spent the last of her bonus money and had no place to sleep. She had just been caught stealing an apple by the unsympathetic motel clerk when Lorna walked into the lobby.

"You want to come along with us? You're much too young to be on the roads like this. It's too dangerous out there. We're headed to northwestern New Jersey, that's near where you live, isn't it?" Maryann gratefully nodded, getting an interested sidelong glance from Jen. Lorna prayed Maryann might exert a positive influence on her granddaughter, or at least keep her distracted during the drive. She reached into her bag for her alarm clock, setting it so they could get at least six hours sleep. She was afraid to sleep longer, not knowing what conditions they might wake up to.

*

The four females slept soundly in their cramped motel beds, the saggy mattresses no roadblock to the relief found in truly exhausted bone-weary sleep. No one noticed when the bed shook or the alarm clock fell off the cracked nightstand. All eyes missed the flicker of the ceiling lights in the bathroom or the fact that they failed to come back on. No ears heard the quiet tick, tick, tick of the air conditioner as it shut down. No one watched out the only window in the room as the neon lights in the parking lot shut off and the streetlights followed, casting all objects in nothing other than the silver wash of the relentless moon.

The night remained soundless, spooking a lonely stray behind the motel as she sniffed for discarded scraps, anxious to return to her litter and hide away from the daytime sun. She raised her head to howl as once again the beds in the hotel gently shook their occupants, who were sleeping soundly while the world imploded around them.


Lorna woke slowly, her consciousness resisting the urge to fully wake. She smiled in her sleep as a lingering dream of Clyde as a young man flitted through her mind, disappearing quickly as she tried to focus on the fact that the alarm hadn't rung.

Springing out of bed, she masked her shock as the light streaming in the window told her it was long past the time to rise. *Damn, we're late and better get on the road instantly.* Waking the girls she gave instructions to hurry.

Playing with the TV remote she experienced annoyance. The TV failed to turn on. The manual switch gave no better results. Peering out the window, she flinched as a noisy flock of what appeared to be army helicopters passed over the road.

Hustling the girls to the rental car, Lorna tried the radio. Nothing. Pulling around the front of the hotel, she encountered a group of men bashing in the windows of an SUV with what looked like an axe. They unlocked the door to raid the contents, before running off into the distance with their loot. Lorna thought it looked like foodstuff.

"Girls, lock the doors, I don't like the looks of this." She headed for the ramp of the freeway, anxious to make up some time. "Jen, I want you and Maryann to spread the lap blanket over the boxes of food. Pile your luggage on top. That's good, thanks girls."

"Gram, are we going the right way? Everyone else is driving the other way."

Lorna flipped her head around to the back seat, trying to keep an eye on the events outside the car. A line of stragglers walking in the opposite direction of their car thickened to a stream; people lugging possessions, children struggling to keep up. They shared one thing in common. They all looked scared shitless.

"I don't know, hon. Maybe something happened up in front of us." The traffic on their side of the road moved quickly, vehicles sparse. Lorna noticed the traffic next to her going the opposite way had finally dribbled to a halt. Slowing down, she pulled alongside a vehicle loaded with people and pets. She rolled down her window and waved, signaling she needed to talk.

"Yes? Can I help you, lady?" The man at the wheel sounded beaten down, his face greenish gray.

"Where are you coming from, sir? Something happen up there?"

"Lady, you gotta turn around. You have to get out of here fast. There's no telling how far the radiation goes."

"Radiation?"

He did a double take, looking at her as if she had just grown another head.

"Lady, where you been? The Russkies just dropped the bomb on Chicago last night. I heard reports D.C. got hit too. Stay away from the cities. You better take cover somewhere. The President ordered strikes. Don't worry, we'll massacre 'em. No telling when it'll be over or what shape we might be in. All the utility grids are down. Watch your gasoline. The pumps don't work." The line started to move. He waved. "You take care now." Lorna sped up the car, trying to locate an off-ramp. Her stomach threatened to roll over from the stress, her shock noticeable to the girls.

"Gram, what are we going to do now? Should we call Grandpa? He'll come get us."

"Grandpa isn't going to come save us, dummy. We're in shit deep trouble." Jen's voice sounded like she was holding back tears. Maryann reached around Jen's tender shoulders, offering her support. Jen leaned her head on Maryann's shoulder, both girls too young to help themselves, but old enough to understand their lives would never be the same.

Lorna pulled off the highway heading east. If the bomb had hit Chicago, which was north, they were far enough away to be safe. Eventually they would have had to turn east anyway. Now they would just meander through the center of the country and the small towns that hold it up.

As they exited the ramp, desperate vehicles decided to enter the ramp the wrong way in their panic to brave the freeway. They, too, came to a standstill. On the side of the road they noticed a crowd of jeering men and boys. Driving by slowly, Lorna witnessed a man on top of a young woman. Her clothes lay strewn on the ground as the man raped her. Two other men stood with their pants at their ankles, stroking their penises as they hovered over the figures on the ground while the rest cheered. What looked to be the victim's car stood nearby with the doors wide open, her purse on the ground and a child strapped in his car seat alone in the back. *Oh, my God.* Lorna sobbed as she pressed the window switch, rolling it down.

"*Leave her alone*, you sick bastards. I'm getting the cops."

"Hey, bitch, why don't you come join us?" They laughed and jiggled their penises at her.

"*Gram, drive*. Get us out of here." Jen sounded hysterical. She glanced in the back seat, at Maryann's shocked face and Jen sitting with her hands over her mouth. She watched in the rearview mirror as they drove away, hoping someone would be brave enough to help the poor woman. How could law and order fall apart so quickly? She pulled off to the side of the road, turned off the ignition and sobbed into her hands on the steering wheel. Suzy threw her arms around

Lorna, crying with her while the two other girls sat stunned in the back seat.

"There, there, baby, it's alright, Gram's okay." She patted Suzy on the head, groping in her purse for a tissue. She wiped her nose, feeling more in control.

"Sorry, girls . . . don't worry. I just let the moment get the best of me." Trying hard to smile, she reassured the girls. "Let's figure out what old Gram is going to do now." She stared out the window, let out a sigh while she wiped her nose again, and took out the map.

"Okay. I see where we can make good time. I think we might be safer if we stay on the country roads. Let's not lose this map, or we're sunk, okay, girls? Maryann, can you hold onto this for me?" She handed the map back to the girls and was rewarded by a brave smile from Maryann, her dark hair a halo of solemnness.

Lorna decided to drive until she dropped. She would hold off on telling the girls that they would have to sleep in the car tonight. She just found the idea of getting out of the car to face any strangers too daunting, too dangerous. Tapping her manicured fingers on the steering wheel, she brightened her voice for the girls. "We all set?"

Maryann cleared her voice from the back seat. "Lorna, I'm sorry, I have to go to the bathroom."

Suzy piped up. "Me too, Gram. I have to go."

Lorna's mind ground to a halt. *What to do?*

"Okay." She started the car, pulling further down the road until they pulled into a winding stone driveway that led to an old farmhouse. Pulling to the side of the drive, she opened her door.

"Girls, we're going to take turns going on the side of this drive. Hop out on your side and go now. Jen, you go after Maryann whether you think you have to or not. Suzy, you scoot over here. Let me help you."

Accomplishing the task amid much awkwardness, they set out again; doors locked and spirits repurposed. They drove for hours, sticking to the back roads, passing vehicles going in all different directions, seemingly like ants disturbed in the ant hill, panicked and directionless.

As the sun began to dip on the horizon preparing to bid goodnight, they found themselves alone on the road with a car displaying Maine license plates, the doors hanging open, the figure of a woman lying on the side of the road. They slowly rolled their car to a stop behind the woman's car. Lorna scanned the area for other lurking figures, still smarting from her cowardly behavior this morning.

"I'm going to check on this poor woman. You girls stay here, lock the door behind me."

"No, Gram, don't go." Suzy began to scream.

"No, please stay here. We can't help her. We need to go." The girls pleaded with her as she stepped outside the car, shutting the door firmly. Slowly making her way to the front of the Maine car, she glanced inside, seeing another baby car seat, but no baby.

As she hurried to the woman's side, she gasped at the woman's face. Raw skin peeled off her face flapped to the sides, her nose was smashed in, her features swollen and purple. There was little doubt she was dead. Lorna bent down to smooth the women's skirt down over her nude torso that evidenced her missing panties. Placing her hands together, she noticed a pale band of white skin on her ring finger, the ring missing. *Jesus Christ, is that all men can think of in a disaster, to revert to beasts? No—not beasts. Beasts don't rape and murder. That's what man does.* She reminded herself never to confuse the two.

Searching the area she found no trace of a baby or the woman's ID. Nothing would be accomplished by lingering. She had to think of the girls.

Skirting back to her rental, the girls unlocked the car and off they went.

"Gram, don't do that again. Don't leave us." Suzy stood up in her seat, stomping her feet, fear turning to anger. Jen spoke stoically from the back seat.

"Gram, you can't just leave us like that for a total stranger. What would Mom say?"

"Jennifer, you should be ashamed. The poor woman is dead. We don't go through life without considering the needs of others."

Jen and Maryann remained silent as they continued further down the road. They drove for five minutes when Lorna felt the car drive over something on the road. Her eyes flicked to the rearview mirror that reflected pieces of wood in the dim light, haphazardly resting on the road. Relief flooded through her as she prepared to seek a place to hide the car for the night. She knew she could drive another few hours but finding a safe place while she could still make out shapes in the fields made good sense.

She drove slowly, scanning the fields to the right and to the left, mysterious shapes far in the distance beckoning; a siren's call. She ignored all, hoping for a clump of trees near the road or a small trail to turn on to, afraid to drive across a field that threatened the car with hidden ruts.

As she continued down the road, the steering wheel suddenly pulled to the left, jerking her hand. As she readjusted the wheel, she felt a thud. The sounds came from one of the wheel wells; a flat? She banged her hands down on the steering wheel in frustration.

"Girls, I think we have a flat tire." She carefully braked the car, rolling to the side of the road. Everyone held their breath as Lorna scanned the area.

"I think I'll be okay. Lock the door behind me." Lorna stepped outside the car. Her driver's side tire was clearly flat. *Why now?* she wondered with exasperation.

Rummaging around in the trunk, she finally removed the tools she needed to change the tire. Now she smelled like the gasoline still stored in the trunk. Dragging the jack and the lug wrench to the front of the car, she wondered how hard it could be to change a tire.

"Now, you don't want to do that nasty job by yourself, do you?" The soft voice came out of the dusk like a warm breath on the back of her neck.

Startled, she turned to face a mild-mannered man, in his early forties, on a bicycle. He wore a pink rugby shirt with khaki shorts and expensive leather hiking boots. Strapped to his back was a large backpack.

She stared into his baby-blue eyes, noticing his wide, amused smile; teeth large and gleaming in the dusk; his thick brown curly hair expertly and expensively quaffed. The only thing out of place was a thick red welt sitting on his cheek like a worm drying out in the late-day sun.

"I didn't hear you." Lorna backed up against the car defensively.

"Sorry, I didn't mean to startle you. Where you headed?" Lorna relaxed as she succumbed to his friendly, nonthreatening manner.

"I'm trying to get to New Jersey to meet my husband."

"Madam, pardon me for saying so but you must be out of your mind. You'll never make it. New York took a direct hit. Where in Jersey you going?"

"I plan to skirt New York City by coming in through Pennsylvania. The northwestern part of the county is where we need to go."

The man shook his head. "Must be a special reason you want to go to all that trouble with your kids in the car. It's dangerous on the roads for a bunch of unarmed women. Don't you know the President said to take cover? There might be more bombs."

Lorna bristled at the inference that she couldn't take care of the kids. "My husband has a huge bomb shelter waiting for us. He said we'll be perfectly safe with plenty of supplies to wait this out. No matter how long it takes." Lorna placed extra emphasis on her statement, reasserting her female control of the situation.

The man, smiling widely, dismounted from his bike. "Well then, we better take a look at that tire of yours, can't have you driving off without it changed correctly. I'm Seth, by the way." He held out his hand to her. She extended hers for a shake, feeling calm strength in his grip.

Relaxing, she bent down to show him the tools. Seth parked his bike at the side of the road. Slipping off his backpack, he reached inside. Lorna held her breath while he searched the large pack to emerge with a high-powered flashlight. Lorna smiled with relief, making room for him at the tire.

Seth changed the tire in no time at all, amusing Lorna with funny quips as he wrestled with the tools. The girls in the car rolled down the windows, watching as he worked, offering heartfelt but useless suggestions, giving Lorna and Seth more reasons to laugh. The experience was a welcome relief from the tension they'd been under since they left Tampa.

"Well, look at that. You must have picked up a nail on the road somewhere." He pointed to the spot on the tire where Lorna saw an unusually large nail head sunk deep in her tire. She thought back to the pieces of wood strewn in the road miles back. There must have been a nail sticking out of the wood. What ass dropped wood in the road? It figured it would be her car that came along first.

"Why don't you pop your trunk and I'll put this inside. You never know, you might need it again. I'm sure you can have it fixed at a gas station . . . oh, sorry, I forgot for a moment." Seth sat back down on the ground, sighing deeply. He rubbed his hands against his forehead as if to push out the memory of the last two days. Lifting his head to face Lorna, she thought she noticed the sparkle of tears in his eyes. In a rush of emotion, the feeling of being in this together overtook her as she placed her arm on his shoulder, patting gently.

"Which way are you going, Seth?"

"I don't really know, Lorna. I'm just trying to stay one step ahead of the bombs. I guess I hoped to find a spot that no one would care enough to bomb, then settle down. What are you going to do now?" he asked.

Lorna glanced at her watch. "I was hoping to find a place to safely park the car when I got the flat. We need to get some sleep and eat something before I can drive anymore."

Seth's face brightened. "Lorna, what do you say if I hitch a ride with you? We can split the driving. That way you won't have to stop to sleep. We can get you to your husband in half the time."

Lorna was taken aback by the proposal yet sorely tempted, anything to get to Clyde as soon as possible. God knew, she could use a capable male presence if the situation turned dire. *Gosh, what to do?* Seth stared at her, a trusting light in his blue eyes, an encouraging smile on his lips.

"Oh, okay. Why not? This will be good for all of us."

Seth gave her a high five and, reaching into his backpack, withdrew a long length of rope to tie his bike to the roof.

After everything was stashed away, Seth slid behind the wheel with Lorna in front, Suzy sitting in her lap. Jen and Maryann fished out some sliced meat and bread from the food stock, passing out water and snacks. It wasn't long before all the women were sound asleep with Seth happily tooling down the road, on the way to Sussex County.

# Chapter 15

As Netty ushered the large group of people with their attendant animals and pets down a wide corridor, she paused in front of the first of two openings, one on each side of the corridor.

"Wil is in one of these rooms. Both rooms house the precious wildlife. They will be split into open chambers, giving them the ability to roam but protecting their privacy."

A voice from the crowd rang out, its bitter tones suggested Peter. "I think it's the height of ridiculousness to expect us to live cooped up with wild animals that will eventually kill us."

Netty halted, turning to face the voice, a serene smile on her face. "Oh, I'm so sorry. I completely forgot to invite you all to leave anytime you choose." She scanned the stunned faces, hearing no objections. "No takers? Well then, allow me to remind you once again. The Hive is here to protect the animals. They are what matters. The Womb is master here. The Elders and the minions serve the Womb. You have no role at all. Allow me to suggest that you keep your complaints to a minimum." Netty took her time to size up the reaction of the survivors, her golden eyes boring deep into their own.

Apparently satisfied, she added, "I'm sure you will be pleased the Womb has decided to use you to care for the animals. You will all become intimate with every single creature before long. That will be your new purpose for life. Servants to those you subjugated."

As a cry and hue erupted, Netty's magical laugh trickled over the crowd. "I know . . . life can be so ironic, yes?"

As the unrest of the crowd rose, Clyde stepped forward. "What's all the fuss, for Christ's sakes? You all love animals anyway. Look at you. Most of you have your own pets in your hands."

Dezi stepped forward, his hands held up in front of his body as if to ward off Clyde's words. "Dude, don't speak for me. I got no love lost for something this smelly and stupid." He pointed his skinny arm toward Tobi and her small herd. "Anything that can poop and piss like these mothers ain't worth a damn thing, and how we gonna feed 'em anyway, babe?"

"Dezi, Dezi, I can see you are a man of little faith. By the way . . ." Netty's eyes bore into his as she approached him, their noses inches apart. Dezi's legs faltered as he tried to stand up to her. Everyone watched as his face turned green, hypnotized and overcome with vertigo. His butt hit the ground with a resounding splat.

"I am sure you just forgot my name, let me introduce myself again. I am Mrs. Wil Capaccino, you may call me Netty." She walked away then turned. "Are we clear, Dezi?"

"Sure, ba—uh, Netty—I mean Netty." His face brick red, he struggled to stand, avoiding her eyes.

She smiled, turning to the crowd. "I can see most of you are starting to flag. Shall we continue our tour?" Waving them forward, she directed them to the next two openings in the corridor. Pointing to one, she explained that it opened on a pool of water for some of the wildlife to play and drink from. The other was for the people. She moved to the opening.

"Does anyone care to join me?" The crowd moved forward into the opening.

Kenya entered slowly, her arm supporting her expanding stomach, her small white shorts now grimy and ripped. As she turned the corner of the opening, she felt a wisp of warmth engulf her perfect face. She glanced at Johno with raised eyebrows then cleared the opening to face the unexpected.

"Oh . . . my . . . God." Her voice whispered in awe as everyone gathered round, jaws dropping to the damp, warm floor. Her stunned eyes moved over every inch of the brilliant glowing cave. Every color in the rainbow represented itself in the swirls of marbleized quartz: emerald, topaz, ruby, diamond, garnet, citrine, amber, coral, opal and moonstone that encased the enormous stalactites and stalagmites hanging from the soaring ceilings and emerging from the warm water that lapped at the edge of an enormous pool, mysterious in its depth.

Shadows from the stalactites cast private silhouettes in nooks around the pool begging the company of lovers. As everyone expressed their amazement, Netty explained the purpose of the cave was for bathing. The warm water was generated from the proximity of an underground river to a minor lava pit that existed hundreds of miles away.

"You will find drinking water in an underground spring that runs alongside my kitchen."

Kenya brightened up at the mention of a kitchen. She had failed to notice any food anywhere and she needed to keep up her strength. Johno's company served as a pleasant distraction but his focus belonged to the elephants in his care. What kind of support could he give her? She craned her neck to see where Kane might be standing. She thought he'd be a more likely source to rely on than Johno.

"If you will all follow me, I think it is time to feed these magnificent creatures." Netty linked her arm with Johno's, nodded to Kenya, and looped her other arm around the neck of the nearest baby elephant, easing the fragile creature back into the corridor.

As they proceeded, Kenya worked her way toward Kane, who was huddled with Chloe and Scotty as they examined the corridor wall. She watched as Scotty pushed his hand through the wall, the gloppy membrane enclosing his hand up to his wrist.

"What do you feel?" Kane's questioning voice contained an undercurrent of distaste.

"Nothing, and I have no intention of going any further."

Chloe reached over to grasp his arm, pulling him back to withdraw his hand. She ran her fingers over his skin, finding it smooth and dry.

Almost to herself, she muttered, "Just another mystery, what's one more in this crazy world I live in?" Scotty pulled her close.

"It's okay, Chloe. We're all here together. I don't think any harm will come to us. I'm grateful that we're here rather than topside, aren't you?"

Kenya intruded. "Hi, chickies, mind if I hang with you? I feel so hungry I could eat a . . . *aahhh*." Kenya clutched Kane's arm as she spied the ferocious cat that had peed all over Scotty on the boat coming around the bend. The tiger's eyes unwaveringly focused on Scotty alone as he stood with an arm supporting Chloe. As everyone turned to watch the tiger, Abby joined them. Echo followed with Baby toting his kitten, the new white puppy trying to keep up.

Scotty shrugged his shoulders. "Don't worry, it's only Caesar. I guess he likes me. He seems to have made himself my guardian." While they watched, Echo approached Caesar. The tiger chuffed lightly. Echo grasped the magnificent coat of the great cat, pulling herself nimbly up onto his back. Baby wobbled over with his kitten, handed it up to Echo, dipped down to pick up the white puppy then, in a flash, joined them on the back of the tiger, who steadfastly failed to even blink.

Kenya stared in horror. "That big stinkin' cat is not normal. We better get him some food before he decides to eat the little guys. Kane, get me out of here."

With that pronouncement, they funneled quickly down the corridor to find Netty and the rest of the group at an opening to a new cavern that glowed with an eerie lavender-blue light. As Kane elbowed his way through the crowd, Kenya made her way to the front. Passing through the opening, she felt a distinct sensation of pressure that dissipated immediately as she passed through. Her eyes popped as she surveyed the cavern before her, the sight overcoming her rational ability to believe.

Johno's little herd had fanned out, their trunks excitedly smelling the air that hung heavy with the fragrance of ripening fruit. Kenya stepped out in front of the crowd, her cumbersome belly weighing her down. She blinked, trying to clear her unbelieving eyes.

Before her stretched a subterranean field that measured the length of three football fields. The rich soil gave rise to an aroma of rich organic loam mixed with a powerful bouquet redolent of every fruit tree imaginable. Her stomach churning, she gazed further to marvel as row upon row of every vegetable under the sun (or should she say, under the earth?) grew to mammoth proportions. The probability of the existence of this amazing sight was outnumbered only by the spectacle of the plants and trees themselves.

She heard a series of trumpets as Tobi's tiny herd rushed forward to gorge themselves on the aromatic sight. Kenya glanced quickly at Netty who smiled wide with delight at Johno and his keepers as they danced with unexpected joy over the discovery and the happiness it meant for all of them.

Trembling, they made their way down to the fields, marveling at the drainage and irrigation system that brought water to the trees oddly sporting strangely exposed roots.

"Necessary for the voracious amount of oxygen they consume. Don't worry, they are well anchored with a prolific root system," explained Netty.

Kenya could certainly understand that. For the trees rose high in the sky like monolithic miracles. Most tree branches grew to the thickness of two men, necessary to hold up the eye-popping weight of the most unusual fruits Kenya had ever seen. A mysterious undulating haze of blue hung over the trees and crops. As she marveled at the size of just one fruit, she realized there was not a one that she could finish eating by herself. Scanning the faces of the crowd, she observed a range of emotions: incomprehension, dawning delight and reverent thankfulness.

Hugs and laughter filled the cavern as the impact of the glorious sight sunk in. It became clear that they actually stood a chance of surviving this catastrophe. Kenya rubbed her belly, tears flowing from her sparkling eyes. She turned to Kane. "Help me down, chicky?" He reached out quickly, lowering her softly, a question on his lips. She patted the ground next to her. "Please, join me."

As others in the crowd noticed them on the ground they one by one knelt to join Kenya in her prayer.

"Dear Lord, as your humble servant Kenya, I send you my blessed gratitude for all you have provided for us. I pray I am worthy of your trust and promise to treat my neighbors as I know you would approve, and the creatures too. I thank you in their stead for the abundance you have provided and the roof over our heads. We'll be eternally grateful for your continued benevolence, your trusted servant, Kenya McCready. Amen."

"Amen."

"Thank you, Lord, amen."

As everyone made their personal thoughts known to God, Netty appeared in the center of the bowed crowd. "Excuse me. Clearly, you do not understand. How can I make this any clearer? There is *no* God. You must realize it is the Womb you are praying to, do you not?"

One of the truckers stood up. "Well, why don't he show himself then?" The crowd hushed, most clearly unwilling to foster an argument with their benefactress.

"Funny, I never thought of the Womb as a he or she." Netty tilted her head to the side in thought, appearing to shake off the diverting subject. She remarked, "Perhaps the day will come when you *will* meet the Womb. I would not choose to look forward to it if I were you."

As she clapped her hands to assure their attention, Kenya watched the monkeys join the elephants, tentatively making their way to the trees for the first time since they had been stolen from their mothers' troops as babies.

"Some of you will be assigned to work here in the field, but you must all know a few things. The sensation of pressure as you enter the cavern is a deterrent to keep our pollinators from getting out. They are the blue creatures you see hovering over the trees and the crops. They are deadly to human skin. They are harmless to all other animal life. They live inside the trunks of the trees. See the bulges on the trunks? They serve as the protectors of the plant life from any humans—just a precaution. I am sure the Womb finds it necessary for some reason.

"All fruit that is not consumed is canned by me or harvested as seed stock. There will be great need once the planet becomes habitable again. If you look closely, you will see plants you are unfamiliar with. They are not all for your palate. The Womb has further plans for new life. They will be in need. You have much to learn. Shall we continue?

"Johno, I suggest you leave Miss Tobi and her charges here to graze. You can collect them later if you wish." With that, Netty turned on her heels, leaving footprints in the soft, warm soil as she headed back to the main corridor, leaving them all to scramble after her.

Continuing down the corridor, Netty pointed to a smallish opening. "This is the kitchen. I do all of my baking there. It is where you will find us most of the time. All are welcome there until your own kitchen is built. I hope you will join us in the morning. I have a special breakfast planned." She moved further down the corridor peeling off to a lesser artery.

"This is where all the other animals will live. One cave is for the cats, the other for the rest. You can explore at your leisure tomorrow. Food must be carried to them as they need it. Each cave contains a water source, ample light and varied topography. They will live content lives with you all managing their upkeep."

As they moved back to the corridor, Wil emerged from one of the caves, joining Netty. He laughed as he observed Caesar shadowing Scotty with his new appendages aboard. "How is the tour going? Ready to hit the lower level?"

He snaked his hand around Netty's waist as she informed him they were headed there now. They walked arm in arm, Wil casually planting a kiss on her cheek as the rest of the crowd followed.

Kenya wondered what was left to show them as she eyed the affection they showed one another; something *more* wondrous?

They halted suddenly, allowing Kenya to catch up and observe a short flight of four stone steps leading to another corridor. They took turns ascending the stairs and advanced down the corridor to stand in a kind of antechamber. Four doors led to additional corridors all made of stone with the thick viscous membrane clinging to the walls.

Wil explained, pointing to the first set of doors. "Sanitary outhouses—one for men, one for women. The other doors lead to sleeping quarters, one for men, and again one for women. Each room has been provided with food and water until morning. You will not find beds but a stone dais for each of you. They look uncomfortable but I assure you it will be the best sleep you have ever had. Sort yourself as you please. We will see you in the morning. Come, Baby."

The golden creature slid down Caesar's broad back with his kitten drooping from his skinny leathery arm to wobble over to Wil. Wil bent down, scooped up the little creature, and secured him to his hip like a child.

"Goodnight." With a nod and a genuine smile, Netty slipped out behind Wil, withdrawing in a swirl of golden light, leaving them all stunned and overwhelmed.

Jose stood. "I suggest we first collect the food and water. We can eat out here and discuss our plans."

Someone shouted, "Plans, you got plans? Seems to me the only plan is to do what we're told or get out. How's that for a plan?"

Little Kimir, who still quietly held his turtle while he clung to Clyde's hand, began to cry.

Clyde spoke up. "Jose has the right idea. Let's get some food in our stomachs and see where we go from there." All agreed as they scrambled to explore their sleeping quarters and collect food before meeting back in the antechamber.

Kenya entered a vast catacomb of various-sized rooms, all positioned for privacy. They held nothing but the stone daises mentioned by Wil. Mama Diaz chose one for her and the girls and deposited their bags on the huge stone. Kenya watched as Karen, the copilot, and Crystal agreed to share a dais.

"What about your pig?"

"What do you mean, what about my pig?" Crystal looked at Karen uncomprehending.

"Where do you want it to sleep?"

"Well, her name is Tulip and she'll sleep with me, of course."

"You mean with us."

Crystal nodded her head, bent down to smooth Tulip's lovely tutu and gave her a smooch.

"Don't worry, she's potty trained."

Karen shrugged, catching Kenya's eye. "I've seen worse."

Crystal stood, giving Tulip an assessing appraisal, checking her out from different angles. "Do you feel okay, girl? Looks like she's putting some weight on. I better keep an eye on what she eats, this is her only outfit. Don't want her to have to go nudie, do we?"

Kenya turned away, spotting Abby in the corner talking to Ginger Mae and Daisy. Heading in their direction, she noticed the older woman's wet face. Ginger Mae sat on the edge of a dais, her arm around Daisy, who tried to wipe away her mother's tears.

"Hey, ladies, I don't mean to interrupt but seein's you all are so deep in conversation, maybe I could take Daisy for you?" Abby reached out to take Kenya's shapely caramel arm, guiding her to sit on the dais next to Daisy who smiled sadly, welcoming her to join them. Kenya slid her arm around Daisy who looked more like a waif than ever with her pale face and thin stringy hair.

"Well, we sure aren't the happiest threesome in the room, are we?" Kenya's bright words fell on deaf ears, depression hanging over Ginger Mae like storm clouds during hurricane season.

"Your face looks a little better, Ginger Mae. The swelling's really going down."

Her face did not look that much better. The stitching closed the long vertical cut like a worm turning in on itself and bruising had spread across the whole half of her face to make her further unrecognizable. Kenya winced, trying hard to meet her eyes. Abby cleared her throat and swallowed audibly.

"Ginger Mae, and you too, Kenya, I hope you have a better understanding of my behavior now. When I met each of you, my preoccupation with the coming catastrophe may have distorted my behavior. If I appeared harsh, please know it was not directed at you. My inexperience and stress gave me no time for niceties. The knowledge I carried became almost too much to bear. I hope you'll both forgive me.

"I'm sure you've heard word of the animals having implants from Echo. Well, I myself was implanted, by Netty. That's how she communicated with me. It also altered my natural behavior in some way. Please accept my apologies. I'm not normally so domineering, I assure you. We need to rely on each other in the coming weeks. I've no idea how long we'll be here or what condition we'll find the world in when it's over." Kenya raised her hand to her mouth in surprise.

"You were under their control . . . an implant? Oh, chicky, that must have hurt." She hopped up to wrap her arms around Abby, hugging her close. "Are you sure you're okay now?"

Abby nodded, very serious. "I'm fine now and we're all safe, that's what matters."

Ginger Mae raised her head. "But you're still one of them." Kenya and Abby heard the bitterness in her voice. "I'm grateful my daughter is safe, but don't think for a minute that I'll turn my back on you or any of the other freaks in here."

Abby rose to her feet with a deep sigh. "It's alright. I understand. We've got plenty of time to get to know each other. Why don't we gather the food and water and join the men?"

Kenya glanced toward the stack of containers and bowls on the stone table in the center of the room to observe Gloria and her mice salivating over the provisions. Eyeballing Gloria's obese anatomy, she thanked God, oops—the Womb—that they could count on plenty of food.

As they all gathered in the antechamber, everyone appeared to naturally gravitate to Jose. He sat commandingly on the stone floor, his darker skin a vibrant contrast to his golden eyes that mesmerized and his huge wings that lay curved against his body. His disconcerting tail sat wrapped around his waist, relaxed and quiet. Scotty and Chloe clustered around the dogs, Echo lounging with the Barney pup, quiet and focused on the food piled in front of everyone.

Digging in, they enjoyed two special items from Netty's kitchen. A loaf of what tasted like an apple walnut spice cake, the spice intriguing with its complex flavor notes eluding identification, and a hearty peach pie.

Tucker, the man with the German shepherd, tore into the food with gusto. "Boy, that lady sure can cook. This'll sure make up for a lot. Nothin' like some home cookin' ta keep *me* happy."

Reaching for a large bean-pod-shaped green thing, Kenya ran her fingers around the outside, feeling a texture like that of her favorite French bread. Splitting it open, she was surprised at the sight of what looked like red meat. But the outside crunched. She wrinkled her nose.

"Here, let me." Kane reached over to rip off a hunk, taking a small bite. He nodded his head, smiling as he chewed.

"It's great." He laughed. "I don't know what the heck it is, but it's delicious."

They all dug in, eating with relish. Kenya noticed little Kimir trying to get his pet turtle to eat by pushing food up to his mouth with no success. The thing looked half dead anyway. She wished they had some greenery to tempt him with. Thinking of the sanctuary turtles, she wondered who would feed them.

As if he heard her thoughts, Jose announced they would need to consider a division of labor. Asking if anyone wanted to volunteer for anything, Dezi spoke up. "I don't care what I gotta do, it just better not have anything to do with any nasty damn smelly critters, hope that's clear." Unfortunately, Penny took that exact time to stretch her legs out to lie down, rubbing up against Dezi. He jumped up as if she was as welcome as a turd in a swimming pool.

"Get that stinking mutt away from me, will ya, for Christ's sake?" He gave a hard long look at Jose. "I'm not gunna tell ya about these mutts again, bro."

Cobby piped up. "Cool down, buddy. You've got to get used to living with the animals. They apparently enjoy a higher status than we do now. You don't want to get on the wrong side of the Womb so soon, do you?" Dezi picked up his dinner, muttering as he moved away from Penny to sit by himself. Clyde eased on over to Jose.

"Hope ya don't mind, Jose, but I noticed your girl Abby seems to have a little bit of pull around here, that right?"

Jose glanced at him cautiously. "Yeah, I guess you could say that, wouldn't *you*, Kenya?" They turned to her with raised eyebrows.

"Well, listen here, chicky, if you're implying that I'm eavesdropping . . ." She gathered her long shapely legs under her, preparing to stand. Changing her mind, she sat still. "For heaven's sake, you can sure bet that I'm gunna keep both these ears open full time. I plan to make damn sure I learn everything I can about what's goin' down here. And yeah, Abby is plugged in like a toaster oven around here. I bet she's even met the Womb. Why, what you want with Abby?"

Clyde stared at Kenya. "Young lady, if you don't mind, this is a private conversation. Can you give me a minute?"

"I'm not going anywhere, chicky, so get used to it."

Clyde took a deep breath and turned back to Jose. "I need a favor. I need you to ask Abby if between her and Netty they might be able to hook me up to talk to my wife. If I can't reassure myself, I'm going to have to leave in the morning. I need to know she's still safe and on her way here. I'm sure you understand."

"Yeah, Clyde, I get it, but you must realize all the cell towers are down by now."

Kenya decided to pipe up. "Since when did a minor obstacle like that stop these critters? Did you forget they live on another planet? They can just snap their fingers and make it happen."

Jose frowned. "I'm sure it's not that easy, Kenya, but I'll look into it for you, okay, Clyde?"

Some of the pain dissipated from Clyde's eyes. "I'll owe ya, man. I'll owe ya big." The men shook hands and Kenya lost interest.

The balance of the meal passed in reasonable good humor, even as Kimir began to badger Scotty about his turtle. He agreed to heal Kimir's pet with everyone watching, their interest a vast improvement over the suspicions and hostility of a few hours ago. Even Tucker's German shepherd began to make advances toward Penny, although the elegant springer spaniel refused to even acknowledge his presence.

Conversation drifted around to the subject of the prodigious fruits and vegetables Netty and Wil had cultivated. They wondered how they grew them so big, what the blue pollinators were, and what the green funky fruit was with the crusty skin that looked like meat, but tasted like French bread encapsulating filet mignon.

The subject of the Womb and the length of their probable habitation in the massive and magnificent cavern never arose. From time to time, someone would use the outhouses.

Kenya left to bring leftovers to the wayward turtles.

Persuading Kimir, Daisy and the Diaz girls to go to bed involved little pleading as they longed for the release of sleep as youth tend to do after exciting events and full stomachs.

The only problem was realized after some hasty whispers by Kimir in Kenya's ear. It seems he was worried about his prayer rug. He must say his Muslim communion and didn't even know where the sun was. How was he to say his prayers?

Clyde rose out of his funk long enough to convince him he would be forgiven for skipping his prayers for one day. A promise to speak to Netty about a prayer rug allowed Kimir to be shuttled off to bed with the rest of the younger survivors.

It wasn't long before the adults tired of the exchange of life stories and the speculation on the horror faced by their countrymen above ground. Chores were discussed and a rotation system agreed upon, even as they agreed they had no idea what might be required of them. Yawns became more frequent as their strength flagged. Saying goodnight, the single men and single women retired to their chosen cubbies, Jose and Abby choosing a private one with the women, hoping to be supportive to his adopted family if they needed him.

As everyone settled down to enjoy their dreamless sleep on their stone daises that bizarrely felt as cushy as a pile of down feathers—many wrongly attributing the sensation to hallucinations induced by the food they ate—the phantom light in the cavern slowly dimmed. An occasional muffled snort or snore sounded from far, far away. A child cried out only to drift again into a dreamless deep.

Time passed as all eyes participated in frantic twitches under paper-thin eyelids, the signs of deep REM sleep emerging as the gelatinous membrane adhering to the cubby walls woke to send tendrils to every sleeping form, gliding soundlessly across stone floors and up the dais to the vulnerable sleepers. No one moved as the insidious ribbons wrapped themselves around exposed legs and arms, up backs of warm, tender necks to disappear, undetected, into the pores of all sleeping survivors, excepting Abby, Jose, Echo and Scotty.

Out in the field, Tobi stood guard over her precious herd, the babies laying asleep on the warm fertile soil, unaware of the invasive substance that easily penetrated their systems through minute pores in their skin. She flicked her tail and flapped her ear as an unexplained tickle interrupted her enjoyment of the giant succulent pear she crushed in her mouth, juices dripping from her enormous maw to drop unseen on the ribbons emerging from the ground, determined to find their way to the sleeping herd.

In the vast cavern of cats, tendrils emerged to sink themselves into the luscious pelts of the huge beasts that slept with bellies full of the green crusty meat-like pods of protein supplied by Wil. They lay sprawled on boulders, cliffs and at the edges of a quiet lake that the tigers dreamed of frolicking in.

Throughout the underground domain, sleeping bodies of all species found themselves visited in their sleep—even the exalted Caesar as he slept lightly at the base of the huge dais occupied by Scotty, Chloe, Echo and her doggy entourage.

The inaugural night, pregnant with unseen subterfuge, passed quickly, membranes withdrawing long before the mysterious light of the next day brightened.

# Chapter 16

Lorna woke to the thwacking sound of choppers flying overhead. She wiped the sleep out of her eyes, trying to stretch without waking Suzy who lay across her lap in the front seat.

"What time is it?" She yawned, glancing over at Seth who stared glassy eyed and slack jawed out the windshield, his foot hard on the gas pedal.

"Seth, are you alright?" She glanced out the window, observing the bulk of the traffic proceeding in the opposite direction. "I think you better slow down. Did something happen while we slept?" Her anxious whisper became more pointed as Seth failed to react. She reached over to touch his arm. As if shot by a bullet, Seth wrenched the steering wheel to the right, causing the car to careen off the road.

"*Watch out!*" Lorna screamed, waking the girls. Maryann sat up in the back seat as the car ground to a halt, stalling out. Seth banged his hands on the steering wheel.

"*Fuck.*" He gave Lorna a vicious glare. "What the fuck did you think you were doing? Look what you made me do." He swiveled around to the back seat. "See what your stupid grandmother did? She almost killed us."

"Now, wait a minute, Seth. There's no need to speak like that. I just woke up and spoke to you . . ." Her voice tailed off, the surprise of his words sinking in. A warning flickered in the back of her mind; the suspicion she may have made an error allowing Seth to ride along with them flashing a red flag. She watched him as she intuited he sensed the shift in her voice. He quickly attempted to bring himself back under control, breathing deep and turning to favor her with an apologetic grin; the old charming Seth back in charge.

"Sorry, Lorna, you just startled me. I must have been concentrating too hard on the long drive we have in front of us. Are you girls all okay back there? How about you, Suzy girl, what are you doing, just waking up? You missed out on the excitement."

He reached over to playfully muss her hair. Suzy drew back to Lorna, trying to evade his reach. He brushed it off as if it hadn't happened, saying brightly, "Well, why don't we get back on the road?"

Lorna nodded slowly, her mind spinning with the thoughts of their vulnerability.

They had been driving for at least ten tedious days; sometimes making progress, sometimes having to backtrack. Many times they were forced to pull off the road and shut off the car, waiting until marauding groups of thugs passed them by. They were losing many hours of valuable drive time each day.

Lorna counted at least six more shocks that rocked the car at various times, scaring the hell out of them. There was no way to tell how far away the bombs had hit. Fortunately, no telltale plumes appeared in the sky, leading them to believe they were far from ground zero.

Yesterday, they were forced to detour around the mob of refugees streaming down the highway from a town far ahead of them. The refugees were migrating away from their town with just the clothes on their backs, stunned expressions preventing them from grasping the serious position they were in without food and water.

Seth refused to stop and ask questions, preferring to leave the road and wait until he could figure out a way around them. When Lorna suggested they might benefit from the intelligence they could gather from the refugees, he looked at her as if she had just suggested he carry the car on his back.

"You must be out of your mind. When the hordes realize we have a car, some brave badass is going to try to take if from us. And what do you think they'll do to us if they learn we have boxes of food? Use your head, woman." Lorna smarted from the remarks but recognized the wisdom behind them.

One unusual bright spot occurred on their second day together. Lorna was nodding off in the car, the monotony making her sleepy when, from inside her purse, she heard the unmistakable ring of her cellphone. She instantly scrambled to answer, knowing it could only be her son or her husband. Rooting through her purse, Seth urged her to hurry.

"How in the world can you get a signal? All the towers must be out."

Feeling the cold plastic in her hand she drew the phone to her ear. "Hello?"

Tears slipped down her face as she recognized the sound of Clyde's voice. "Oh, my God, how are you? Are you safe? Yes, yes we're fine. We have a Good Samaritan with us . . . no, he's fine . . . Seth. He's helping us to find you. What . . . what do you mean, Clyde?" Her voice became measured, concern coating her words.

"But that's not possible." She laughed. "Well, if you say so, it just sounds fantastic . . . Healing powers, wings? Yes, dear, I believe you if you say so . . . no, I don't know much. The cities are burning. We know at least half a dozen bombs have been dropped. No, we haven't seen any sign of the authorities. No ambulances, a few choppers. Clyde, people are killing each other." She started to cry again. "No, stay there, love . . . I need to know you're safe. We'll come to you . . . promise. Clyde . . . Clyde, are you there . . .?" She glanced at her phone—it showed a dead battery. But the battery had died days ago. Sniffling, she returned the useless cell to her purse out of habit.

"That was Grandpa? Where is he? Will he come get us, Gram?" Jen's anxious voice sounded tiny and close to tears. Maryann tried to comfort her, murmuring sounds to reassure her. *What a good kid, thank heaven we found her.*

Lorna tried to hold on to the last echo of Clyde's voice as Seth intruded, demanding an explanation. "Well, what was that all about?"

"That was my husband, calling from outside the sanctuary. He said it would be a onetime deal—whatever that means." She turned to Seth, excitement shining in her eyes. "They have food, lots of food. He said they're growing it." Her voice filled with amazement. "I don't understand how this can be but he said he's with other people and animals, lots of animals." Her voice reduced to a halting whisper. "He said . . . he said a woman with wings saved them. She cloned a dog—and something about a healer."

"Cloned a dog? I think you got the message wrong. Did you have a bad connection? The whole thing sounds ridiculous."

"I know. But he's safe. And they have plenty of food. They're growing it. This must be a big place. Oh girls, I think we're going to be okay." She glanced again at Seth as a pensive expression ran across his face, lighting a fire in his blue eyes. Lorna turned away, refusing to have her happiness dimmed by Seth and his ambiguities. She pushed back her filthy hair, refusing to let it trouble her as she remembered how wonderful it was to have heard Clyde's voice.

It was only on their third night together that Lorna's uneasy feeling about Seth began to surface. They all agreed it would be a good idea to get off the road and rest. They hadn't bathed in days and the girls were getting testy from the amount of time they were forced to spend in the car. Searching for a while, they finally located a deserted motel. Most commercial buildings they encountered were either boarded up and deserted or guarded carefully by gun-toting rednecks and trigger-happy business owners, all trying to preserve what they could feel and touch in a disintegrating world that made no sense. Occasional bodies testified to the new rule of law: Shoot first, ask questions later.

It didn't take long, once the bombs had started, for the fires to come. Horizons glowed at night with the voracious flames that consumed all in their path. It wasn't just the bombs that brought the fires. It was busted gas mains and careless campfires, unleashed firebugs and plain malicious thugs taking advantage of the situation to create mayhem. Again, they found they were forced to go out of their way to skirt coming conflagrations.

The motel Seth found appeared to be deserted and boarded up. They approached it cautiously, searching for signs of life, praying the road that ran in front of the motel was far enough off the beaten path to offer a safe haven for the night.

Seth and Lorna developed a procedure. He would park the car down the road with the hood up, the women locked inside. He then crept back to the motel to reconnoiter, using the broken down car as a plausible excuse if he were caught. It sounded weak but it was all they had. When he ascertained the coast was clear, he came back and waved them forward, the hood banging shut as Lorna rolled into the parking lot.

Their first successful night brought a welcome release of happiness for the young girls. They argued about who would take the first bath. Seth warned them about the amount of water available. To preserve as much as they could, they would plug the tub, letting the water pour in until it stopped. They managed to collect enough water that had remained standing in the pipes from other showers to bring back to their tub to properly wash.

But no one wanted to be the last one in of course. Seth had played the gentleman, waiting in the bedroom with Lorna as the girls took turns with their baths. Unfortunately, Lorna would have to be blind not to notice him lingering in the bathroom with Maryann and Jen as he teased them about who was next. *Is he flirting with them?* Dismissing her active imagination, she banished her suspicions. Seth had already showed them what a good guy he was, agreeing to help them get to Clyde.

Now she began to have her doubts again. It was becoming clear that the tension and conditions they faced were wearing everyone down, including Seth. She fretted as she wondered if she just expected too much from him. Maybe she needed to cut him some slack too.

"What do you think?" Seth slowed the car as they approached a one-story motel, seemingly deserted.

"Yeah, looks okay, let's check it out." Seth stepped outside the car, raising the hood for their cover story. As he walked toward the motel, he turned his head back to the car, entirely missing the man that crept from behind the hotel with a shotgun in his arms. The dirt pinged with a warning shot, sending Seth fleeing back to the car.

"Son of a bitch, he almost got me." He slammed the car door, started the engine and turned the car around. Slamming his fist on the steering wheel he shouted at Lorna. "See what you made me do? You distracted me and I didn't see the gunman. I could have been killed."

"What do you mean I distracted you? You were already out of the car. And if he wanted to kill you he wouldn't have given you a warning shot."

Seth froze. His hands gripping the wheel tightened so hard Lorna could see them turn white. He turned to her so slowly she was confused. "What's wrong, Seth?"

He stared right through her as if he didn't see her. Taking his hands from the wheel, he grabbed his pinky with his other hand, bending back until it popped. Shaking out his hand, he put his foot back on the gas pedal and moved on down the road in silence. Suzy looked up at her grandma; her face blank, lips trembling. She felt Jen's hand on her back looking for reassurance. She held tight to Suzy and sent the girls in the back a hushing motion, unwilling to challenge Seth.

From behind the wheel came Seth's tight voice. "We need a new plan. I think we need to find a vacant house." He suddenly turned to Lorna, all smiles and charm. "How 'bout that, girls? Want to stay in a nice house tonight? I should have thought of that sooner." He turned back to the road, a satisfied smile dancing from ear to ear.

*What the hell?* Lorna trembled inside, trying desperately not to show any emotion, as she realized they had to get rid of this guy before something bad happened.

Seth cruised through the residential neighborhood of a modest town looking for a likely house. Some were boarded up; others were obviously occupied with shades drawn.

They quickly found their situation was no different than at the motels. Seth soon located a modest white split level at the end of cul-de-sac, conveniently set back from the road. Parking the car, Seth turned to Lorna, his relaxed and handsome face smiling with confidence.

"This looks like the one. I'm going to go check. I'll come back to get you girls when it's all clear." Sliding out of the seat he bent down to pluck out the keys and, giving the girls in the back seat a quick wink, he reached for his huge backpack, sliding it on his back. Lorna watched him approach the house, slipping the car keys in his pocket.

Disappointed, Lorna realized this definitely was not the time to be without a spare key.

"Gram, Seth is a little scary, don't you think?" Jen piped up from the back seat.

"Gram, I don't like Seth. He's a bad man."

Even Maryann added her opinion. "Lorna, can't we just leave him here?"

Lorna turned uncomfortably in her seat. "He just has a bad temper, girls, let's keep him happy for a while longer. I'll wait for the right chance. I need to get the keys away from him first." Groans were heard all round, the girls as frustrated as Lorna. Jen sat back, smelling her underarms.

"My pits stink, can't wait to take a bath. Do your pits smell, Suzy?"

"*No*, I do *not* smell." She reached back to punch her sister. "You smell like doody."

"Ewww, you have maggots in your hair, Suzy." Soon all hell broke out, the girls doing what sisters do: They fought, they squabbled. The time passed.

Before long, Lorna realized Seth had been gone for over twenty five minutes. *What could be taking him so long?* She became anxious. If something happened to him, he possessed the keys and they'd be stuck. *Damn.*

As the girls continued to fight, she glanced down at her hands, lamenting the condition of her nails. She wondered if she might find a bottle of nail polish inside the house. She didn't plan to steal it, just touch up her manicure. She hoped they might find enough water to take a decent shower. Hot water was something she probably could say goodbye to. She turned to the window again to watch for Seth. Doing a double take she observed him running out the front door of the house to the car. He was not wearing his backpack.

"Girls, girls, stop that. Seth's coming, I think we're in." They watched as he made his way to the car, then slid inside and started the ignition. He noticed their inquiring expressions.

"Come on, ladies, it's time to celebrate."

"What took you so long?" Lorna sounded accusatory even to her own ears. She quickly reached out to pat his arm and amend her tone as his eyes darkened. "We thought something might have happened to you."

"Nope, all's good." Pulling into the driveway, Seth directed the unloading of the car. They had learned quickly never to leave anything behind at night. If marauding gangs spotted anything in the car, they would help themselves, leaving busted windows and flat tires. They had started to hide the car when they found a safe place to stop, not wanting to find it missing in the morning.

Lorna carried a box of food into the kitchen. As she placed it on the kitchen table, she noticed a half-eaten peanut butter cookie in the trash. Who would throw that out with food such a desperate issue? Reaching in the garbage can she withdrew the paper plate that held the cookie, revealing a blood splattered dishtowel hidden underneath.

Pausing to stare at the blood soaked rag, she reached out to touch the towel. Drawing back, she swallowed hard as her fingers encountered wetness. She stared at her fingers, trying to discern the meaning of the damp blood on her fingers.

Scanning the room, she looked for Seth's backpack. Not there.

She ran to the front door to observe Seth horsing around with the girls as they unloaded the car. She might have a few minutes before they finished.

Running wildly through the house, she looked for Seth's backpack. Relieved, she found it in the sweetly decorated master bedroom, lying on the bed like an obscenity.

Sitting on the big bed, she quickly unzipped it, rummaging through clothes, water bottles, small tools, nails . . . *nails?* She withdrew a handful of large headed nails wrapped in a plastic bag. Her heart beat faster.

Moving on she withdrew a large item that turned out to be a woman's purse with a colorful scrap of silk tied to the strap. The silk felt as if it were knotted around a small hard object. Unknotting the silk, she recognized the items, blood draining from her face.

Why would Seth be carrying a pair of ladies panties threaded through a set of wedding rings? She held the rings in her hands as a beam of sunlight caught the large diamond, sending refractions of light around the room in dazzling patterns.

Snapping out of her paralysis, she hurriedly put the rings back as she had found them. Unable to resist, she opened the purse to discover the usual female items: car and house keys, cosmetics, two plastic baby diapers and a wallet . . . baby diapers?

Opening the wallet, she searched for identification. Reading the address on the driver's license, she felt a creeping coldness grip her heart like a fist: 7 Prince Henry Dr. Ladenport, Maine. *Oh, my God, the dead woman on the side of the road with the empty baby seat.* Lorna ran her finger slowly over the plastic of the baby diapers. *Where's the baby?*

Feeling as if she had been kicked in the stomach, Lorna hastily stuffed the items back into Seth's backpack. Smoothing the backpack down, she placed it on the floor. *Is that where I found it?*

"What are you doing, Lorna?"

She jumped up off the bed, her face stiff with shock. "Uh, I thought I might lie down and take a nap."

He stared at her, searching her face as she held her breath. Suddenly, he broke out in a big grin, his eyes twinkling, compassion in his voice. "I bet you're beat. Why don't you get something to eat with the girls? I have them filling our water bottles. I found the homeowners have a well that they water their lawn from. It's too bad the house isn't hooked up to it. While you eat, I'll bring water into the tub in here. We can take turns when the girls are ready."

Lorna raised her hands to her face, wondering if it looked green. She fought the urge to vomit, nodding her head at Seth, trying hard to make her stiffening lips smile and to act naturally. He took her arm, guiding her down to the kitchen with him, every fiber of her nerves screaming for her to run.

Lorna felt as if she had been sucked down Alice's rabbit hole in a vicious dream that refused to let go. Her mind raced as she tried desperately to devise a plan to get the girls to safety.

"Maryann, have you seen the car keys?"

"No, Lorna, last I saw them Seth had them. Want some peanut butter?" The girls were eating peanut butter out of the jar with tablespoons, having run out of bread and crackers long ago.

"Let me see if I can find some crackers for you. Anyone check the pantry?" Lorna stood in front of the small pantry, noting the absence of crackers but discovering many canned goods they could use. She absently wondered if she could be wrong about Seth. Maybe he had just found the woman's purse somewhere. Yeah, that could be the answer. She moved into the laundry room. Sometimes people built another pantry in there.

"Find anything yet, Gram?" Lorna opened the laundry closet, turning to the kitchen to answer when a bad smell of feces assailed her nose. She swung the door open to discover the dead body of a woman in her late thirties and a young boy of about twelve. Both throats grinned their bloody evidence at her, sheets of congealing blood betraying Seth's obvious handiwork. Lorna slammed the door, running to the kitchen sink to vomit as Seth returned from the master bedroom.

"Gram, you sick?"

"Want some water, Lorna?" Maryann held a jug out to her with a glass in her hand.

She reached for a chair, sinking down, her head spinning as white noise took over her mind, paralyzing her. Gripping the glass from Maryann, she held tightly with both hands, fearful her trembling would betray her to Seth. *Oh my God, please help me.*

"Lorna, you really don't look good. What's wrong?" Seth knelt in front of her, feeling her forehead, which sent Lorna back to the sink to dry heave, her stomach completely empty. She brushed surreptitiously at the tears forming in her eyes as her fear manifested itself, and prayed that Seth wouldn't notice.

"I just need to lie down," she whispered. "I feel a bit feverish. Girls, why don't you come with me, you can start your baths."

Seth rose, placing his hand on Suzy's shoulder. "I'll come too."

Lorna whirled, her hand shaking. "I think we can handle this alone." Her whole body shook, forcing her to sit again.

Seth grabbed her under her arms. "No, I insist. Let me help you." She threw a silent panicked plea at Maryann, mouthing the word run. She watched Maryann glance at Jen, confusion across her face, as she felt Seth aggressively guide her to the hallway and down to the master bedroom, the girls trailing behind. Suzy tried to wiggle her way between them.

"I want my Gram. Gram, hold my hand, please Gram?"

"It's okay, baby. Gram's fine. Okay, Seth, I can take it from here."

Unexpectedly, Seth escorted her to the master bath. "Here, Suzy, you stay with your gram. Jen, you can come in here." As the girls funneled into the bathroom with puzzlement clear in their eyes, Seth grabbed hold of Maryann, steering her back out to the bedroom. "Not you, my dear, I can use some help."

Lorna's heart tripped madly. *"No, you leave her here."*

Seth stood eye to eye with Lorna, neither blinking. Grabbing Jen he faced Lorna again. "Which one?"

She blinked, not understanding. He screamed at the top of his lungs, face turning purple, enunciating carefully.

*"Which . . . one?"* Lorna thought she would pass out. *Please Lord, get us out of here.* She made a quiet mewing sound, her face pleading as she held tight to Jen, who cried for her mama. Seth smiled with triumph.

"I thought so." He pushed Maryann back across the master bed, rushing forward to punch Lorna squarely in the face, forcing her and Jen back to the bathroom. Blood spurted out of her broken nose as she heard the astonishing sound of a hammer as Seth drove nails into the bathroom door, sealing them inside. Suzy and Jen stood rooted to the spot as they watched with silent tears, the blood gushing from their gram's nose.

Lorna grabbed for a towel, gathering the girls in her arms, as they heard Maryann scream from the bedroom. They huddled down on the floor, the girls holding their ears as they tried to block out the banging and screams that Lorna prayed for Maryann's sake would end swiftly.

Maryann lay stunned, face down on the bed. She could feel Seth wrap something around her left arm fastening it to the bedpost, forcing her to flip over or risk injury.

"I'm so glad it was you. I can tell you'll be more fun. She gave you up pretty easy didn't she?"

Maryann couldn't make her mouth work, fright stealing her voice. From out of nowhere came Seth's hand, gathering up her dark hair and yanking her head up off the bed. She screamed. He slapped her in the face; she screamed again. Reaching down he grabbed the front of her dirty shirt, ripping it down the front to expose her braless young chest.

Maryann sobbed. "Noooo, please, why are you doing this? We've been nice to you." She watched his blue eyes dance as he eyed her quivering breasts.

"Maryann, this is just another chance for you to be nice. And I'm the guy that's going to show you how." He suddenly thrust his lips down on hers, cutting off her breath. His hands were everywhere; kneading her breasts, trying to pull off her pants. She tried desperately to prevent his hands from gaining traction, but she had only one arm to work with.

"Stop it right now." He stood up from the bed and slammed his hand on the nightstand. His eyes met hers and he smiled. "I'm going to make sure you like it baby, don't you worry." He pulled off her shoes and her pants from the bottom of the bed. She was helpless to stop him.

She could see him as he removed his clothes, his erection bursting from his underwear. He suddenly ran his hand up her legs to her crotch, following slowly with his tongue. She fought the desire to pee as he slobbered in her groin. She held her breath as he suddenly stopped to peer up at her.

"If you aren't going to play, Maryann, I'm going to have to change the rules."

"I don't know what you mean. Please let me go. I haven't done anything to hurt you. Why?" She began to sob louder. "I don't understand."

From out of nowhere his fist landed on her cheek. Her eyes slipped back in their sockets as she tried to push the stars away.

When the pain came from the rape, it felt hot—like a poker—but far away. He thrust and thrust, grunting like an animal, disgusting her. Her mind drifted as his fist came down on her face again yanking her back to feel the pain in all its wicked viciousness.

"I told you, little bitch. I'm forced to change the rules now. See what you made me do?" She felt a new stab of pain then a rush of agony. She opened her eyes to see him standing over her with a bloody knife in his hand. *Where did that come from?* His erection bobbed as if mocking her.

"You're a lousy lay, you know? Can't even get a man off properly, can you? Never had a real man before, did you?" His face moved so close to hers she could smell his sour breath.

"Doesn't matter now, there's new rules in play. You won't like this, Maryann, but you had your chance. I'm very fair. I like to give the ladies a chance first. *But they always fail me*," he shouted in her face, spittle from his lips reaching out to remind her of her helplessness.

Maryann had no idea how long Seth's mad behavior continued as she vacillated from confusion to terror. She knew from the agony all over her body that it must have been hours. She could feel the bedcovers soak up the blood from her many wounds as she regained consciousness from time to time.

She woke once to find the body of a young boy in the bed with her, his arms removed and, to her astonishment, lying on her torso. Sweet waves of unconsciousness claimed her once again.

It must have been hours later when she felt water on her face return her to her vile reality. Seth stood at the bathroom door, his face sweaty with dull, glazed eyes, but fully dressed. She tried to open her mouth but found only agony. Blood bubbles formed as she attempted to talk. Her mouth surged with blood as she weakened. A tear managed to make its way down her cheek.

She watched as Seth tore the nails out of the door caging the other women inside. She heard screams as he disappeared inside, then a sudden silence. More tears ran down her face as she knew how unaware they were of the fate awaiting them. She heard shuffling at the bathroom door but failed to find the strength to move her head to look.

As Lorna and the girls skirted the bed like zombies, Maryann watched the horrified pinched expressions on the faces of Suzy and Jen.

Then Lorna appeared with her face gray and full of shock . . . and a little something else. Was it shame? Relief? *Oh . . . yeah, Seth wanted Lorna to pick.* She remembered now. *Guilt.*

Blood bubbled up again as a bitter breath made its way out her mouth. It was the last breath before she slipped back into the miraculous land where pain failed to follow, unable to hear the two words whispered as Lorna shuffled past . . . softly . . . tenderly . . . ashamed.

"Forgive me."

# Chapter 17

Morning announced itself slowly with the phantom lights of the Hive rising like the steadfast dawn now fated to become an abstract memory. The group roused just as slowly, most unwilling to fully wake to face the extrinsic reality of their new existence.

Tiny Teddy, Chloe's obstreperous monkey dog, sat on her chest, eyes riveted and focused on Chloe's every twitch, waiting for her to awaken and fuss over his needs.

She finally woke, Scotty's birthday gift slipping down to tangle in her hair, the gold coin glinting as she pulled herself together for the next day. She followed the others as they gathered in the antechamber.

"I don't know about you guys, but I feel fantastic." Cobby raised his hands over his head, stretching and doing a squat.

"Damn, I gotta agree with ya there." Clyde yawned, watching as Johno and his keepers slapped one another playfully on the back. Peter just watched, saying nothing. Dezi sauntered around the room flexing his scrawny arms, obviously expecting comments.

"Well, well, how 'bout it, ladies?" He winked in their direction. "I'm offering my services if any of you babes have trouble sleeping."

Crystal laughed. "Why do you think we slept so well, Dezi? You were putting us to sleep last night." Everyone laughed, taking turns in the outhouse and planning swims in their dazzling bathing cave.

Bonnie and Emma shyly approached Chloe, offering to help her walk the dogs. Chloe turned to Billy and Tucker.

"Would you guys like to come with us? We can look for a regular spot for the dogs to go." They happily agreed, leaving the room with the girls, the German shepherd and Honda the poodle trotting behind. Kenya approached Ginger Mae,

"Morning, chicky." She leaned over to rub Daisy's arm affectionately. "Why don't you let me introduce her to some of the animals from the sanctuary? Not the cats—the turtles or the goats, maybe the bird. It might give her a sense of purpose."

Ginger Mae nodded, watching them as they left with Crystal and her potbelly pig. She quickly noticed Mama Diaz checking everyone out.

"Has anyone noticed a complete change of attitude this morning? I feel great, and happy." She paused, waiting to get their attention. "Do you all remember what's happening above us? Millions are dying. How can we feel this way? It's not normal."

Guilty eyes cast themselves down, faces drawn as they remembered the carnage taking place above them.

At that moment, Netty entered the room, her golden glow and the sparkle from her eyes preceding her. She stood quietly, her soft cotton wrap allowing her wings and tail to move freely as her delicate bare feet stopped at the door.

"Good morning, everyone. I hope you are all anxious to join us for breakfast. Wil needs to cover a few items with you then we will leave you to your own devices. We have a few more supplies to dispense. Perhaps you can choose a few to handle the supply closet. I think you will need three strong men. After breakfast you will leave with my husband. I also need to know who wants to work in the kitchen with me until we construct one for your own use."

As Netty spoke, the group walking the dogs returned, Kenya and Daisy bringing up the rear.

Netty clapped her hands and the refreshed but wary group followed her out to the main corridor where she led them up the incline from last night that led to an opening from which aromatic smells wafted. The crowd started as they heard the muffled roar of a lion, followed by a barrage of elephant trumpets.

Netty reached out to restrain Johno and his men. "Don't worry, Johno. They are fine, just a territorial dispute. The cats are unable to harm another animal—or human for that matter—while they are in the Hive."

From the back of the crowd came a disdainful chuff. Everyone turned, reminded of the ever-present Caesar as he slapped his powerful paw on the hard, smooth stone of the cavern floor, his laser eyes watchfully focused on Scotty, Chloe and the dogs as if to dispute Netty's words.

Scotty spoke up. "Oh, don't worry about Caesar, Echo says he's harmless."

He turned to Caesar, approaching softly to give him a tentative pat on his magnificent head.

"See?" Breathing more easily, the group entered Netty and Wil's kitchen, Caesar plopping down outside the entrance.

As the group funneled in, they stood dumbfounded at the scene in front of them.

The cavern was much smaller than any of the previous spaces, the ceiling only about ten feet high. The walls featured the ever-present thick undulating membrane, yet two of the walls sported iron bars with wide metal rungs from which hung intricate and colorful handmade quilts, clearly priceless antiques. Rag rugs of all shapes and sizes with coordinated colors hugged the bare floor. But most surprising was the fireplace that burned brightly, flames dancing flirtatiously, enticing the group closer as the aroma wafting from the huge iron pot hanging from an iron arm bubbled its spicy brew.

A bed of what appeared to be cloth stuffed with straw sat to the side of the fireplace with Netty's golden creature and his kitten cuddled up, watching them solemnly.

The furniture in the cozy room consisted of several rocking chairs and three plank tables with benches tucked underneath. A smaller intimate table for four was to the side of the room where Netty's kitchen worktable sat with piles of the green crusty pods and smaller pieces of sliced peaches, their smell seductive. All the furniture appeared old, handmade and covered with layers of hand-rubbed patina. The vintage room, clearly a step out of time, looked well lived in and eminently suited their two perplexing benefactors.

Their attention suddenly shifted to two resplendent pit bulls that stood at attention in one corner of the room; Netty's baking ovens hidden in the corner with them. Ears at attention, their tails wagged ominously as Echo and his tiny white puppy tottered toward them.

Scotty lunged forward, scooping the hapless buddies into his arms and Echo, struggling in his arms, wriggled to be free.

"Brother Scotty, put me down. Do you not know these dogs?"

Netty stepped forward, tears in her golden eyes. She swept Echo and puppy Barney away from Scotty to deposit them on the rug in front of the pit bulls, who knelt in front of Echo with bowed heads, their strong muscled bodies quavering. They looked up at Scotty and made tiny crawling gestures toward him. Netty's musical voice rang out. "Do you recognize anything hanging from the mantel?"

The crowd turned to the mantel. The only incongruous item was a large sledgehammer bolted to the stones along the right wall of the fireplace. Scotty stared, his memory searching, picking at a dawning comprehension.

"No . . . it can't be." He searched Netty's eyes for the truth, understanding as she wiped away the tears. Scotty walked deliberately to the pit bulls as Echo wound her arms around each of them.

"We did this, Brother Scotty. The Womb is pleased with us. We saved them. They would have died."

"But I saw them die. I watched the sick bastard bust their skulls." Scotty looked into the eyes of the sweet, happy creatures that intently engaged his attention. He felt them try to communicate their thanks to him. *How did they know?*

"They know much, Brother Scotty, they were saved by the Womb."

"These are the dogs we watched get killed. How can they be alive now?" Scotty's nose crinkled his puzzlement.

"King . . . Queenie." The dogs rose and padded over to Wil where they jumped up on their hind legs, bracing themselves on his chest. Wil bent to hug them.

"Don't you understand? When it comes to creating life, there is nothing the Womb cannot do—including the salvation of the spirit. As long as the rescue is made in a timely fashion. These dogs were the only two that could be saved from the butchers in the dogfighting ring the night you and Echo went to the woods."

Wil glanced at the fireplace. "We keep that sledgehammer to remind us never to forget the brutality of man. It makes our mission easier whenever we get depressed about the new future of this planet." Wil's bitter tone did not go unnoticed.

"Gee, dude, a sledgehammer? Isn't that a little extreme?"

Billy Susseman, the red-headed trucker, shook his head as he stroked his poodle. Wil turned on him unexpectedly.

"Not extreme enough." Bitterness intensified as Wil's expression hardened. "We have no love lost for men of this planet. Sick greedy evilness runs through all of us. Some control it better than others. Pity the victims, and I don't mean just the creatures."

Wil's face twisted with hate. As Wil's outburst shocked the crowd, King and Queenie whined, sending Netty to Wil's side and Baby shuffling to him for comfort. They stood huddled as a united family, clearly bereaved over something. Netty's arms embraced him as Wil scooped up Baby, holding him close.

As the crowd grew silent at the display of emotion, Netty broke away to busy herself in the kitchen. Wil turned to face the crowd with a sigh, rubbing his hand across his glowing eyes.

"Please forgive me. It's been a mighty long time since we . . . died. I have trouble forgetting. Thank the Womb for our salvation."

"Can you tell us what you mean about the new future of the planet?" The question came from one of the new truckers, the one with the German shepherd who up until this point had remained in the background just taking it all in.

Wil turned to him. "And who are you, young man?"

"My name is Tucker. Tucker the trucker, and this here is my boy, Fire. He goes everywhere with me." Tucker patted his large German shepherd while his suspicious eyes stayed tethered to Wil, who seemed to dismiss him, suddenly staring into the distance, apparently lost in the vicious memories of his past.

Shaking his head, Wil grimaced at the shocked faces before him. "Sometime, perhaps, we will tell you our story. And I will get to your questions later, young man. But for now, I think it is time to take our seats to enjoy Netty's breakfast. Shall we?"

He extended his arm to point the way, inviting everyone to find seats at the large farmhouse tables. As everyone funneled to the tables in anticipation of a hearty meal, Netty called from the kitchen, dispelling the lingering tension from Wil's revelation and heading off any further questions of the Earth's future.

"I can use a hand here. Mrs. Diaz? And how about you, Gloria? Crystal? You can leave your sweet pig by the fire with Echo and the dogs. She will be fine."

Breakfast became a celebration as the women placed large earthen bowls of unidentifiable food on the three tables. Platters of colorful crunchy vegetables joined the unfamiliar bowls of spicy foods that tasted like magic if you could just figure how to capture it. Cold pitchers of icy clear water washed the hearty meal down parched throats. Netty offered tea and fresh fruit pie in a surprising buttery flavored green crust.

As Chloe, Bonnie and Emma cleared the tables, Dezi, Karen, and one of Johno's men helped Netty wash the dishes. A sense of wellbeing and languid comfort permeated the group.

The only responsibilities anyone thought about was to feed the wildlife. Wil made sure the assorted dogs and pets were fed. Baby and Echo watched from a perch on the wall near the dogs, their arms stuck into the wall as if absorbed by the thick membrane. As Wil and Netty failed to comment, the group at the tables looked away, swallowing their discomfort. When Kenya decided to ask what the heck they were doing, Netty casually replied, "They are eating. The Womb provides for them."

"Oh, okay." Kenya turned green as she gazed at the golden creatures.

Turning back to the table they watched Jose rise. He cleared his throat, a hesitant smile managing to sprinkle reassurance around the tables.

"Wil, Netty, we would all like to thank you for your hospitality." Nods and murmurings from the group forced Jose to pause.

"I speak for everyone when I tell you how overwhelmed we are to be here. I'm sure most of us will need a lot of time to adjust our thinking to our new surroundings. It's not just about learning who our ancestors are, contrary to all we have been taught. It's the loss of a way of life, our hometowns, our families and friends, our jobs. We need some time to mourn. I hope you understand that."

Wil and Netty sat on a bench near the fireplace, Baby curled at their feet with little Barney tucked in next to his tummy.

"We understand completely. We went through something just like that many years ago. It will be difficult. It took me several years to stop mourning. But I had the help of someone who loves me."

She slipped her arm through Wil's. "Many of you are without spouses and children. You were deliberately chosen because of that. The people sitting with you at these tables will become your family and your loved ones. You will build new relationships. You will study. You will prepare yourself for the time when the planet will ask for your help. You will surface when it is safe again."

"Can you give us any idea when that will be?" Karen, their copilot, spoke loudly over the din caused by Netty's remarks.

"Study? What do we need to study?"

"I don't need to study anything," Billy said as his hand rose to his nose to squirt nasal relief into his nostrils, easing his asthma.

Wil rose, approaching the tables. "Please, please, calm down, everyone. I have a suggestion. Let me lay out some of the responsibilities you will be faced with. It will give you something constructive to think about. Why don't we plan to get a few months under our belts then reassess how you are doing? I think for now we will continue to use Netty's kitchen, postponing the plans for your own. Sound good?"

As the group gave tentative nods, Wil continued, "As I mentioned yesterday, we need teams to feed the wildlife, perform sanitation duty and enrichment detail. This is serious work. The Womb will not tolerate irresponsibility. You must all remember—the wildlife comes first. They are sacred.

"Netty needs help in the kitchen. She is looking for four assistants who will make the assignment their permanent job."

Dezi shot his hand up in the air, interrupting and getting shushed by Abby. "Are you volunteering, Dezi?" Wil raised an eyebrow.

"Damn straight, anything to get me away from those dumb, smelly beasts."

"I wouldn't say that too loudly if I were you, young man." Wil's voice cut deeply through the din, instantly sobering the crowd. "As a matter of fact, you are precisely the kind of human who needs to learn tolerance. I do not believe the kitchen is suited to you any more than caring for the wildlife is. But you must learn. Be grateful for the chance.

Turning his attention to Johno and his men, Wil addressed them, "I realize your job with the baby elephants is labor intensive. I am hoping you will consider taking on some helpers to spell you from time to time. It will be very helpful if you can impart some of your wisdom to the rest of us."

Johno nodded, bowing his head respectfully.

"I need three or four of you to work in the fields with me. It will be your responsibility to cultivate new plants that the Womb wants us to grow as they are presented. It is also your job to tend to seed retrieval and storage, along with selecting the produce Netty and her crew will need for meals and for canning.

"I need three men to work on a new project. Jose, I am putting you in charge. I will give you the keys to the supply closet and we will tour it later. You and the three men will also take charge of a daunting task. I need our new library cleaned and organized. Anyone who is not working in the kitchen or the fields will lend extra hands as needed. That means those who feed the wildlife will have to take a turn helping to clean the library. These sound like simple chores but I assure you they are not."

As Wil continued to outline responsibilities, Scotty, Chloe, Kane and Kenya put their heads together, quietly conferring as to where they hoped to be placed. Scotty took the lead. "Guys, I don't know about you, but I want to work where the food grows. Did you see that place? It feels like magic. The monkeys and elephants will hang out there. It will be a great place for the dogs. Chloe, you need to be careful with Ted. He's so small, there may be dangerous areas for him in other places. The growing fields are bound to be safer." Looking up at Echo as the others considered his plan, he caught her eye as she languished with the dogs by the fireplace.

Auras whispered, seeping into his mind. "I am happy, Brother Scotty. My Barney is small and new. My mission is no more. My family grows. We can now plan for new life. That is our destiny. My brother Baby asks me small questions. He is damaged but can still function. He is productive in the field. We will join you." Scotty's head reeled from the breath of Echo's provocative comments.

"New life, Echo? Is someone planning to make babies?"

"No brother. There will be no babies."

Echo fell silent, turning back to her posse of Baby, little Barney, the pit bulls King and Queenie, Penny and Teddy, Mimi and the two new additions: Fire the shepherd and Honda, the poodle. Scotty looked up to see Wil join Netty at their small table, leaving them to sort out who would do what.

# Chapter 18

Ginger Mae hiked up her pants that had slipped down over her hips for the tenth time that morning. As she sliced into a three-pound apple for the pie Salina Diaz was making the green dough for, she wondered if she had finally managed to shed the five or six (okay . . . *ten*) extra pounds she had fought to lose before she found herself living in the great cavern of the Hive. She estimated a good six weeks had flown by since Abby had saved them. So much seemed to have changed in the short period of time.

She glanced up as members of the Hive wandered into the kitchen to either confer with Abby and Netty or try to cop a preview of the goodies Netty and her crew of kitchen staff were preparing for dinner.

Salina Diaz (she insisted everyone use her first name) quickly became a leader in the kitchen, her skills at organizing and overseeing for her own blended family in the past an asset that she put to good use. Netty's kitchen became the hub of the Hive. A warm and inviting sanctuary where all could pretend life was normal. It was where the survivors did their planning, their voting, their disciplining, their questioning, socializing (flirting) and of course, their gorging.

And gorge they did. Apparently the new and delectable foods they ate contained less garbage calories than the food processed and sold to them in the grocery stores above. Ginger Mae didn't know how that could be but as she eyed her fellow group members, she noticed many of them looked slimmer. Especially Gloria, who had confided she was diabetic. Clyde, who walked around like he had a load in his saggy pants, matching his saggy spirit and Billy, the red-headed reluctant trucker, who now thanked his scrawny balls (incessantly to anyone who would listen) that he chose *this* gig to fill in for a friend.

Gloria had a few days' supply of insulin with her when they arrived at the Hive. When the women saw her inject herself in their sleeping quarters, they wondered what would happen if Gloria went into a diabetic coma or got sick. Would Netty provide medical care? Would the phantom Womb assist or even care? So far, though, Gloria appeared to be fine and had dropped quite a bit of weight.

By the end of the second week, everyone had reluctantly swallowed the fact that they were here for the long haul.

How long? No one wanted to put a voice to that question after evaluating Wil's shocking revelation given upon their arrival. There were only so many traumas and upheavals a person's system could take. Everyone feared another shock might drive someone over the edge, someone like Clyde.

As week after week passed, the likelihood of Clyde's wife and grandchildren joining them looked more and more remote. He refused to give up though. Ginger Mae didn't fail to notice how Salina Diaz took pains to make sure Clyde got a little extra helping of anything he appeared to favor at meal time. Even so, his weight continued to slip away.

Putting down her knife, she finished peeling the fruit for Salina's pies. Searching for her tattered handbag, she took a break at the small oak table favored by Netty and Wil at meals. As she fished in her bag for her mirror, she felt the little black and white dog they called Mimi scratching at her leg for attention. She knelt down to gather the love-hungry girl in her arms, noticing the cloud of cataracts on her eyes was missing.

Mimi had failed to join Scotty and his young gang with the rest of the dogs in the field. She was older with short legs and almost blind. Besides, she was turning into the original chow hound. Wherever the food was, you could find Mimi. So Netty's kitchen became her new home. Lots of food . . . lots of love.

As Ginger Mae gave her a kiss on the head and set her back down on the floor, she felt a kinship with the damaged dog. Glancing around to see who might be watching her, she turned to the wall to take her mirror out and examine her face. Looking critically at her scar and the distortion of her lip that had been so poorly stitched, she tried not to flinch at the ruin of her face. She still couldn't get used to the unfamiliar countenance that looked back at her. A lonely tear traveled forlornly down her damaged cheek as she remembered how she used to fret about losing her looks—the kiss of death for an aging working girl.

So much had changed. Their lives had been turned upside down in such a profound way that *she* had become the mute one while Daisy flourished and blossomed. Daisy's intellect quickly became apparent to all as she followed Jose and Abby around like a sponge, soaking up knowledge wherever she could.

Jose currently had her working on a special project in what they called the library. Ginger Mae wondered when they would be able to unveil their project, as she was more than curious why Daisy always came back early with Jose and his men for dinner; filthy dirty, covered in thick grime and dust.

She looked up as Dezi walked by, giving her hair a playful tug as he carried a jug of water to the fireplace to fill the dog's dishes.

"Come on, babe, put a smile on that pretty mug of yours."

And she did. He always made her smile. Some people rolled their eyes at Dezi but, over time, Ginger Mae realized he was just like her. The only difference was his damage was on the inside. His base, sassy bluster and sexual innuendoes were a transparent cover, his way of dealing with his damage. She knew he would tell her his story someday. They were becoming close friends as he was the first one who didn't treat her like a toxic victim. He saw who she was beyond the notorious skirmish with the dead Armoni.

She had learned a few things about life while she plied her trade in the exclusive hotels and apartments of New York City. Every once in a while she would get a request from what she referred to as *an unfortunate*. It might be a man with an extreme illness or a disfiguring disability. Some of them were born that way. Many found they would never have an easy time with the ladies so they turned to a professional rather than risk rejection.

These were her personal VIPs, the ones she saved her honest tenderness for, the ones who were privileged to glimpse the real Ginger Mae Shrute.

She glanced back at Dezi as he conferred with Salina Diaz regarding the produce she wanted him to collect from the growing field. You couldn't tell for sure from the outside but Ginger Mae knew . . . Dezi was *an unfortunate.*

Ginger Mae spotted Karen entering the kitchen. She spent most of her time working on the project at the library. She stopped in the kitchen each day to pick up lunch for the crew who seemed to get inordinately filthy for a bunch of people organizing books.

Smiling to herself, Ginger Mae noticed that Karen, like herself, was not a true blonde. Her roots were growing in. Well, her own were probably just as bad.

Holding up her mirror, she checked them out. Oddly, her hair appeared to be growing in darker than normal, not a single sign of the creeping grey strands that seemed to have multiplied every time she was due for a touch up.

Shrugging her shoulders, she let the mirror slip back down to her ruined mouth. As she took a final peek, she did a double take. Her finger reached up to her mouth to slide over the worm-like puckered raised scar that ran the length of her face. *How can that be?* The scar felt smooth, the puckering gone. She peered closely at the scar, verifying the new smooth texture.

Something else caught her eye, another subtle change. For several years she had noticed a fine network of lines developing around her eyes. Nothing serious, just enough to force her to stay out of direct sunlight with her johns, just enough to annoy her. She had been forced to cut back on her expensive Botox shots to save money for Daisy's future, but the tell-tale lines had now disappeared.

Ginger Mae's eyes darted around the room, anxious to know if she was being watched. Deciding to keep this to herself for now, she quickly slipped the mirror back into her purse. Salina Diaz approached from her wooden workbench, a box laden with lunch for the field workers in her arms.

"Ginger Mae, would you care to take this to the kids in the field?" She placed her hand on Ginger Mae's shoulder, her tenderness a constant in Ginger Mae's life. Nodding her assent, she gave Salina a lopsided smile of gratitude and headed out the kitchen with the box.

Ginger Mae strolled along the cavern corridors that were becoming second nature to her. She no longer flinched at the sight of the mysterious live membrane that lined the walls. Just weird and ugly interior design in a very strange home she was now grateful to live in.

Approaching the opening to the water cavern housing the big cats, she slowed, listening for the chuffing of bears at play. She wondered what had possessed the bears to take up residence with the cats. Their cavern luckily contained a lovely underground lake that allowed the cats and bears to claim their own play areas, but she didn't remember any accounts of lions, bears and tigers getting along like this. She wrinkled her nose as the ursine and feline smells hit her. Funny how the smells no longer revolted her.

Moving on, she shifted the box she carried to a more comfortable position. She still had a ways to go, winding around the serpentine corridors and dodging clumps of elephant dung that littered the corridors no matter how often they were cleaned.

Turning another corner, she met up with Johno and his men. They were walking the baby elephants with the juveniles and young tusker on their daily foray to the growing fields.

"How are you this fine day, Ms. Ginger Mae?" Johno's grin split from ear to ear, his affable nature irresistible even to the sullen Ginger Mae.

"I'm fine, Johno, you and the boys coming around for lunch?"

"Yes, madam. You'll never see us passing up a meal. Just need to drop the babies off in the field first."

Ginger Mae stretched her head down the corridor the group had just emerged from, getting bumped by two rambunctious babies in the process.

"Where's big Tobi? She's not with you?"

"No, I let Emma and Bonnie keep Tobi busy. I want to try to keep her away from the fields for a while. She's been a little destructive lately. She keeps digging her tusks into the ground. It makes Scotty and his crew mad. She seems to be looking for something. Her trunk flings the dirt around like she's angry. Wish I could figure it out."

"But Johno, you've known her all her life. Did you ever see her exhibit this behavior in Africa?"

"No, madam, but after Tobi grew up enough to join the wild herds I only saw her when she came back for visits, usually at night during feeding time, of course. She loved to come back to say hello and see the new babies. Most of what she did during the day is a mystery to me, though. I assume just the normal things wild elephants do. Always on the move, looking for new browse and moving from waterhole to waterhole."

"Well, I hope she works through her problem soon, for everyone's sake."

Gently swatting away the searching trunks of the sometimes demanding babies, Ginger Mae lifted her box higher. Within a few more feet, the group found themselves at the opening for the growing field. She held her breath as she stepped through, feeling the odd pressure that kept the small lavender-blue pollinating creatures from accidently escaping their cavern and their vital job.

As she gazed out into the field that gradually rose up to the rear of the cavern, creating an artificially far horizon, she spotted Kenya lounging on a hillock, her pregnancy at its maturity, delivery just a few weeks off. Johno broke off to escort the babies to a safe spot near a row of strange fruit trees that appeared to have been planted within the last few years, young enough not to attract the deadly pollinators. Lugging her box to Kenya's comfortable hillock, she collapsed next to her.

"Hey there, chicky. Hope ya all got something sweet in there today, my cravings are just not going away."

Kenya was fast becoming a source of comedy for her. The poor girl was so goodhearted but her self-interest was transparent. She just could not accept the fact that the world was different now. She could enthrall Ginger Mae for hours with her big plans to find the right baby daddy for her and her baby as soon as they 'got out of this smelly underground tunnel with the wanna-be angels'. Ginger Mae did not fail to notice how tolerant Abby, Netty, Wil and Scotty were around her. Her impending birth was the probable answer, giving her a pass on her deep-seated denial.

Kenya no longer sported her filthy white short shorts. Like the rest of them, the clothes they'd been wearing upon arrival had quickly been reduced to rags. It was a pleasant surprise to find a smaller cavern beyond their sleeping quarters piled high with all kinds of clothes. Most, but not all, still had tags on them, as if they had been recently purchased from a clothing store. She knew that was probably a stretch as piles of racks that had formerly held clothes lay heaped, broken and twisted on one side of the room. When asked where the clothes had come from, Netty just smiled and said, "The Womb provides".

Kenya rummaged around in the box of foodstuffs until she found something to her liking. Out in the field, Ginger Mae could see the others were making for the hillock in anticipation of their lunch break. And of course, that included Echo and Baby with their doggie entourage.

They quickly found that no matter what responsibility they assigned Scotty and Chloe, the two golden creatures insisted on accompanying them, which meant the large pack of dogs would follow too, and the infernal tiger, Caesar. Everyone agreed the growing field was the best place for the troupe. From time to time one of the other survivors would join them, just to relieve the monotony. Ginger Mae had to admit, as well as their bathing caves, the growing field was a beautiful place. If you could overlook the dangerous pollinators, that is. She had no wish to get any closer to the strange, venomous creatures.

As Scotty and Kane approached, she could see they were lugging their large water tank. Many of the survivors kept their drinking cups tied to a loop on their clothes—you never knew where you might be at any given time in their vast network of connecting caverns and caves. Many contained water sources but they had learned weeks ago to keep barrels of water in strategic locations. The practice of dipping their hands into the water to take a drink came under protest early on. No one wanted the dirt from the animals' keepers or feeders in the drinking water, hence the dangling cups. Luckily, the growing fields had their own water source from a brook that meandered strategically through the rows of trees and vegetables. Nicely convenient.

"Hi, Ginger Mae, thanks for lunch." Chloe sat down next to Kenya, reaching into the box for her lunch that she shared with her scamp, Teddy. He was an adorable dog but what an ego: He spent far too much time making sure everyone knew he was the big dog in town, not even backing down for King and Queenie, the royal pit bulls that remained her personal favorites.

Ginger Mae noticed Chloe still had not shaken her fragile air. By now everyone in the Hive knew about her bizarre kidnapping by the famous politician, Omar Nasir, and how Scotty's golden creature had killed her uncle who had carried out the actual kidnapping and had planned to shoot them all. She shrugged, knowing Chloe's story was no more bizarre than her own. It wasn't like she hadn't seen the golden creature kill anyone before.

Life truly was stranger than fiction. She knew her story featuring the psychotic Armoni had gotten around. No one had bothered to ask what she had been doing with him to begin with. They must all just think she was part of his despicable plot to rob Abby and Jose and kill their creature. How much lower could her self-confidence get?

She stood quickly as Echo and Baby approached, still uneasy in their presence.

The creature that belonged to Netty and Wil gazed at her, its luminous eyes lingering on her face. She watched as the creature turned to the one called Echo, placing one fragile digit on her chest. Together, they turned to Ginger Mae as if to assess her. She felt a strangeness overcome her as her vision clouded with an aura felt deep in her mind. She trembled with confusion as she heard whispers, unable to make out words. The whispers stopped as the creatures gave her a slight bow and backed away with the rest of the dogs to join the crowd around the lunch box. *What the hell was that?*

As Scotty and Kane reached into the box, they nodded their thanks, sweat dripping off their muscled arms. Scotty's wings remained tamped down under his shirt but his tail was free and relaxed. Not everyone was used to the changes in the bodies of their benefactors, but Scotty behaved just like one of them. Just a kid who had found himself innocently caught up in something he hadn't asked for. He clearly wanted to be normal like the rest of his friends. It was much easier getting accustomed to his changes compared to the others but it was a slow process.

As a matter of fact, she only saw Abby and Jose at meals these days. They spent most of their time with Wil or at the library. She wondered when they would get to see what was so special about the library. Efforts to pry information out of Daisy got her nowhere. She bent down to retrieve her box. They had to make it last as long as possible. Nothing was wasted here.

Lingering in the beauty of the growing fields, she heard the trilling laughter of little Kimir, who was being chased among the rows of tall, succulent vegetables by Billy, the trucker who had become a survivor due to the vulgarities of fate when he had volunteered to fill in for a buddy who had originally been vetted by Ginger Mae.

Kimir still cried at night for his mother and father. They all tried to distract him during the day to keep his mind off his loss, and he appeared to bond well with the truckers. Perhaps it was because they felt like outsiders themselves and found an affinity with the young boy.

She waved goodbye to Kenya who had commenced holding court with the boys. Ginger Mae observed the young girl's skin and hair appeared more luminous and lush than ever, even as she stroked her burdensome belly, clearly not far off from delivery. She watched as Johno waved to Kenya from the hillock where the baby eles frolicked. Glancing back at Kenya, she observed the young girl wave back and toss Johno a provocative wink. *The irrepressible Kenya just might find herself with a surfeit of suitors once that baby comes,* thought Ginger Mae. She bowed her head and, waving to the kids, she backed out into the corridor, anxious to hurry back to the kitchen to continue her duties.

As she traipsed the corridors, she thought about the golden creatures. Had they been trying to talk to her? She knew they had some way of communicating that only a chosen few could understand. Why would they be interested in her? Had she misread their behavior? It had been so subtle, maybe she had imagined it. *Don't be stupid, Ginger Mae.* She dragged her box carefully around a corner. *I didn't imagine anything. They're up to something and it might involve me.*

As she approached the kitchen, she found herself so preoccupied with Baby and Echo that she failed to notice a figure standing in an alcove past the kitchen opening. The blank face of the figure focused on her, unable to turn away. With teeth clenched so hard they made grinding sounds, the figure backed deeper into the alcove, remaining undetected as Ginger Mae disappeared into the kitchen.

"Ginger Mae, you're back. Can you take over for Netty?" Salina Diaz nodded her head toward Netty who dropped the huge iron spoon she was using to stir the pot bubbling at the fireplace.

Netty hurried over to the cart that was loaded with the food they had spent the morning cooking. Everyday Netty disappeared with the cart, not to be seen again until dinnertime when she returned to the kitchen with Wil . . . sometimes after dinner was finished. She often wore the air of distraction upon her return. They were all aware of the fact that when originally questioned by Salina, Netty had responded in an uncharacteristically abrupt fashion, refusing to answer the innocent question and mandating the subject never to arise again. *Just another one of the strange mysteries of Netty and Wil*, thought Ginger Mae as she contemplated Netty's now familiar winged back disappearing through the kitchen opening, to evaporate into the Hive with her cart of food.

Ginger Mae quickly stirred the stew pot Netty had been working on, its bubbles exploding tiny burps of spicy mystique into the air.

As she stirred, she scanned the bygone room, marveling at how easily the harmony in Netty's kitchen flowed. Even when the dogs were underfoot or Crystal's pig rearranged the rugs with her snout, the room almost made her feel like she had a real home here.

"Hello, guys." Sassy Emma Diaz breezed in to kiss her mother on the cheek, grabbed a box, and filled it with food to take back to the keepers who were watching the rhinos and the rest of the elephant herd. Ginger Mae noticed how one of Johno's young keepers watched her every move as she filled the box he would help her carry. The light in his eye meant one thing to Ginger Mae. Emma was well past the age at which most women in Africa would have had their first child. And this young man was no different than many of the men in Africa who thought a woman's job was to be available for sex at all times, often whether they wanted it or not.

She eyed Johno's young keeper from the corner of her eyes, wondering if a problem may be in the making. Did any of the keepers from Africa have AIDS? What would they do if someone got really sick? They were damn lucky Billy's asthma had subsided after he ran out of medication in his inhaler. Everyone assumed the air must contain less contaminants than the air above ground, certainly no pollen except from the growing fields. But if the pollinators couldn't get out through the pressure lock at the entrance, it must also keep out the pollen.

As Emma left with the keeper—*what's his name anyway . . . Elias?*—Salina stood with her hands on her hips, her apron saggy and filthy from washing vegetables as she watched them disappear through the doorway. They could hear Emma's girlish giggle carry back into the room in response to something said by the keeper. Emotions flickered across Salina's face. Ginger Mae interpreted pride, love and fear. Yeah, Mama Diaz was no fool.

Ginger felt a tap on her shoulder. Bending her neck, she confronted her closest ally, Dezi, standing behind her with his skinny ferret face plastered with supplication, his voice hesitant. "Hey babe, do you mind if I ask you a question? I kinda need a favor."

"Sure, Dezi . . . what's up?"

"Well . . ." Dezi bowed his head then glanced up. "You know how these stinky damn beasts drive me nuts, right?"

Ginger Mae could not stop herself from smiling. "Yes, Dez, I think everyone knows."

"Well, I think I'm going to go postal and start slapping them around if I don't get away from them for a while."

Unfortunately for Dezi, his lack of skills other than truck driving had put him at a distinct disadvantage when chores had been assigned. He had been faced with a choice of hard labor in the library or being the official animal census keeper of all animals. Dezi had chosen the latter, hoping he could just stand back and count, moving on from cavern to cavern until they were all accounted for. It had taken him all day. Many did not see the wisdom of the exercise but Wil and Netty had insisted on it. The warning from Wil regarding the wrath of the Womb in the event of just one creature being unaccounted for was enough to make them all tremble. If Dezi's daily count came up short, they were all tasked with sending search parties out to comb the endless passageways and caverns until the missing creature was located. It had only taken a few false alarms to put Dezi on the bottom of the popularity list in the Hive. They had also made him very exacting at what he did.

And, as luck would have it, Dezi found it impossible to just peek in a cavern and count. The cats and bears were very boisterous, hiding behind rocks, readying themselves to playfully pounce on unwary victims. Dezi became their favorite plaything, although they were careful never to seriously hurt him, no matter how he varied his schedule to fool them. His cuts and bruises healed rapidly but he knew they sensed his disdain and disgust.

Dezi fared no better with the rest of the creatures. He was kicked, spat at, urinated upon and nipped. No one else elicited this response from the wildlife. Even the dogs stayed away from him. Oddly, from time to time, Baby would approach Dezi during dinner to stand quietly at his side. He would eventually feel the creature's presence and nod hello, receiving an enigmatic golden touch on his skinny arm from Baby who would then re-join Echo and Barney at the fireplace with the other dogs and Tulip, the pig.

Raised eyebrows from other diners would stare at Dezi then refocus on the abundance of tasty confections that were birthed in Netty's kitchen. After all, it wasn't like they hadn't seen anything odd in the Hive before. Their whole lives were now the exact definition of odd.

"How exactly do you want me to help you with your problem, Dez? You know I'm pretty much stuck in the kitchen all day."

Dezi took a deep breath, true desperation now bleeding into his eyes. "Well, doll, that's the thing. I was hoping you might want to swap jobs for a while. The animals don't bother you. Please, Ginger Mae?" His voice cracked with strain. "You would sure be doing me a solid."

Ginger Mae looked into his eyes, clearly feeling his desperation and the deeper layer of what she sensed made him an unfortunate. She stopped stirring the kettle, wiping her hands on her limp apron. "I don't know how well you'll do in the kitchen, Dez. We'll have to get the okay from Salina and Netty."

Seeing the grateful anticipation of salvation in Dezi's eyes, she took him into her arms and gave him a comforting hug. "Of course, I'll be happy to help you out, hon."

Dezi held her harder, lifting her up and swinging her around, exclaiming loudly, "I love ya, babe. You're my girl."

As Dezi set the laughing Ginger Mae back down on her feet, she caught sight of Peter standing on the other side of the room dipping water from the bucket into a cup. His mouth hung wide open. Pretending not to notice, he quickly bent down, turning his back to Ginger Mae, but not before she caught a glimmer of something unidentifiable in his eyes. *Hatred? Anger?* she wondered. *Or hurt?* Dismissing Peter's hatred of her, she took Dezi over to Salina to discuss their new plans.

Netty and Wil trudged silently down and around the twisted corridors, dragging a wagon loaded with food. They made the trip daily and the food would last until their next trip tomorrow. Baby sat in the wagon, his kitten now almost fully grown and less willing to be dragged around by her golden furry mentor. Netty glanced back, deciding to leave the cat behind next time. She had too much weighing her down to have to worry about a squirming cat eager to escape Baby's worshiping hands. If the cat took off and got lost, they would never hear the end of it from Baby.

Netty smiled as she admired Baby in all his gloriousness, his wings as alive and functioning as her own. It was now perfectly clear the Oolahans were the ancestors of humans. Netty didn't need a DNA test to tell her that, although she was quite capable of performing one in the Womb's laboratory.

She and Wil had learned to be accomplished in the biological arts of creating life. Looking at Baby, Netty's heart lurched for her precious creature. Baby's destiny would always remain unrealized. He should have been able to work alongside her and Wil in the Womb's lab. Unfortunately, when the Womb had transferred their souls and memories into their new bodies, the only thing left to work with in Baby's mind did not include the regeneration of his damaged areas from his landing on earth so long ago. And the damage wrought by Eli's viciousness as he stomped on Baby's head, splitting his skull to leave only brain splatter, had not helped either.

"Helloooo? Neeeettttty? Where did your mind wonder off to? I have been trying to get your attention."

Wil smiled down at Netty as they continued their trek, the wagon now throwing off a harsh squeak that bounced around the echoing membrane-lined walls. Netty looked up at his dear, sweet face, trying to smile. She watched as Wil's brow furrowed, worry the only expression on his handsome guileless face. *Goodness,* she thought, *he still takes my breath away, even after a hundred and twenty years.*

"Love, I can see something is troubling you."

Wil steered them to a ledge, set the wagon down, and swept her up into his arms where she clung to him, trembling. As they stood, wrapped in each other's arms, a frantic aura shot through their minds. They turned to see Baby standing in the wagon with skinny leather fingers reaching out spasmodically, his arms waving as the whispers cried forlornly.

"Sister . . . Brother . . . me . . . me." With love in her eyes, Netty leaned down to embrace Baby, lifting him into their arms where they huddled together.

"Sister sad." Baby traced the contours of Netty's face with his tiny fingers.

"No, Baby, I'm not sad." Wil removed Baby from Netty's arm, placing him back into the wagon.

"Well, why the long face?" Wil asked.

"Oh, I don't know, I guess I am just worried about our future. We have so much to deal with. I never expected this to be our lives." Her hand drifted down to stroke Baby's fur as she spoke.

Wil's face clouded with anger. "I know . . . I should have shot that bastard you were married to when I had the chance."

"It is so strange. I know a century has passed but it will always be like it just happened yesterday. I will never forget what that . . ." Netty choked. "What that degenerate deviant Eli did to Baby. When I feel stressed about the challenges in front of us, my mind goes back to that moment." Netty rubbed the side of her temple.

"I wish I could just burn that image out of my mind but it will not go away." Turgid auras intruded, startling them both. They turned to Baby, expecting whispers. But Baby sat silent, his auras turning black.

Wil shook his head at Netty, putting his finger to his lips, giving a subtle shake. Ashamed and crestfallen, Netty squatted down to nab Baby's escaped cat, depositing it back in the wagon. Baby quickly grabbed the cat, holding it close and shutting his eyes. Subject closed.

As Wil and Netty resumed their long journey, from behind their winged backs Baby's eyes opened and narrowed, flashing rare chaotic emotion. With an inscrutable toss of his antlers, Baby appeared to stew, his posture purposeful, despite the slight tremor of his delicate hands disguised in his movement as he resumed the deliberate stroking of his cat.

Netty and Wil rounded a corner to stand before a stout rough-hewn wooden door sporting a bright new lock affixed to a strong bolt embedded into the cavern wall. Baby quickly let his eyes dim, resuming his benign demeanor.

Netty glanced back at Baby, her bearing suddenly hopeful. Will wrapped his arm around her shoulders as she forced her melancholy mood to vanish. She clasped her hands together with excitement as she watched Baby, receiving a slow nod. Turning to Wil she received the same signal. The cavern echoed with her dull pounding on the door as she squared her shoulders, the temperature suddenly cool. Wil hurriedly removed a key from the twine around his neck, hidden from view by his tunic.

Time stood still as they held their breath, waiting for the door to admit them. Ponderously, the door creaked open, the sound amplified by the acoustics of the cavern. As Netty stepped forward, her hand raised for a greeting, she felt a prick at her neck. Glancing back at the shadows of the membrane-covered cavern wall, she dismissed her premonition, attention focused on what lay behind the door.

The furtive figure melted into the shadow of the cavern wall as the rough door swung open and Netty's voice rang out with quiet reverence. "Good afternoon, Father."

As Wil and Netty ushered Baby and their wagon through the door, the shadow heard a scream followed by shrieks. The last image observed by the shadow presented a payoff as it watched the small group being ushered into a brilliant light-filled space by a huge, darkly robed effigy.

In a blink, the ponderous door closed and the lurking shadow was left with the lonely silence of the cool vacated corridor.

# Chapter 19

As the survivors slowly trickled into Netty's kitchen for dinner, they were surprised by the early return of their benefactors from their mysterious daily disappearance.

Salina, Dezi and Ginger Mae snagged Netty's attention as Kimir and young Bonnie took the time before dinner to play by the fire with the dogs. Echo and Baby watched from their usual stoop, arms swallowed into the membrane that clung to the kitchen wall, ingesting their own variety of nutrition through the pores of their skin.

As Dezi and Ginger Mae worked out the details of their new responsibilities, the rest of the group took seats at the tables, adhering to the spots chosen weeks ago. Dezi's stint in the kitchen fell on him immediately with the serving of dinner and the cleanup, unexpectedly freeing Ginger Mae to enjoy the company of the other survivors for once.

She felt a worm of anticipation and nervousness stir in her bowels. This was the time for everyone to socialize, relax and let down their hair. She didn't normally participate in the hilarity, being self-conscious and somewhat ostracized by the facts of Armoni's death that had made the rounds and, of course, her appearance. It never occurred to Ginger Mae that the community's reluctance to embrace her might be because of her own reticence.

Pouring herself some tea, she scanned the crowd, missing the foursome: Scotty, Chloe, Kenya and Kane were late again, probably dawdling in the bathing cave. From behind Ginger Mae, thin arms snaked around her waist.

"Hi, Mommy, I'm home and I'm starved."

She turned to survey her dirty daughter. "Daisy, I thought we agreed you would wash up before dinner. You can't sit down to eat looking like this." Daisy's thin hair clumped in stringy lumps of grime and her fingers were encased in tiny white gloves; a requirement of her job and as grimy as the rest of her. Her eyes sparkled with an otherworldly fire as the passion for her task threatened to cascade over them both.

"But Mommy, Mommy, I was so engrossed in . . ."

"Shhhh . . . I know, baby. You can tell me later."

Ginger Mae's heart set to bursting with pride as she marveled at her six-year-old prodigy. Already, Daisy's vocabulary far outstripped her own. *What in the world is she doing all day, getting filthy, yet coming back to me with a vocabulary and knowledge that increases daily?*

"Ginger Mae . . . allow us."

Ginger Mae gratefully turned to confront Netty who stood with Abby, hands outstretched, inviting Daisy to join them. She felt a twinge of jealousy as Daisy slipped her dirty hand into Abby's, her childish face scrunched up with pleasure.

"We're on our way to the baths to collect our wayward young people. We will see that Daisy bathes at the same time." Without waiting for her permission, the two winged beauties turned away, Daisy walking proudly between them.

Mildly irked, Ginger Mae took her tea to a table not yet fully occupied. She sat deflated as she reluctantly watched the interplay between her fellow survivors.

Young Bonnie, sweetheart of the group with her sunny personality, infectious laugh and chubby cheeks—pinchable enough to get the oldest of the men in the group blushing—rose from the floor where she tumbled with the dogs. She ran to her mother, who stood ready to pour tea at another table.

As Bonnie chattered to her mother, Ginger Mae watched Salina bob her head in assent, all the while her searching eyes resting on the entrance to the kitchen. Ginger watched Salina's eyes light up as Clyde lumbered into the room. His somber expression flickered subtly as he met Salina's gaze. Turning toward him, Salina scooted Bonnie away as she patted a spot for Clyde at a table, resting her hand on his shoulder as he sat holding his mug up for his share of fragrant tea. Salina paused as he sipped the tea, refreshing his mug with a top-off before she moved on, peeking back quickly to see if he still watched; her smile dispirited as she noted he had turned away. *Why in the world would she do that to herself? We all know he's praying his wife makes it to the Hive.* Ginger knew what a women in love looked like. The only thing Salina had in store was a broken heart.

Her interest wandered. She watched as Karen sat next to Cobby, a huge smile on her face. She mouthed something Ginger Mae was unable to catch but she didn't miss the meaning of Cobby's interest as he cuffed her playfully with his fist, laughing and smacking her leg like he would with another man. They had much in common, both navigators: one of the skies, the other the seas.

Ginger Mae couldn't blame Karen. After all, he was the most attractive man in their group: knowledgeable, masculine and possessing sex appeal galore. But everyone knew Cobby treated Karen just like one of the boys. And Karen still felt like enough of an outsider to let it slide . . . for now. Ginger Mae knew women. And Karen didn't strike her as the type to play the buddy for long. Ginger Mae planned to watch this one real close. She hadn't missed the sidelong peeks Cobby threw at Abby when he felt safe. As of yet, Ginger Mae thought Abby entirely unaware.

"Yo, John." Everyone turned as Crystal sauntered over to plop down next to Johno.

"Miss Crystal, my name is Johno. I have reminded you of that many times." Johno's wide smile stayed in place as he held on to his eternal patience with Crystal.

"Yeah, yeah. Now John, I just got back from the baths and I heard the kids yammerin' about how ol' Tobi is a tearin' up the groves with her tusks. Just wanna give ya a friendly heads up. They're gunna be all over ya when they git here."

"Yes, Miss Crystal. I know big Tobi is acting out. I must speak to Miss Abby. She may know of a remedy. Thank you for your concern."

Crystal let out a belly laugh that echoed around the room with her mirth.

"John, you know better than letting that big ol' lady be the boss. You need a firm hand with 'er."

Johno looked weary as he bristled at her advice. "Miss Crystal, I have been an elephant man my whole life. I know my eles and what they need. They respect me. I'm not about to change the way I care for them nor will I be changing my name to suit you. Why don't you spend more time with your pig? She keeps eating and eating. If she puts any more weight on she won't be able to walk."

"Now, John, ya know I don't mean anything by it. Just passin' the day with ya. Lighten up."

"My name is Johno." He shook his head and nodded to the fireplace where Tulip was exploring the butts of any dog that would hold still.

"Miss Crystal, I caught your pig with Tobi again this morning. Can't you keep him away from the herd? The babies are much too boisterous. He will get hurt."

"Now Johnny, you know damn well my baby is a girl. Why you gotta insult her like that?"

A sudden squeal sent Crystal over to the fireplace to referee, allowing Johno to turn to his keepers with relief.

Scanning their faces, she saw one missing. With a frown, she searched the room. From Ginger Mae's seat, she could only infer that that he was with Emma—who hadn't come to dinner yet. *And we've only lived here a few weeks. What if this turns into a few years? Hormones are going to explode.* Ginger Mae jerked her head up with a start. *A few years? Holy shit. Am I already accepting this? What if it's much more than a few years?* Ginger Mae racked her brain, searching for any crumb she might have heard about bombs and radiation. The realization of what they were up against began to slowly dawn.

Cackles and shrieks from the young bathers emanated from the baths. From inside, hollow echoes bounced off astounding stalagmites that rose from the tepid water to sparkle and glitter with their precious stones melded into the swirls of the composition of the aged stone.

Piles of recently washed clothes littered the cave floor where the water lapped, eager to reclaim the clean clothes while their owners frolicked innocently behind the striking stalagmites that afforded complete privacy to shy bathers and bashful lovers.

Chloe carefully rinsed suds from Scotty's wings as they soaked in the warm waters, well hidden behind an outcrop of jeweled stalagmites.

Dreamily, she remembered Netty's simple explanation of where the fluorescent minerals and jewels had come from. They had been taking their second dip in the warm waters when Netty and Baby had stopped in to enjoy the sight.

"I hope you appreciate the efforts made by the Womb on your behalf. Echo told us how you treasure beautiful stones and gold."

The four young people splashed happily as she spoke.

Scotty shouted out to Netty as she made herself comfortable on the dry rock ground on the edge of the warm water, Baby looking spooky through the wisps of fog as he settled in her lap.

"The Womb did this for us? I thought it didn't care about us?" He slowly made his way over to the twosome, his wings dragging him down as they collected water in the soft down of his undercoat.

Netty patted the seat next to her, an invitation. She absently stroked Scotty's soaked wings as she explained. "It isn't that the Womb doesn't care about you, Scotty. It's just that the Womb has given up on our species. We brought it on ourselves with our bloodlust and selfishness. How much longer could the Womb stand by as the planet was raped and the other creatures of this remarkable earth were brutalized for sport and profit?"

She hung her head mournfully, then faced Scotty with signs of tears on her pale face. "And what of those who deliberately inflict pain on other creatures? What of the savage subjugation of women in your third world countries? What about the country of China that rips the skin off the backs of the Womb's most glorious creatures and grinds their body parts up to foolishly enhance their own idea of virility? Do I need to go on?"

"No, Netty." Scotty noted Baby flashing his eyes, wild intelligence replacing the soft complacency he always exhibited. Scotty looked closer but Baby had settled down, his normal placid expression firmly in place.

"I feel just like the Womb does. We are the scourge of this planet," Scotty spoke from his heart. Netty reached over to clasp his hand.

"I know you feel that way, Scotty. We have watched you for some time now. That is why we prepared the Hive so it would be comfortable for you."

She waved her arm to encompass the beauty of the bathing cave.

"But where did you find all of these luminous rocks and valuable stones?"

She smiled down at him. "That was the easy part. Remember the gold and diamonds Echo obtained for you? That was us. I mean, really the Womb. We knew from Echo what you desired. It was a simple matter to reach out in the ground until the Womb found the material. And we didn't have to look far. Just about ten miles from here is a place called the Franklin Mines, in the town of Franklin. It was the largest supplier of zinc in the world during World War II. Oddly enough, it was also well known for the largest collection of some of these stones. The fluorescent minerals are a specialty of the mine. It wasn't hard to find and obtain exactly what we needed. The Womb left quite a catacomb of caverns in the mine, much like here, but not as beautiful, of course. The Womb can go anywhere in the world and obtain anything we want. It's too late now, though. All manmade things are tainted. Radioactive."

"Scotty," Chloe's plaintive and petulant voice called out to him. With a wave of her hand, Netty excused him to return to his sweetheart.

"Come here, you."

Scotty turned and scooped Chloe into his arms, tilting her face up to his. His worrisome eyes examined her face, still showing tight signs of the trauma from six weeks ago that still gave them all nightmares.

She was finally beginning to hate her erstwhile father, glad her Uncle Brooks had killed him as he lay groveling on his study floor. And they were all very happy Echo had killed Uncle Brooks after he had shot Teddy. *Where would we all be without Echo?*

"Thinking about Echo?" Chloe remained expressionless as she searched his face for answers.

"How did you know?"

With that question, Chloe broke out in a smile. "I don't know much about anything anymore, but I know everything about you."

She hugged him close. Scotty could feel desperation in her straining arms.

"Not only did you save me but I love you."

"Echo saved you too."

She smiled again, acknowledging full well she couldn't have Scotty without accepting Echo.

Scotty had stopped holding his breath long ago as Chloe and Echo tried to make peace with one other. He couldn't blame Chloe for getting the creeps as Echo adjusted to Scotty's commitment to her.

The first night he had asked Echo to find another bed to sleep on had been a doozy. That meant Barney had to go too. The two creatures were inseparable. It took two day of silence from Echo, strange stares at Chloe, and long explanations by Scotty before Echo began to get it. There was no similar interspecies love on Oolaha. As individuals, Oolahans were just one of a whole consciousness. They didn't mate either, of course. Scotty wasn't sure Echo understood that he didn't love her less, but she did make room for Chloe's permanent presence in their lives.

Caesar was another matter. No matter what they did to coax Scotty's fierce enigmatic guardian into joining the other cats and the bears, he wouldn't budge.

The only place Caesar gave Scotty some space was in Netty's kitchen. But when anyone decided to leave, they were forced to clamber around the five hundred pounds of focused feline that sat in the corridor awaiting the sight of Scotty.

Caesar never actually harmed anyone, so after a while the grumbling stopped. Scotty himself, after recovering from the shock and unusual sight of a huge tiger continually stalking him, began to feel special. He finally got over his trepidation and established a firm relationship with the big cat, often approaching Caesar to stroke his enormous gleaming head, three times the size of his own.

His self-esteem grew through the admiration of Chloe and the respect accorded him as the object of Caesar and Echo's attention. He no longer railed at how his changes set him apart. It was clear to everyone that his changes gave him an advantage, a closer link to Netty and Wil who were still a bit feared as the conveyors of the new laws in their strange world under the ground.

Scotty realized he had come far from the bullied and pilloried child of the mean streets to a handsome young man with abilities and confidence enough to develop into a leader of their foursome. He and Kane had bonded quickly during their mad dash to safety. Their relationship developed deeply, both viewing the other as brothers, much to Cobby and Abby's delight.

Scotty often wondered how deep Kane's affection went toward Kenya. He shook his head as thoughts of her flirtatious behavior elicited sympathy for Kane.

They all looked forward to the baby's birth, which by Kenya's calculations should happen any day. Maybe the baby would mature Kenya. Her priorities were bound to change as the responsibilities of raising a child under these circumstances hit home. An alliance with a stable man would offer the best chance of survival once they got out of here. He hoped that would be Kane, if that's what he wanted.

Scotty had to admit, some of the best laughs he had ever had resulted from some hilarious observation of Kenya's. Her combination of slick sassy street talk and tender idealistic sensibilities left them in stitches all day. A damn good thing because she was worthless as a worker; although Chloe wasn't much better and she had no excuse.

"Elias, no. Let's stay close to the bank. We're running late. It's dinner time."

Elias's low seductive voice cast murmurings across the water. Scotty watched from behind his sheltered outcrop as Emma and Elias swam by, his arm wrapped around Emma's waist as she struggled to pull them back toward the bank. Her laughter rang out in protest as he dragged her behind a stalagmite, his mouth locked firmly on hers.

What could Scotty say? It was none of his business. Emma and Chloe were about the same age. It was only natural she be attracted to one of the other single guys. Elias was older and very mature. Hard work does that to you.

They all listened avidly as the elephant keepers related tales of the atrocities that had become a way of life in Africa. Scotty didn't doubt for a second that Johno and his men had hit the lottery when Abby had decided to add them to the rescue. They had survived through the destruction and now enjoyed life in the Hive with the same distinct advantages they all shared. They were alive and safe.

Scotty heard a groan from behind the other stalagmite. The splashing in Emma's direction stopped. All was silent except for occasional murmurings.

"Yo . . . I'm over here, Scotty." He turned back to Chloe, her fingers entwined in the chain of her necklace that held the antique gold coin he had given her on her sixteenth birthday.

He ran his fingers over hers. "You like?"

"I love. Where did your mind drift off to?"

"I'm just thinking about how far we've come since your birthday and my unveiling to you. Do you realize if you had freaked out, we wouldn't be here? There wouldn't have been enough time to convince you I was normal. I would have just left with Abby and I'd have lost you with the rest of the population when the bombs came."

"What makes you think that Sarasota got bombed?" She wrinkled her nose, turning her face to the side, clearly not liking the thought. "When this is over, I plan to go back home. And you're coming with me. There's nothing in Sarasota that would present a target or anger any of the United States' enemies. Our houses will be there just waiting for us."

Scotty swept her hair from her eyes, sadness written in his every gesture. "Babe, don't you get it? How will you make it back there? Walk? Through cities teeming with radiation? You can't think like that. It's over. Civilization as we knew it is gone. This is our home now. We have it good here." He pressed a thumb to the first tear that slid down her cheek.

"But I don't want to live here forever. I don't really know these people and I wouldn't choose some of them for friends anyway."

"Chloe, you have to get over that attitude. We're safe here and we have everything we need." Her tears we dripping fast now. "Don't you like the growing fields? I love our job, I thought you did too."

"It's not that. I just want to go home."

"How can you call that monstrosity you lived in home? Isn't home supposed to be where your heart is? The Nasirs weren't your parents even though they did love you. Your father was not who he pretended to be. Your Uncle Brooks wasn't either. Do I need to tell you how they murdered your real parents?"

Chloe sobbed openly now. Her arms tried to push Scotty away, his scalding words slicing at her heart.

"Come on, Chloe, it's been six weeks now, we've been over this before. I thought you understood. We need to make a new home here. And those people that you haven't even made an attempt to get to know? They are our new best friends. Think of them as extended family. They're the ones who'll be there for us when we need them."

"Why would I ever need them? I have you." She wiped her nose with the back of her hand before rinsing it off in the warm bath water.

"Chloe, I can't be everything for you. You need to learn to toughen up and stand on your own two feet. I'll always be here for you, but we need to interact more with the rest of the group. There's no telling what our lives are going to be like when we surface. We'll need help. And you need to spend more time getting to know Jose. He's your brother, for God's sake." She made a sour face. "What if you get pregnant? Don't you want help with the baby?"

"Pregnant? Ew, I hadn't really thought about it."

"Well, we better. It's bound to happen."

Sobering, she looked into his mesmerizing eyes, vertigo hitting her hard. They each shut their eyes, giving her respite from the golden image. Resting her head on his shoulder, Scotty heard her voice regress, feathering out in childish whispers. "Do you want that to happen?"

Scotty wondered if he detected a touch of coyness in her tone. From the other stalagmite, they heard a sharp slap. Emma's voice could be heard, spewing angry exclamations with undertones of hurt, the exact words indistinct.

Scotty and Chloe tabled their discussion to crane their necks around their outcrop. No sooner did they crank their necks around, then Emma swam past, all flailing arms and thunderous looks. Were those tears on her face or just drops of water from her angry splashing?

Watching Emma return to shore, they decided to follow, surprised by the appearance of Netty and Abby with Daisy in tow.

Glancing curiously at Emma, Abby hustled Daisy to the water's edge to bathe.

"Hi, gang. Emma, why don't you come sit by us?" Abby watched as Emma hurriedly dressed and sullenly made her way over to Abby, where she sat glumly.

"Hey, Ab. Surprised to see you here. We were just heading over to Netty's." Scotty watched his sister drop the hands that were cleaning the dust off Daisy. She stood looking past Scotty, her face wary.

Abby called out, "What's wrong, Netty?"

Scotty turned to see Netty's face devoid of color as she stood frozen watching Chloe dress.

Netty stretched out her hand and held it in mid-air. The moment was spellbound as all watched the tableau between Netty and Chloe, who stood mortified to be the object of attention.

"Where . . .?"

Netty moved as if in great pain toward Chloe, her arm still raised as if frozen yet frightened to touch something. Scotty watched, confused. He recoiled as he witnessed a gamut of emotions flicker over Netty's face: shock, anger, bewilderment and hatred. Netty stood face to face with Chloe as her voice hissed the question.

"*Where* did you get that necklace?"

Chloe shrank back from the uncharacteristic assault from Netty. She looked around helplessly for someone to intervene.

"I asked you a question, young lady."

Scotty stepped forward. By then Netty's frozen hand woke to clutch firmly at the golden coin wrapped in its platinum bezel, still hanging from Chloe's gulping neck.

"Netty, it's mine. I gave it to Chloe as a gift. Why do you ask?"

Netty turned her attention to Scotty. She jerked her hand back from the coin as if burnt. Her eyes flashed in acute contrast to her suddenly slack face, vacant and devoid of life as she slowly sank to the ground. She bowed her head, letting tears slip through her shuttering fingers as she cradled her face.

In the distance, Scotty could see Elias rise from the water to furtively slip on his clothes and make his way to the entrance, vanishing into the corridor without a word. All other eyes remained focused on Netty.

Abby wrapped a towel around Daisy and hastened over to kneel at Netty's side. Wordlessly, she cradled the older woman in her arms. Abby's touch appeared to sober her, the sobs stopping to be replaced with bitter choking embarrassment.

"Sorry . . . oh . . . so sorry." She struggled to regain her composure, gently patting Abby's hand as it gripped her shoulder.

"What is it, Netty?"

"My dear, you don't need to concern yourself with my travails."

Abby reacted as if struck. Scotty and Chloe watched Netty absorb Abby's reaction to her words. Clearly, the two of them shared a close relationship.

"I'm sorry, Abby. I didn't mean to be so harsh. It's just that I thought I had put all this behind me. It's been so long . . . the coin, just . . . I can't explain." She reached out again to Chloe.

"Do you mind, young lady? May I have a look?" Chloe looked at Scotty then tentatively pulled her necklace over her head, extending it to the shaken Netty.

They watched as Netty's wings wrapped themselves securely around her huddled form as if to protect her from pain. She turned to Scotty, her breath hitching loudly. "Scotty, did you find this coin in the woods . . . near the big rock that shelters the entrance to the Hive?"

Scotty nodded quietly, unwilling to let his voice break the fragile moment.

"This coin . . . was so momentous to me at one time." She looked up with the coin in her hand. "It used to belong to the man that—" she choked "—that murdered me. That had Baby and Wil murdered."

Scotty, Abby and Chloe recoiled in shock.

Emma stood stunned. In the ensuing silence, she spoke, "But Netty, you're alive. I don't understand. Who was this man?"

So quietly they strained to hear, she whispered, "That man . . . was my husband."

Scotty heard gasps from the women.

Emma spoke up again. "But Wil is your husband."

Netty graced them with her beautiful smile, now laced with bitterness over her haunting memories.

"Yes. And Wil is my first love, my true love, my eternal love. But there was a man in my life before Wil . . . my first husband, Robert Doyle."

Her voice pitched even lower, her whispers weaving a web of sickness and dread, "He was the most evil, venal and violent human being a young girl could fall prey to. I was very young, very innocent. I thought I was over it. I have kept it bottled up for so very long. Wil and I try not to dwell on why our lives were so changed. The pain can be quite . . . debilitating. " Netty's golden eyes swirled with emotions as she drowned in the torment of her past.

Slowly, haltingly, Netty related the dismal details of her life with Robert; the rapes, her theft of the gold coin and the horrible details that had led to their murders.

"It was the Womb that saved us. We are forever grateful." Netty now clasped Abby's hand in her own, drawing strength from the younger woman's adoration. She handed the coin and chain back to Chloe. "This coin gave me courage when I needed it. I pray that it brings you some luck, Chloe."

With those sincere words, Chloe took the coin, re-hanging it around her neck. Abby appeared to have a question desperate to leave the confines of her lips. She squirmed as Netty turned her attention back to her. Scotty knew his sister well. She must have something damn uncomfortable to ask Netty or she would have just asked by now.

"My dear . . . out with it."

Abby's own golden eyes swirled deeply into Netty's. "Well . . . I understand from Echo that once we're healed and changed we might have immortality. I wondered if it was true. According to your story, you and Wil must be well over one hundred years old, even though you look to be the same age as me."

Netty rose, pain still evident on her otherworldly face. She sighed deeply. "Yes, you, your brother and Jose are all as immortal as Wil and I. We hope it also extends to Echo and Baby. As long as your head is not severed, or a limb removed so quickly that you bleed to death before it can regenerate, we have no limit to our lives that I am aware of. But why don't we just take things one day at a time? I have learned life works best that way." She peered into their faces, pausing as if taking their measure. "May I rely on your discretion? Will you protect my privacy with the others?"

"Yes."

"Of course—"

"You don't need to ask."

Everyone rushed to reassure her, tripping over their words to pledge their allegiance. Netty finally rose, shaking out her wings and her hair falling into place as if to say the intimacy had never happened.

"I think it's time to go to dinner. Shall we?"

With her arm intertwined with Abby's, the two unearthly women left the room, Daisy somberly trailing along behind them.

# Chapter 20

As Scotty and his crew entered Netty's kitchen with Emma surreptitiously scooting to her seat, Caesar backed out of the kitchen and took up his post outside in the corridor. He padded around in a circle until his massive body found the best resting place that would enable him to monitor the comings and goings of all the survivors. He knew he must be ever vigilant. If any harm came to The One, all hope for the human race would be gone, even the small glimmer of hope there was.

The Womb had entrusted him to help allow them a last chance. If he failed, the Womb would be philosophical, blaming the loss on a fate that could not be denied. But he had no intention of failing. He refused to let the Womb down.

They all had worked too hard to see that The One secured the best mate possible. Caesar's eyes closed gently as his ears took over, sensitive to every breath that emanated in the kitchen. He projected a long wait tonight. Caesar jerked his head up as The One suddenly appeared with a platter of his favorite nosh and a bucket of cool water.

"Here you go, big boy, I see in the excitement at the baths we forgot to feed you."

Caesar leaped to his feet, bowing his neck to the voice that was the most important sound in their new world to him as she turned her back with a smile and disappeared into the kitchen.

Sounds of merriment drifted out to the lonely cavern hallway as a shadowy figure made its way from the kitchen. Caesar sniffed out the shadow, nothing new to him as it made its nightly trek, solitary and silent past the big cat. Ignoring the shadow, Caesar turned his magnetic attention back to the sounds of the kitchen and the feminine fragrance left behind by The One.

\*

Hilarity ensued as Dezi dropped his armful of crockery after tripping over Netty's braided rug that had been rooted up by Crystal's pig. Tulip had sure acted strange all night, particularly restless and rooting more than usual. Dezi received a chorus of boos and catcalls as he cleaned the floor of the broken shards, ears burning with resentment and embarrassment.

"It's damn time you take this stinkin' barnyard pest outa here, Crystal."

"Aw, hon . . . now you know it was your own fault. You gotta watch what your doin' if ya wanna work the kitchen. Don't be such a clod. You know Tulip rates higher than we do. You wanna chase her outa here and piss off the Womb?

Dezi's furtive eyes darted around as if he suspected the Womb might be listening.

"Tulip . . . what's you up to there?" Crystal stood up and rushed to Tulip as she collapsed in front of the fireplace. All the dogs turned to sniff wildly at her. As Crystal knelt down to examine her stricken pig, she let out a scream. "Oh my dear Lord! *We're gunna have a baby.*"

Sweeping the dogs aside as everyone rushed to Crystal's side, they could clearly see tiny feet emerging from Tulip's abdomen. Her udders were swollen and unmistakably ready for birth.

"*Here it comes.*"

As the anticipation rose, the dogs became excited, knowing something unusual was transpiring.

As the second set of feet emerged, Crystal stood. She bent over to watch, helplessly wringing her hands and appearing about as useful as a vagina on a bumblebee. A dark figure jostled the spectators aside.

"Please, please move back. Get these dogs out of this space . . . *now.* Scotty, could you and your gang remove the dogs, please? Salina, get me some warm water, some towels and a clean knife."

Johno finished elbowing his way through the crowd. He shook his head at Crystal who by now was useless.

"Woman, would you please just remove yourself? I will handle this." And he did.

Calmly and rhythmically he readied towels to receive the eleven piglets that came into the world in exactly fifteen minutes, the last one looking small and shriveled.

He worked, fully prepared to receive the numerous afterbirths that he discreetly passed to Wil for disposal. The piglets easily found a teat to suck on for the critical first swallow of colostrum they needed to kick in their immune systems and ensure their survival.

Amidst all the jockeying for position was the eleventh piglet that lay unmoving in the towel. It failed to fight for a place at the milk trough with its littermates. Johno placed his finger on the tiny body, feeling for precious life; the tiny body cool.

A hopeful twinge played on his expressive dark face as he lifted the runt to a teat on Tulip's utter. A squeak broke the tension as the runt proclaimed her life still hung on.

"I do not think he will make it," determined Johno. "He is the runt and will not be strong enough to fight his littermates for a place at the table. I can feel he is cold. He may be nursing now but he will most likely be dead by the morning."

"Aw, what a shame. Nothing we can do?" inquired Crystal.

Bonnie sprang up from her position on the floor. "We can't let the poor thing just die. Life's precious down here. We don't have so much that we can afford to lose any." Bonnie hovered on the verge of tears, her love for all the creatures clear in her tearful voice.

Suddenly, a low voice wafted from the back of the crowd around Tulip. So soft it cut like a sword amid the other rambunctious voices.

"I'll take him." And louder. "*Give him to me;* I'll take care of him."

And, to the surprise of all, Dezi stepped forward. In his hands lay a soft tiny cloth. "Give him to me, I won't let him die. She deserves a chance."

As the crowd parted, a few titters were heard. Without glancing around, Dezi knelt to receive the piglet. Johno looked into Dezi's earnest face, so out of character, his swagger missing.

Dezi held out his hands, cradled with the soft cloth. "Come on, Johno, I can do it. He needs someone. *We can't just throw him away.*"

Nodding his head in agreement, Johno placed the cold piglet, half the size of Dezi's hand, onto the cloth.

From out of nowhere, Netty's hand rested on Dezi's arm, her other hand extending a bottle filled with a milky substance, a nipple tiny enough to fit in the piglet's faintly searching mouth.

"This is all you will need. I have warmed it for you. There is more where this comes from. Just ask me when you need it. I am here for any advice you may wish to consult me on." She gave him a smile of confidence.

"Now *wait* just a gosh darn minute. You don't even like animals, Dezi. Why should I trust you with the lil guy?" Crystal stood with her hands on her hips, ready for a confrontation.

Quickly, Bonnie cut her off. "Give him a chance, Crystal. I'll help Dezi." Bonnie threw him a quick glance, looking for assent. Seeing surprise but no objection, she hurried on. "Dezi and I will do a good job. You know I can do it. We'll make sure the little tucker gets all the attention she needs, won't we, Dez?"

Bonnie edged over to Dezi where Ginger Mae and Daisy now peered over his shoulder at the newborn.

"Come on, Dez. Let's get out of here before anyone changes their mind." She quickly edged him out the kitchen door, Ginger Mae and Daisy following behind. Within a second, Gloria joined the exodus.

"Well, if that don't beat all." Crystal stood with Johno as the other newborns suckled happily with the proud mom.

Johno patted Crystal on the back. "They will be fine. If the little one wants to live, he will have a chance with their care."

"But Dezi? Ah just don't reckon I will ever understand men. He hates animals."

"It is okay, Crystal. Did you not see his face? This little rejected creature means something to him. Let them be. Come . . . let me pour you some tea."

With that, Johno ushered Crystal back to the table. Scotty and Chloe released the dogs and they raced to cluster around Tulip and her babies. Echo and Baby joined them from their posts on the wall. The royal pittie pair, King and Queenie, presided over the piglets as if they themselves were responsible for their births. The other truckers went back to their usual gossiping.

Glancing around the room, Scotty saw Elias watching Emma and Salina talking. Peter entered the kitchen having missed the excitement.

"I'm going to go talk to Peter," Scotty decided. "He looks like he needs a friend. You guys want to wait for me here?"

Kenya spoke up. "I guess so, chicky. You want to stay here for a while, Kane?"

Kane ran his hand over Kenya's huge abdomen. "Hope Tulip might give you some ideas?"

Kenya groaned. "Right now, I sure don't give a zombie-ass nigga what Tulip is up to. I just want this kid a mine *out*. I should a had this babe two weeks ago."

Chloe spoke up. "You feel okay, Kenya?"

"You kiddin' me, chicky? I feel stoked, like I could boogie down all night. But my monster bump don' agree. Y'all think it might be stress?"

Chloe's eyes popped. "Stress? You don't even *know* stress. Kane and Scotty have been doing your share of the work since we got here."

Kenya arched her exemplary eyebrows. "Sounds like you got something stuck in your craw, baby doll. You got something you want to say ta me?"

All eyes swung over to Chloe at her unexpected attack on Kenya.

"You think y'all want to carry this beach ball around for me for a while, I sure be happy to do your work for you, chicky."

Indignation stabbed at Chloe with every word. Before anyone could respond, Salina sat down accompanied by Emma.

"Everything good here? Kenya dear, how are you feeling? Any pains yet?"

Scotty could hear the undertones of worry but he knew Mama Diaz well. *Maybe the others won't pick up on it.*

"I'm just nifty, Ms. Salina. Still hangin' in there."

"Well, you boys look after her. If you start to feel any pain . . . of any kind, you send the boys to come get me. You hear? Chloe, that goes for you, too. This young lady's baby is very important to us."

Salina rose. Sliding her arms around her quiet daughter, she and Emma returned to the mixing counter to plan tomorrow's meals with Netty.

Chloe picked up Kenya's hand, clasping it in her own. "I'm sorry I ragged out on you. I'm under so much stress myself, but I'm getting better. I just don't envy the position you're in with the baby. We're still just kids after all. All this is still so new and scary without having a baby to take care of . . ." Her voice tailed off.

"Well, chicky, you just better make sure you don't get knocked up yourself then."

Chloe cast her eyes down. "Yeah, I know what you mean. Easier said than done when you're in love."

Salina sorted through the ingredients she would need in the morning, giving Emma a further chance to come clean with the truth about what had happened between her and Elias. She rested her eyes on Clyde who sat across the room sipping tea next to Peter, where no conversation would be required since Peter never spoke to anyone unless forced to.

The room was settling back down to normal, Johno holding court with Crystal and the other keepers, Elias sullen and flicking occasional glances toward Emma, who ignored them all. Truckers Tucker and Billy decided to head out to swim and Cobby sat conferring with Wil and Jose as Cobby's eyes trailed after Abby, drawing away quickly when he saw Salina watching. He completely missed the lovelorn eyes that belonged to Karen as she too watched his interest in Abby.

Salina's eyes lingered on her daughter, ready to do some gentle probing. Scotty ran over, his wing brushing the side of her table.

"We're heading out now, Mama D. Do you need anything before we go?"

"I don't think so, sweetie. Just make sure you keep your eyes on Kenya. The baby will come any day now." Scotty gave her a kiss and ran off with the other kids.

Salina turned to Netty. "He's such a good boy. I can well understand why he was chosen to be The One, no matter what it means. Do you have any thoughts, Netty?"

Netty looked up. "I'm as mystified as you are, Salina. All I know is that the Womb insisted I implement some specific orders relayed through Baby. It is rare that Baby offers explanations. He is even more subdued than he was before we were all mur . . . died."

Netty picked up the pace of her labors, clearly uncomfortable with the discussion. With a tight smile, she moved off to the sink, leaving Salina alone with Emma.

With a tired motherly sigh, Salina turned back to her daughter, her patience at an end. "Kenya's delivery date is well past. She's very uncomfortable. Even as we'll gratefully welcome the baby, the road for her will not get easier. What a shame."

Emma lowered her head until it almost rested on her chest. "Mummbble . . . Elias . . . did not agree . . . sorry . . . mummmmbble."

Salina lifted Emma's face with her finger, gazing deeply into her eyes, assessing the hurt that can only come from a rejected love. "If you need to tell me something, Emma, please spit it out. I can't hear you when you mumble. How can I help you unless I can understand you?"

The hot tears Emma so fiercely labored to hold back broke over her lids. Salina gathered her up in her arms, sending a withering flash of motherly contempt to Elias, who stalked out of the room without a backward glance.

"Have you and Elias been intimate, honey?

Emma gave her mother a disdainful look. "If you mean, did we get it on, well, yeah, Mom."

Salina's crestfallen face left Emma antagonistic. "I cared about him, Mom. He said I was smart and pretty. He understood me."

"You are smart and pretty, Emma. Too smart to fall for lines like that."

"Well, I didn't know then. I'll be a backyard crumb snatcher before I *submit,* as he calls it, to him again."

Salina found the next question difficult to choke out but she had to know. "Did you take precautions? Did Elias?" She tried to sound casual.

Emma looked askance. "Christ, Mom. A little personal, don't you think?"

"Where did you learn to speak to me like this? I didn't raise you this way." Salina's voice was raised and startled glances were thrown their way. Calming down, she stroked Emma's hair, the glossy texture silken under her fingers. "Baby, I'm just worried about you. We live under rather extreme conditions right now. I don't know what's in store for our future. We might be down here for quite some time. You don't want to bring a baby up in these conditions, do you? We need all of our strength to stay strong for what may lay ahead. After the bombs stop and it's safe to come out, the world will be far different and I have no idea what to expect. We need to be ready for anything. An unexpected baby would really complicate things. I don't want to see you in the same position Kenya's in."

Emma raised her head defiantly but her voice lacked less passion. "I think what Kenya is doing is brave."

Salina rolled her eyes. "I think you got the message. Let's see how brave Kenya is when she's screaming her pretty head off in labor. If Elias gives you any trouble or makes any demands, will you let me know?"

Now Emma rolled *her* eyes. "I can handle it, Mom."

Salina looked deeply into the eyes of her oldest daughter, cradling her tender unblemished face with her worn hands. She banished the thoughts of what a happy trouble-free baby she had been. "I love you, Em. No matter what, I will always be on your side. You can come to me with anything. Bonnie too. Make sure you keep an eye on her for me, okay? I would never survive if something happened to either one of you."

Emma's arms snaked around her mother's neck for a quick hug, followed by a peck. "I know, Mom. We both know. I gotta go find Bonnie now. I want to see what she and Dezi are up to with this new piglet of theirs. We good?"

She smiled as Salina swatted her butt. "We're always good. Now off with you. See you at bedtime."

Nighttime came quickly to the hard-working and tired survivors. Sleep was never a commodity they searched for with difficulty. It was more like a drug undulating through a healthy body, claiming conscious thought like a seductress, softly enticing her victim to her solicitous embrace, promising oblivion as cavern walls dimmed, animal excrement lay fallow, and all living creatures, save winged ones, were visited silently and unobtrusively to render unto their innocent flesh the mechanism by which the Womb had chosen to send its tendrils to invade.

Body functions took their course: an occasional groan, a soft expulsion of breath, the unexpected fart. Sounds of the sleeping . . . the unaware. Throughout the caverns, similar scenes were being replayed with the creatures. All was restful, all as expected. Cool air wafted through cavern hallways, sweeping away the daily odors of a busy Hive.

Echo's mesmerizing eyes drew open as a light probe pierced her unconsciousness. The time was near. The probe danced in her brain as she rolled away from My Barney to behold Baby at the doorway to the alcove.

"Sister, we are ready."

"I am ready too, Brother. Time to saddle up as my Brother Scotty would say."

Baby reacted with a faint blink, his golden eyes sparking. "This is our secret, Sister. No one is to know. Not even your Brother Scotty."

"Yes, yes, Brother, this will remain a secret." Echo stood, following the noiseless Baby through the alcove into the corridor where old Tobi and her ragtag herd—babies and all—awaited.

Without any communication, Echo mounted Tobi's proffered trunk, which she raised high to deposit Echo on her head. They would be moving quickly and silently like elephant ghosts in the night, just as their ancestors had done for thousands of years in Africa. Only this time their mission was not to protect the babies from nightly prowling predators. No, they would be following Baby to a source they needed to sustain their lives; a source that had been eluding a frustrated Tobi for weeks.

Lifting off, Baby shot into the air, his fluttering wings enabling him to move so much more quickly and easier than his wobbling step allowed him to. He had become quite adept at walking since arriving on this planet. Gravity was heavier on Earth than on Oolaha. But now that his wings had repaired themselves, the Womb had reasonably allowed him to retain the ability to fly, another privilege stripped from the minions upon the discovery that they were creating life on their own with their DNA.

Baby realized early on that the more you differed from the creatures around you the more suspicious they became. Humans were no different. So he walked when he was around them. Why upset them by flying? He remembered how upset they had appeared to be the night they had chosen the Hive as their home when they saw Sister Netty fly.

Baby led the elderly but spry Tobi and her small herd for a mile deep into the bowls of the Hive. When he landed, the herd found themselves in front of a large boulder that appeared to mark the end of the corridor.

Tobi allowed Echo to clamber down with the assistance of her trunk. Turning to Tobi, she sent an aura to probe inside Tobi's giant head, to proclaim, "At one time I had my own vehicle, a Carriage, and had no need to sit on the backs of others. But I thank you for the privilege anyway, great creature."

Echo's golden eyes flamed as she felt a deep rumble in the pit of her being from Tobi's response.

In the past, Echo had yet to find a reason to use her wings. My Barney had no wings so what was the purpose? She wanted to stay close to Barney, not create distance by exemplifying their differences.

As Baby approached, his wings crackled with their unexpected use, motioning for the restless herd to follow. As they rounded the boulder, an opening to a large, dark cavern could be seen, much like the opening to the Hive from the ground above. As no membranes halted their way, the procession ventured in, milling at the bottom of the passageway that led to a gentle but great rise of the cavern floor.

Tobi waved her trunk madly as if to taste the air. In the distance, they discovered the pathway split into two directions at the crest. The vastness of the cavern rose ten stories from the crest, the floor appearing to fall away on the right side. The temperature felt a full ten degrees cooler.

Suddenly, Tobi let out a scream and a great trumpet, marshaled her charges, and took off, her herd following as if pursued by demons. Baby began to waddle forward.

"I must follow, Sister."

Echo gauged the distance to the crest, shook out her wings, tested their strength, and remarked, "Now is as good a time as any, my Brother." With those words, Echo took to the air. Baby followed, leading the way to catch up with Tobi and the herd as they veered toward the left pathway.

When the two creatures set down, they discovered Tobi and the herd placidly eating the dirt at the back of the hard-packed cavern wall. Tobi set her yellowed and splintered tusks to scraping at the enormous wall. Trickles of the dirt she dislodged were quickly sucked up by questing trunks, the minerals in the soil a necessity for the digestion and survival of the pachyderms.

Echo and Baby eased their furry bottoms down onto the hard, cold floor to observe.

"The matriarch knew. Tobi knew." Echo's eyes threw golden refracted light on the wall, not distracting the elephants in the slightest.

"Yes, Sister. The Womb knew she would smell her own earth and know it for what it was."

"African earth. Was the trouble great?"

"No, the Womb has obtained much for the human survivors. Why would anything be too great for the creatures? It just took longer to bring this here. They will be happy now. The Womb keeps them healthy but Tobi does not know this. Her instinct to travel great distances for her minerals would never change. She will now pass it on to the rest of the herd. They will be happy with the trek. It will represent a challenge they can conquer, a must for Tobi's mental health. She will no longer take her frustrations out on the growing fields. There will be peace for her. As you know, that is all that matters to the Womb."

Baby swiveled around to gaze down at the end of the other pathway, very visible from their higher elevation, yet allowing them to remain hidden. The view took on perilous proportions as they observed the catastrophic drop from the sudden end of the right-sided pathway, a drop that widened into a bottomless chasm.

Echo's fragile leathery arm shot out to signal silence. She sent an aura to the shadow that had resolutely stalked them from the moment they had left the sleeping rooms.

Baby stood. "We must go." His aura dimmed, yet dismissed the shadow as of little significance. "Sister, we must go now, the time is near for the exchange."

Baby's aura buckled in Echo's mind, a reminder that Baby had agreed to share with Echo the burden of his deep responsibility. A responsibility he had guarded with absolute secrecy for a very, very long time.

Leaving the elephant herd behind, Baby and Echo flew unobtrusively over the lurking shadow at the top of the right pathway. Slipping through the entrance behind the huge boulder, they flew back the way they had come; down empty corridors lined with the ever-present membrane, the air warmer and the light improving.

Veering off a side passage, they approached another cavern, this one easy to find if you knew where to look. Echo estimated they were two miles from the sleeping rooms. He had no doubts about the unlikelihood of any survivors accidently discovering the cavern. Their activities were more concentrated in the other direction. Who had the time anyway?

The Womb made sure they were kept busy with responsibilities. It kept the restlessness at bay. Restlessness worked on a man's brain until he tied himself up in knots; and then trouble started. The Womb felt it best to keep them busy of their own volition rather than step in with drastic measures.

"We are here, Sister."

Baby wobbled over to the entrance. As Echo followed, a low moan emanated from the bowels of the smaller cavern. They stood in the darkness listening to the breathing sounds of a creature. *Is it more than one?*

Another low moan, cut off by a faint whimper. Echo joined him to stare, transfixed by the sight before her. Turning to Baby, she watched his eyes narrow, a perplexing smile playing contemptuously across his golden face. Turgid auras threatened to bring Echo to her knees with pain, generated from Baby's highly emotional state. She reached out to place a leathery finger on Baby's cheek. The auras calmed and brightened. The moment passed.

Now for the perfunctory business that routinely brought Baby to this spot. He stood ramrod straight as his antlers split. He held out his hand as his mind shouted a call. From inside the bowels of the cavern came three blackish red projectiles, almost too small to be seen. They landed on Baby's hand, lying motionless as three similar objects dropped from his antlers to replace the spent ones, flying back into the bowels to reach their targets. A fresh round of whimpers and actual screams told them the replacements were successfully at work.

Echo watched as the spent projectiles returned to their home in Baby's antlers. Baby stood motionless, his aura again chaotic and painful. Echo went to his side and held him until he regained control. They lingered another few moments, savoring the sounds from inside. Then, with one last finger to Baby's face for reassurance, they turned and whirled up into the air to surreptitiously return to the sleeping rooms.

Time passed quickly for the survivors. They kept busy with the perpetual cycles of their chores, eating, sleeping and getting to know one another. Strangely, Kenya's baby failed to appear, making the poor girl more morose but still very healthy. The older women survivors conferred regularly regarding their helplessness, wondering if Kenya needed a doctor.

Oddly, Netty failed to chime in as they tried, unsuccessfully, to elicit her opinion on the medical resources she might command from the Womb, if necessary.

Dezi and Bonnie bonded closely over the care of the piglet. It was touch and go for the little guy. There were many long nights and juggling of chores to stay on top of her feeding.

Dezi insisted the piglet sleep with him to stay extra warm. Eventually, they managed to wean him off the bottle and on to solid food. They named him Chance.

Everyone marveled at the change in Dezi. He carried Chance around in a sling while he kept up with his chores in the kitchen. No one said boo about the cleanliness issue because they knew Dezi kept his prince cleaner than most of the men kept themselves.

The only time he left Chance with Bonnie was when he bathed. It became clear that Bonnie and Dezi were a nanny team but clearly, Dezi was the dad . . . Chance was *his* baby boy.

Ginger Mae marveled at the changes in her own life. Her new duties brought her into contact with more of the survivors than ever before. Something about her exposure to the creatures melted the shell she had erected around herself, enabling her to hold up her head and smile. Soon, her eye contact improved enough that she found herself offering the first greeting and an uplifting comment.

She found her natural delight in the innocence of the creatures she was forced to tabulate fostered a bond with them. They knew when to expect her. If her duties delayed her, she found them restless when she arrived. They would calm down at her appearance, expecting a treat or a stroke, gentle murmurings and lilting encouragements; all healing the traces of the mental anguish her experience with Armoni had visited on her.

Clyde began to recover from his mourning and accept the likelihood that his wife and grandchildren had perished in the conflagration. Salina was only too eager to provide the proper medicine.

And, as the weeks passed, Gloria lost more weight, revealing the bones of her soon-to-be shapely silhouette, her diabetes apparently banished.

Several of Johno's keepers perpetually vied for her attention, although she seemed more interested in one of her fellow truckers. It seemed that Billy's asthma had cleared up completely, giving them a reason to convert their commiserating into celebration, creating a common bond that foreshadowed more than friendship.

Crystal and Johno's contentious bickering about the proper methods of wildlife care and just about anything else, refused to abate. Her disinclination to recognize his given name and his subsequent indignation enjoined her to christen him Johnny. Nothing he did to dissuade her worked.

The days slid into weeks, which slid into months. Not much changed: Baby continued his now companionable sojourns with Echo; Tobi and the herd flourished with their nightly constitutional; Netty and Wil endured their afternoon penitence.

The project that Wil, Jose, Clyde, Cobby and Daisy worked on continued. Ginger Mae noticed a maturity developing in her daughter. Her vocabulary grew at an accelerated rate, yet there occurred no abatement in the filth she wore as she returned from her day's work. The only childhood moments Daisy indulged in were when Kimir tired of playing with the big guys and finished with his prayer rug kindly fashioned by Netty, and decided to revert to a little boy who liked to show off in front of the only person he could impress: Daisy.

Then there was Peter. He remained taciturn and unsociable, and lurked as an occasional nebulous shadow, seeing all except the most fundamental element of the survivors' existence. But that was bound to come in time . . .

# Chapter 21

Lorna woke, cramped and thirsty. Her stringy hair lay lank across her greasy forehead as she tried to sweep it back with her filthy hands; her nails were split, broken and encrusted with dirt. Who thought about washing anymore? She was lucky to be alive. Water was the new gold. And no one ever wasted gold, they hoarded it . . . if they were lucky enough to have any to hoard to begin with.

She dragged herself off the filthy floor of the bathroom that had been her bedroom for the night to check the door and found Seth had yet to remove the board he always nailed across. She uselessly smacked her palm on the door and slid back to the floor, a futile gesture of defiance.

Defeat settled around her shoulders like a tattered cape; the effort to raise her head again was overwhelming. Picking absently at the sores developing on her face and her upper shoulders, she diffidently examined the blood she found mixed with the dirt under her nails.

Exhausted, she wondered if Seth would allow her the time to scrounge for some antiseptic in the next town they passed. Probably not. His plan of keeping to the woods had kept them alive this long.

From the other corner of the antiquated tiny bathroom, she heard a groan. Slowly she dragged her emaciated body over to where Jen rested and attempted to cradle her granddaughter's head on her meager lap. She stroked Jen's limp hair, feeling crusty growths beneath its once lush thickness. *We might all look like Biafran refugees of the distant past but we're still alive,* she thought, a spark in her soul refusing to give up. *Seth will ensure I at least survive. I'm his ticket into Clyde's bomb shelter.*

Bitter tears dropped down onto Jen's unconscious figure as Lorna thought about her husband. Would she ever see him again? Would they actually survive long enough to get to Sussex County? Would she remember the directions Clyde had given her?

The once glamorous, confident and competent Lorna found herself reduced to a quavering, subservient creature that would do anything to stay alive. Half the time she existed on the plane of the insane, trying to think only about getting through the next day. Where to steal water, where to steal food, and what straggler she would turn her back on next as Seth stole their supplies and immersed himself in his deadly amusements, leaving silent inert bodies behind with the fading echoes of screams and desperate pleading in Lorna's ears.

Her stomach plummeted as she forced her memory to turn away.

"Gram . . . where are we?" Jen's eyes slowly opened as the hesitant whispered words foretold her dissipated strength. Lorna bent down, her worn hands gripping the sides of Jen's sunken face. She leaned in to shower Jen with grateful kisses.

"Thank the Lord, you're okay. I didn't know if you were going to come back to me."

"What do you mean, Gram? I'm fine." Jen struggled to sit up, but the task overwhelmed her. "What's the matter with me? Why can't I get up? I feel weird."

She looked down at her clothes, seeing rags. Raising her hands, she discovered the sores that had erupted weeks ago. "Ew, Gram. What's wrong, where's Mom?" Her eyes flitted frantically around the room, horror registering as Lorna tried to calm her down. "Christ sakes, where the heck are we?" Her voice broke, terror taking hold.

"Shush, Jen. We don't want Seth to hear us."

"Seth? Who's Seth? And where's Suzy?"

*Oh, my God*, thought Lorna. *She can't remember.* Tears began again as Lorna wondered how Jennifer could have amnesia. Was it because of her coma?

Lorna allowed her mind to regress back to one of their more hateful evenings. The evening Jennifer had fallen ill. She had unexpectedly slipped into a catatonic state after watching Seth bludgeon a child to death in front of his restrained parents. He had slapped the mother silly as she sobbed, listening to her child's screams of pain and terror, her husband powerless to do anything. It hadn't helped when Seth had taken the woman to the car for his amusement.

*That was what, two weeks ago? When we still had the car?* Lorna ached with the memory of what Seth had done to the woman's husband after he'd killed her. *Poor man, he looked like he didn't want to live any longer. The family had been just a few days from starvation anyway.*

Seth recovered very little from their belongings. Lorna remembered that Jennifer's sanity had begun to slip right after she had refused the cookie Seth had found in the child's bag. His crack about how she would grovel for a juicy piece of the kid's thigh before too long was the final straw for the tormented young girl.

Seth wanted to leave her behind but Lorna would have none of that. She refused to budge without her. Seth's threats failed to move her. She was not going to leave Jennifer behind like they had Suzy.

Lorna's vision clouded, her head dizzy as she hurriedly shoved all thoughts of what had happened to Suzy from her mind. If she and Jennifer were to survive this ordeal, she must hold it together.

"Gram, where's Mom and Dad? I don't . . . I don't feel so good. I want to go home."

Thinking fast, Lorna manufactured a tale. "Sweetie . . . don't you remember? We were bombed. The Russians, Iran, or maybe Pakistan, who knows, maybe all of them, they all hate us anyway. Suzy's with your mom and dad. We're on our way to meet Grandpa."

Jen scanned the decrepit room and the piles of rags they slept on. "But we're hurt. And why . . . why are we in this room? Can I call Daddy?"

Lorna thought of her tall, successful son, his dear face already fading from her memory. Who knew if he and his wife still lived? Probably not. She patted Jen's limp hand, too numb and dehydrated for more tears, and wondering what to say next.

"Gram, I need a glass of water." Jen's voice rasped, her tongue swollen and pasty.

*What to do?* Seth kept them on a leash with the water bottle. Only a sip at a time; never enough to quench their thirst, but enough to keep his meal ticket alive. He refused to supply any water to Jennifer, probably hoping she would die. Lorna was forced to cut her ration in half, saving her last swallow to feed it to Jennifer from her mouth.

"Grrr . . . pluk . . . cak . . . cak, Gram . . ." Jen's voice tailed off. Lorna shoved her hand under Jen's rags to feel at her skin as she watched her granddaughter's eyes flicker and close. She felt the tender flesh at the hollow of her throat, sunken in but warm with a faint beat. Still alive.

Lorna allowed her head to fall back, her emotions fried and spent. She stared up at the yellow-stained ceiling of the bathroom in the small deserted restaurant they had found way off the beaten path four days ago. It had appeared to be a safe place to hole up.

Seth had removed the for sale sign in front of the saggy building, ripping it out of the ground to hide it in the overgrown weeds. No sense inviting any stragglers like themselves to take refuge. Let them wonder if it was occupied and move on. Most would be unwilling to take the risk.

If it appeared you might carry food, water or weapons, you were a target and your life would not be worth shit, nor the life of anyone else in your party. Seth was far from the only predator afoot. He was just more accomplished . . . more experienced . . . more eager.

Now they had a roof over their heads, they rested. They needed it desperately as they'd been running for days. Ever since they had lost custody of the car that horrible night they had left Suzy behind. Lorna wished she could take a burning poker and just burn out the part of her brain that tormented her with the memories of it.

She remembered their first mistake. Seth had decided they needed to get off the back roads to make better progress. They knew they had to hook up to Route 80 eventually, then it would be a straight shot almost all the way to Sussex County. Lorna refused to give Seth any more information after that.

But the highways were littered with the carcasses of vehicles with empty gas tanks. They heard rumors of refugee gangs and ragtag groups calling themselves tribes that took up housekeeping in their useless cars, marking out small territories to highjack any trespassers that passed, looting their meager belongings and sending them on their way empty-handed to die.

If any brave souls decided to challenge the raiders . . . well. Evidence of death and murder lay piled on the sides of the road. From the size of the piles it appeared the killings had escalated. It was sometimes easier to slaughter your prey outright rather than risk them coming back with reinforcements to rescue their belongings.

It became worth the risk. Without their belongings (food, clothes, weapons), no one stood a chance anyway. Their world now existed far beyond that of dog eat dog. Civilization teetered on the insane edge of human eat human, and Lorna did not plan to be around when that erupted, even if she must carry Jen on her back the rest of the way to Sussex County.

That fateful day had begun as miserably as the last. They had piled into the car with all the stolen loot from the cabin they had slept in, not that there had been much left after the inhabitants and other looters had got to it first.

But they had found a blanket and a few kitchen items they could use to trade with. That's how they had got their intelligence. Seth would take one of the girls with him as he approached an innocuous group after staking them out to reassure himself of their safety. He had found that by trading a small food item, usually crackers or cookies, a pot or a pan (he didn't want to use water or anything containing protein), he would obtain information that kept them away from trouble spots, hostile gangs and radiation.

They hadn't been able to avoid radiation completely though— Seth said it extended far into the adjoining suburbs of some of the hot areas they skirted.

Lorna wondered what kind of long-term toll the radiation sickness would take on them. As of the moment before they lost Suzy, they had still had their health except for Jennifer. The sores had sprouted quickly, Seth even getting sloppy nosebleeds. Was that because he had kept them locked up so much while he did the raiding?

As emaciated as they were, they still had energy and health enough to keep food down when they hit the jackpot. And they had still managed enough strength to make deliberate, if paltry, progress east every few days. Seth was certain the medicine socked away in Clyde's bomb shelter would help them if they were careful not to absorb large doses of the deadly fallout.

They all knew far too well what *that* looked like. Lorna squeezed her eyes tightly but failed to block the images of dying city dwellers who had survived the bombs only to perish in pain and vomit, their lifeblood draining from their pores as they refused to let go. The children were always the worst. Some lay quietly, others cried weakly, pining for their already dead mothers and fathers before they too took their last breath.

They were lucky that Seth's guidance had allowed them to miss out on the hundreds of thousands that had died in their boots along the main thoroughfares and highways. Three things ruled their lives: food and water, avoiding trouble, and moving east to salvation.

Lorna and the girls had lived in debilitating fear and shock after the discovery of Seth's true nature. The girls had been tormented by nightmares for over a month, Lorna by guilt.

All the time Seth had behaved as if they were on a jaunt. No mention had ever been made about Maryann or the events of that fateful evening. Lorna and the girls had instinctively known it was better to cry silently, Lorna's terror-stricken eyes cutting off any questions that might be overheard by Seth.

Which was most of the time as he never let them out of his sight unless they were locked up. Lorna often tormented herself with the question of what would have happened had she not snooped in Seth's backpack. Might they have avoided the incident?

Tying her stomach and nerves into knots never gave her an answer. So Maryann had become another victim of the holocaust . . . unknown, unremarked and unmourned. Just another slice of Lorna's memory she wished to excise.

As time had marched inexorably toward the catastrophic events that had almost destroyed them all, Seth and Lorna had been aware of their dire need of gasoline. They had both known they had about as much chance of finding some as they had of raising Lazarus from the dead, although they kept their opinions to themselves.

Seth's psychotic habit of pretending they were on the way to a party grated on Lorna's nerves. So much so she rarely spoke, refusing to play his fucked-up mind game.

It didn't stop *him* though. So there they had been, tooling down the access road that ran parallel to the interstate, Lorna dosing off and on, Suzy curled under her arm, and Jen stretched out unconscious in the back seat, twined between the stacks of valuable detritus they had collected.

Lorna and Suzy had been startled awake when the car had run over something in the road, something big by the feel of the bump. The car had swerved first one way and then another as Seth had tried to keep it on the road. Suzy had painfully gripped Lorna's shirt, her fingers cutting into her skin.

"Ah, *fuck*. Son of a fucking rotten bitch." Seth had slammed his palms down on the steering wheel in frustration.

Carefully, softly, Lorna had asked what had happened.

"We just got a flat, *again*. I hit something. Now we're going to have to change the tire. And we were making good time. I wanted to get up on the freeway before we ran out of gas. We need to reach a good spot to pull off for the night before it gets dark. Now this fucking tire's going to put us behind." He had slammed the car door.

"Get the fuck out here, Lorna, you're not going to sit on your ass while I do all the work."

Lorna had clambered out of the car, first imploring Suzy to stay inside. As Seth had opened the trunk, she had watched him appraise the best of the tires he had been collecting for the car. *Or should I say stealing? I guess it doesn't matter anymore. I'd steal too if it would keep the kids safer and get us closer to Sussex County.* Flats had become a common occurrence with the amount of off-road driving they had been forced to do in their efforts to stay unobtrusive.

Rounding the passenger side of the car, she had scanned the road, spotting a pile of rags. She had walked toward the rags, holding her breath against hope, praying . . .

"Get the fuck back here, Lorna."

She had turned to see Seth's purple face, spittle collecting on his lips as he had screamed at her again. The familiar dread had seeped into her pores, setting her nerves on end. *Oh my God, he did something bad again, I know it.*

Ignoring Seth's protests, she had continued on. She had heard his furious footsteps behind her as she had approached the blood-soaked rags, the fixed stare of a young boy with his bloody hands still holding his dying dog by the leash. The large short-haired dog's tail had wagged uncertainly as Seth had grabbed her arm and turned to viciously stomp on the dog's head; once, twice, until the tail lay limp.

"You stupid bitch, didn't I tell you what would happen if you gave me any trouble?"

He had slapped her hard, her face numb, stars swirling in the darkness of her mind. As she had wiped blood from her split lip with the back of her skeletal hand, he had continued to rail at her, demonic eyes flaming.

"We don't have time for this. How would you like me to dump Jennifer right here by the side of the road?"

Lorna's gaze had turned back to the two motionless lumps on the road as the enormity of what had actually happened registered.

"You ran them down deliberately, didn't you, Seth?" Her voice had pierced the cold air, low and deceptively calm.

"Get the fuck back to the *car,* Lorna. That tire isn't going to change itself."

Lorna had balled her fist, unwilling to let it go. "You sick piece of garbage, I will not allow you to kill anymore."

Seth had shut his mouth and stared at Lorna. He had looked her up and down, slow and insolent. The gleam in his eyes had brightened as his face had lit up with a brilliant sick smile.

Suddenly the click of a dozen rifles had sounded, the clicks themselves no less shocking as their bullets might be. A voice had carried crisply across the cool air. "Are you going to answer the nice lady, Seth? She wants to know if you ran them down deliberately."

Seth's face had drained of color as they were surrounded by a motley group of men of various ages and states of emaciation who had appeared up on the ridge that separated the access road from the freeway: lean and hungry looking men.

A tall man in his late forties had nodded his head toward the dead boy. Another shorter man, his beard wild and matted, had scrambled down to lean over him. His hand had gone to his face, now awash in anguish. His broken voice had carried back to the tall man, who appeared to be their leader.

"Doc, it's too late. He's gone, Dukie too."

The man called Doc had clenched his teeth and ambled down the ridge to make his way to Lorna and Seth. The other men had closed in. With a nod from Doc, two men had slipped behind Seth, wrenching his arms behind his back, and had snapped on a pair of plastic cuffs. Doc had turned to face Lorna. He had given a measured nod.

"Madam, I presume from the conversation we just overheard that you and ol' Seth here are not exactly friends?"

Lorna had tried to consider her answer but her thoughts had raced so fast she couldn't formulate a plan. With her heart tripping madly, she had decided some version of the truth would be best. She couldn't afford to piss off Seth, there was no telling what he would say or do. What if he told the men about Clyde's shelter? They might want to try to break in themselves.

Lorna had stolen a glance at Seth. *If only I could use these men to break away from him.* She had quickly considered her dilemma, remembering they were almost out of gas and would be forced to carry Jennifer the rest of the way. *Can I do that on my own? In my condition? Oh Lord, I think I'm going to need Seth after all.*

"I'm Doctor Benjamin. Just call me Benjamin, or Doc . . . or royally pissed off."

His stern but respectful countenance, precise diction and clear intelligence had suggested to Lorna that she might be able to leave here peacefully if she was careful. Doc Benjamin had motioned with his hand to his men who hastened to remove the remains of the boy and his dog.

"But I am a reasonable man, so I will ask you again, who are you and what is your relationship to Seth here?"

Lorna had begun to quaver as she had seen the car door open in the distance. *Oh no, baby, stay in the car.* She had watched as Suzy had stepped out of the car to see what was going on.

"Keep your mouth shut, Lorna. I'll handle this." Seth's voice had clearly carried a menacing undertone. With that, Benjamin had leaned over to give Seth a backhand, knocking him to the ground.

"Did you hear me ask the *lady* a question? Is your name, *madam*? Do you need some help with your *hearing*? *Avery* . . ." he called out.

A behemoth-like Avery would have stood out no matter what the prevalence of food was. But Lorna's attention had been drawn to the equally enormous machete gripped in his ham-like paw.

"I want you to help Seth here with his hearing. I need him to understand who I'm speaking to."

With those instructions, Avery had bent over, reaching down to tug on Seth's ear. With one deft stroke, he had removed the ear, his machete slicing deftly through skin and cartilage. Lorna had not been sure Seth had understood what had happened, even as blood had flowed down the side of his head to mix with the dirt and blood left by the boy and his dog.

To Lorna's mortification, Seth had begun to cry, and Benjamin's men had hooted and jeered. Lorna had cringed, knowing that if they got away with this, Seth would take his humiliation out on her and the girls. She had shouted out, her words tumbling off her lips. "My name is Lorna. I'm traveling to find my husband. Seth is a traveler I met on the road some months ago. He's helping me drive. I'm so sorry about this accident. But it *was* an accident."

Doc Benjamin had looked straight into Lorna's eyes as she spoke, causing her to squirm. His eyes had followed her every twitch.

"I must have misunderstood your conversation with ol' Seth here. I thought you were accusing him of deliberately running our boy down."

"Oh, no sir . . . I mean, Doctor Benjamin."

He had moved closer to Lorna, so close she had been able smell his ubiquitous rancid breath. Exhaling her own, he had backed off quickly.

"It was purely an accident, sir. No harm was intended. We're horrified and stressed by our actions. I didn't know what I was saying. I'm sure you can understand that."

Doctor Benjamin had looked from Lorna to Seth.

"I rightly can understand that. But you killed a promising young boy. And that dog of his could have fed my men and the women for a full day. As soon as you compensate us for our loss, you can be on your way."

Lorna had breathed a sigh of relief as Seth had continued to whimper on the ground. "Oh, right . . . of course. We have water and pots . . ." She had watched Benjamin's unyielding expression. "And a few blankets . . . I'm sure you could use those. Uh . . . *wait*." She had lifted her hand in vain for the men had spotted Suzy.

Benjamin had given Lorna an enigmatic glance, ripe with expectation. "I think we should have no problem coming to a suitable arrangement."

With that, the men had turned toward the vehicle. Benjamin had put his fingers to his mouth and given a piercing whistle. From over the ridge had flowed a torrent of women—young women . . . with blank faces. They had run to the men, lining up behind each of them. Some girls as young as twelve and possibly less had stood at attention behind the men who had cultivated possessive grins. Some men only had one or two girls, some five or six. Benjamin had none.

"All right now, you know what to do." And off they had run to the car. Like locusts, they had ripped every thread of cloth, every bit of metal, all of their food and water *and* their map out of the car. One of the older girls had run back to Benjamin.

"You better come see this, Doc."

With that, the entire group, minus Seth, had moved over to the vehicle. As Lorna had hurried behind them, Suzy had run into her arms, eyes big and frightened. Lorna had paled, catching a lingering glance from Dr. Benjamin as he had made his way to the back seat of the car, their possessions now strewn about in small piles.

"Who do we have here? Is she sick?" He had hurriedly backed away from the car.

As Lorna had realized Benjamin was a *doctor, duh,* she had begged him to examine Jen. With a nod, he had pulled a breathing mask out from a pocket, waving for the rest of his gang to hasten and do the same.

From out of their rags, they had all removed a breathing mask. Jealously, Lorna had waited while they put their protection in place. All kinds of diseases were circulating. Many were airborne. In the breakdown of civilization, one of the first things to go was hygiene. When toilets didn't flush and soap was nonexistent . . . Seth's plan to stay away from other people by sticking to the back roads and woods had kept them from catching any of the numerous viral diseases that had decimated towns like wind blowing over matchsticks.

Twenty minutes later, Dr. Benjamin had climbed out of the car.

"I can't see anything wrong with her. She shows no overt symptoms of anything. Without lab work, I'm just guessing, though. Most of my work before the bombs was just guesswork anyway. I don't even think I've ever met a real doctor."

"You're not a *real* doctor?"

Benjamin had looked affronted at her admonishment.

"Well, I *am* a physician's assistant. I worked in a hospital for almost twenty years. Don't you know there *are* no more doctors? *I am* the doctor. I'm the best you can get."

Tiring of the discussion, Benjamin had signaled the women, who picked up Lorna and Seth's possessions and scurried over the ridge out of sight.

"Whoa, hold on there. You can't leave us out here with just our car."

"I'm not going to. Keys, please?"

"I don't have them."

As Lorna had watched, a man had run back to Seth to rifle his pockets. Other men had eased Jennifer out of the car and laid her out on the ground. Lorna had raced to her side.

"Get your hands off her."

Benjamin had flicked the recovered keys to another man. Lorna had stared as he drove off with the car. All had been quiet as they waited for the car to return. Ten restless minutes had passed before the car had returned, stopping in front of Lorna. Stuck in the open back had been a child's wagon, modified to carry possessions with a tightly secured board, creating a large platform from which to load.

"You have got to be kidding me." Lorna had watched as the modified wagon had hit the ground and the vehicle had driven off again.

"On the contrary, dear woman, you don't know me so I will forgive you. Does it look like I am a kidder?" Benjamin's eyes had bored into her own, then he had glanced again at Suzy. "Please help Seth to his feet, gentlemen."

He had signaled to his men. Seth had hobbled over to Lorna, his cheeks tear-stained, his pride in Benjamin's pocket. Lorna had tried not to look at the blood leaking from his missing ear.

From over the ridge had run one of the young girls who, with an encouraging nod from Benjamin, had proceeded to quickly bandage Seth's ear. She had stepped back and run off back over the ridge. Benjamin had inspected her work.

"Not bad, she's improving." He had turned to Lorna. "I think we may be even now. I think it is time for you to move on . . . before I change my mind." He had smiled encouragingly.

"But we won't survive without our things. I demand you return our water." Lorna had stood tall. From nowhere, Benjamin's arm had shot out to grab Lorna's arm in a death grip, the pain forcing her to stagger and drop to her knees.

"My dear, I'm sure my pleasing affect and melodiously educated voice has convinced you there is some way you can reason with me. I assure you that will not happen. You are beginning to test me and I don't care to be challenged. That is a mistake. Avery?" The giant had come to attention.

"I want you to remove my gift of the wagon and take your machete . . . what is the young lady's name?"

Lorna had paled, all blood rushing from her face. She had felt as if she would faint. Benjamin's fingers had dug deeper into her arm, the pain fighting with the mind she had thought she was losing.

"*Her name,*" he had roared.

"Jen—Jennifer." Lorna had forced the word but it had come out as a whisper.

"I want you to take your machete, Avery, and slit Jennifer's throat."

Avery had moved toward Jennifer.

"No! Please. Come on, Seth, Suzy. Let's get Jen into the wagon." She had turned to Benjamin, who released her arm. "We'll go. Thank you for your . . . your gift." She had bowed her head, pushing Suzy and Seth over to the wagon.

Before they had been able to take an extra breath, Benjamin's men had appeared behind them.

"Just one minute, my dear. Your transgression requires further payment."

Lorna had spun around, suddenly frightened by the proximity of Benjamin's men.

"Further payment?" Her voice had squeaked with incomprehension, her features stiff and glacial.

On a signal from Benjamin, the men had surrounded Lorna, separating her from Suzy. They had passed the little girl from hand to hand, rushing her toward the ridge.

"Grandma, *don't let them take me,*" Suzy had shrieked.

She had fallen to the ground, her fingers digging into the dirt, trying to claw her way back. "No, no, no, Gram, Seth . . . *don't let them take me.*"

One of the men had reached down and thrown her over his shoulder.

"Nooooooo . . ."

They had quickly disappeared over the ridge as her little girl's screams had faded into the dark. Lorna had dropped to the ground sobbing. Avery had knelt with his machete to Jennifer's throat.

"Look at me." Benjamin's voice had cut through Lorna's sobs like the edge of a stiletto. She had raised her head slowly.

"I suggest you and the worthless Seth put the other young lady in the wagon and be off."

"But Suzy's only five years old. Paleesee," she had begged pitifully. "We can't just leave her. Take me instead."

"*You?*" He had sounded incredulous. Laughingly he had added, "I admire your spirit, my dear, but you are simply unsuitable. I assure you, she will be well trained with the rest of the girls. The training is quite rigorous but most come through without scars. The young are quite malleable. There have been a few suicides but they would have proved unsuitable anyway."

Lorna had wiped her tears with the corner of her torn shirt. "Suicide? Unsuitable?" she had numbly asked. "But why? Training? What are you going to do to my baby?" Lorna had rubbed her hands through her scraggly hair, her split nails raking down the sides of her face. She had doubted if she could take anymore, her mental reserves bankrupt.

"Don't worry, my dear, I will personally take her under my wing. Unlike my men, I have yet to take a woman as my concubine. She will be my first."

With the shock permanently imbedded in Lorna's face, Benjamin had turned on his heels. As he had slipped over the ridge, his last words had echoed in her ears, never to be forgotten.

Seth had spoken up for the first time, as if nothing of any great significance had just happened, his voice regaining strength as he spoke. "Well, time to get the show on the road." He had tried to lift Jennifer, to no avail.

"Are you going to just sit there and mope or are you going to help? They might decide to come back. I'm sure they saw me as a threat and might want to force me to join them. That would leave the two of you alone. You really need me now."

"Oh yeah, I'm sure they're scared of you."

Lorna had tried to stand, her legs weak, her stamina beaten down, her thoughts and prayers on Suzy.

"What did you say?" The gleam of control had been back in his eye.

She had witnessed his hands draw up into a fist. Unwilling to be a punching bag for a cowardly psycho again, she had pulled herself together, thought about how they could rescue Suzy, and had stepped forward to calmly face the man who she knew she would be forced to kill before she found her way to her husband with *both* of her granddaughters safely in tow.

Lorna's neck had developed a crick and she adjusted her position on the bathroom floor, withdrawing her feeble hand from under Jennifer's rags, her granddaughter clearly back in the grip of a deep coma.

She had yet to find the proper moment to fulfill her promise made the day they had lost Suzy. *Lost*? Was that the word she was using to convince herself that she needed to let Seth live? Without his cunning, she would never make it to Clyde and salvation. Her heart shriveled as she wondered what she had become.

Inching closer to Jen, Lorna caved into despair and closed her eyes.

**The End**

Dear Reader,

I want you all to know how heartfelt my appreciation is that you have taken the time to read my books. Being an author is one of the most torturous professions out there. Many of us live on the thanks of our readers alone. If anyone cares to leave me an honest review on Amazon.com, Goodreads.com, Smashwords.com, Kobo.com or Barnes and Noble, I would be ever so grateful. Some of you are unaware that Amazon, in particular, promotes books based on the amount of reviews a book gets.

Don't be afraid to make suggestions or criticize the writing. How else is one to improve? I look forward to your comments!

Yours fondly,
J.K. Accinni

# Introduction to
# Species Intervention #6609
# Book 5

# Evil Among Us

## Synopsis for Book 5: Evil Among Us

Will the two groups of survivors finally meet? Will Seth become a threat to those in the Hive who have discovered the mystery and the shocking ramifications of their good health? Who is the Father that Netty and Wil visit every day? What secrets and despicable deeds are Baby and Echo hiding? Why is poor Kenya's baby taking such a long time to arrive? Can the bloodthirsty nature of man be suppressed enough to satisfy the Womb?

And what about the hapless Suzy? Her abduction by the bloodthirsty barbarians will have enormous ramifications for the entire planet.

The survivors in the Hive live and love in happy ignorance until a well-loved member of the group disappears, unraveling the mystery of the Kreyven, secrets hidden by Netty and Wil, and the horrible truth that teaches the survivors that even the most loving and benevolent creature can have its moment to seek revenge.

A complete blast from the past, *Evil Among Us* will answer all the questions readers hungered for in book one, *Baby*.

# Prologue

The brown sky rained dirty ash onto soundless trees denuded of life and flattened as if a giant fist had descended to pummel them from the gray and wintery sky. The horizon was blank; the most famous skyline in the world gone, leaving devastation, twisted metal and death.

There was a complete absence of color, life or warmth. The crushed horizon smoldered with a palette of black and leaden barrenness; benumbing and bone-crushing godforsaken loneliness.

The crumbled remains of the Bronx Zoo flinched under the sight of its once-proud sign, bent and misshapen. Precious wildlife reduced to ash. Minute bone fragments of the Womb's proud creations scattered in the wind.

Yes . . . the premonition directed to a naïve Abby by the transformed Netty Doyle as an Elder of the Womb came to pass over six months ago. No longer just a premonition but a cold ugly reality. Bloody reality. Hopeless reality . . .

The evil death that rained down on the Earth from the very hands of man that had been entrusted to protect it had done its job effectively. Just as man had idiotically planned while stupidly believing the time would never come. What was the old cliché? Man plans, while God, the Womb, laughs?

No one laughed now. Those who survived the early bombings found death at the hands of the next waves of horror, mass hysteria, depraved lawlessness and disease. If the plague, revisited from the Middle Ages, didn't get you, then dysentery, dehydration or starvation did.

Now that the population existed only in miniscule numbers that huddled deep in rare, clever concealments, human feces no longer littered every landscape. The smell of raw human sewage no longer carried on the perpetual wind that harbored its own invisible death to man and beast.

Yes, the wind that struck terror in the hearts of even the strongest, the most psychotic, and the most resourceful, carried invisible radiation along with the powerful spawn of dirty bombs. Even the most infectious microbes searched on the wind for unlucky hosts, the final death knell for the hapless humans and creatures in every corner of the once green planet.

What did the leaders of the most powerful countries in the world think would happen if one of them were foolish enough to hunger for absolute supremacy through the means of nuclear power? Did they think the world would come rushing to their feet in supplication? Only Homo sapiens would conceive of such a barbaric maneuver.

Yes, Homo sapiens: the species that, unlike any other creature, harbors a conscious ego. The ability to manipulate its environment and the complete disregard for the balance of nature and the other creatures that shared the formerly glorious planet.

And where now were the exalted leaders from the United States that bled their constituents so readily into poverty over the last 245 years?

Where were *any* authorities for that matter? How long would the politicians survive in their hunkered- down, taxpayer-funded concrete and steel monoliths in the ground? How many years would pass before their food ran out? Five years? Ten? Fifty? Could they hold out for *one hundred years*? If they could, what shape would the Earth be in? Questions, nothing but questions: long answered and prepared for by the most expensive experts taxpayer money could buy. For all the politicians in all the countries that assumed they would survive . . . the Womb laughed again.

# Chapter 1
# 2057 AD

Five-year-old Suzy lay on the dirty cot with her leg chained to a metal spike embedded in the cold ground, muddy from the drizzle and constant footfalls of the men who came to confer with Doc Benjamin. Many attempted to catch a glimpse of the now notorious young captive who promised salvation for all from the devastation closing in on them as they maneuvered around the poisonous cities like army ants, ducking and weaving, destroying and obliterating everything in their path.

Their numbers now counted in the hundreds. For every man there were five to ten women, all young, most under the age of twenty. And all owned by an individual man. Virtual slaves.

They did the work during the day, setting up the extensive camp and cooking the meals, and were forced to extend comfort at night. If they refused they were beaten, starved and left without shelter, such that it was. It didn't take long for a young girl to be broken. Most were still mourning the loss of their families who had been robbed and murdered by the very men they were now forced to view as their protectors. Some existed in a state of perpetual shock, unable to answer questions or respond to threats as they were repeatedly raped or beaten. But they were alive. They were amongst the lucky few; if you could count their existence as living.

The only things that kept them from going over the edge were their sister captives. The strong and resilient ones knew their best chance of survival was to nurse the weak ones on the off chance they could increase their strength enough to overcome their captors.

It was a hopeless plan, doomed from the onset. The strength of the men only increased as they gathered food from their victims, stray livestock, and indispensable salvage in their march across new territory, pushing further and further east to their destination. But it was this trifling spark of defiance that the girls nursed, unwilling to let the fledgling ember of purpose be extinguished and so threaten their tenuous hold on thoughts of independence and freedom.

Suzy cringed as Doc Benjamin approached with Avery at his side. Avery claimed to be a veteran of the last few wars the United States had been sucked into by conservative politicians who hungered for the international conflict that enriched the pockets of the multinational corporations; in turn enriching their re-election coffers. He claimed to be an expert in electronics, rigging up a communication system between the men that rivaled anything the few rag tag groups of authorities had in the beginning.

Now, most in authority were either part of Doc Benjamin's group or dead. Stupidly, the principled ones had failed to adjust quickly enough to the new rule of eat or be eaten. Not literally, of course; it hadn't come to that yet. But unfortunately, their ethics didn't have room for flexibility, leaving their stripped corpses ignobly and anonymously behind in the dirt with the rest of Doc's victims.

Suzy tried to keep her eyelids squeezed tight as Avery approached. He was a lumbering giant of a man. His shaved head with its knobby protrusions and his dead, flat eyes that glittered as he watched the young girls laboring around the vast camp did nothing to dispel the aura of restrained violence. He hadn't touched her, but his excited grunts and the soft sobbing that were usually accompanied by sharp slaps and occasional screams could be heard around camp. That alone convinced Suzy that even though she didn't understand what was happening, she knew it was only a matter of time before she was the recipient herself.

"When ya gunna let me have the little one? You promised it was my turn the night we took her." Avery eyed Suzy's thin form, apparently asleep on the ramshackle cot, his voice unexpectedly squeaky and high pitched. The whining tone made Doc Benjamin cringe with annoyance. He turned to eyeball Avery. With the long suffering patience of a mother who's close to being on her last nerve with a beloved child, he sighed.

"Avery, you know she's our ticket to the bomb shelter her grandfather has. We need to keep her happy and cooperative. How long do you think that would last if I turned her over to you? Didn't you get the last two women we liberated?"

Doc sidled up to Avery. A quick glimpse of steel flashed in his eyes, unseen by the giant. He playfully slapped Avery on the cheek; his hand stinging while Avery remained unperturbed, still caught up on what he felt was an undeserved slight.

"Yeah, but Doc, they both didn't work out. I had to dispatch the mother the first night when she tried to claw my face after I broke her kid's arm. And you know that was an accident. She just didn't get it when it was her kid's turn to be my bed warmer."

The whine in Avery's high-octave voice was trying Doc's patience. He snaked his arm around the giant's waist. "It's time to break camp and get a move on. Why don't you see what's keeping my breakfast? Tell the women to send a sweet for the girl. I need to have a talk with her when she wakes up." The giant's face sagged.

"But—"

"No buts. We don't have time to go over the inventory right now either. It'll keep. Just check on the livestock and make sure the men eat before they start to round up the herd again. We need them to keep up with us. What good does it do us if they get lost on the way to Lily Pond Road? It took us a long time to make it here to Sussex County. I'm not about to lose them after all this." Slapping Avery on a thick, meaty cheek a second time, he turned him around and sent him on his way, patient resignation in the slump of Avery's huge slabs of shoulders.

As he waited for his breakfast, Doc leaned back on the vehicle he and his men had confiscated from Suzy's grandmother and the worm, Seth. *What was the woman's name? Laura? No Lorna . . . yeah. Seth and Lorna.* He stewed over his error in letting them go. He should have killed Seth on the spot, but something about the old lady had made him pause. Not to mention the comatose young teen in the back of their car. There was no telling what illness she might have been carrying.

In his haste to get away, he had let the one person who could save them all slip through his fingers. His fists tightened in anger. How was he going to keep his horde under control if he continued to make bad judgment calls like that? His decision to follow Seth and the grandmother to Sussex County was called into question continually. He'd heard the whisperings.

He glanced over to Suzy's sleeping form. *Too bad the kid doesn't remember where her grandfather's bomb shelter actually is. It must be huge if they're growing crops inside.*

And she said they had medicine and something that cures people. At least they'd pulled the name of the road out of her. Now they just had to figure out where Lily Pond Road was. He absently fingered the ugly sores with their hanging scabs on the underside of his arm. No matter what he did to treat them, they refused to heal.

Doc peered up at the gray sky through a gap in the lean-to, wondering how long it would be before they saw the sun again. It had taken them months to get this far and they never did catch up to Seth and the grandmother. It made him suspect they had wandered off the route or been killed on the way. Perhaps the tribe had arrived before the twosome. After all, Seth and the old woman were on foot, dragging the sick teen. His horde had many vehicles. Even slowing for the multitude of stops to scavenge for gas supplies, females and anything else they might find useful at some future date, they had made decent progress.

When they had traveled off Route 15, the main artery leading into Sussex County, he had quickly established camp in a town called Franklin, just to the east of Sparta. They had decided that going further northwest to the town of Andover, which had at one time been nothing but rich farmland, was the wrong direction. There was no point in going further. He cursed under his breath as he remembered entrusting the map they had liberated from Seth and Lorna's car to one of his most reliable men.

Thompson had passed it on to his wife, one of his only men to have a spouse in the tribe. Unfortunately for them both, she'd lost the map during a mad scramble out of a town in Pennsylvania after they'd discovered dead bodies covered with bulbous growths and dried blood. They'd dropped everything they'd just scavenged where they stood and bolted, with Doc threatening to shoot anyone who held on to their tainted bounty. He didn't know what disease had struck the hapless inhabitants of the town, but he knew it could be most anything. His forethought regarding the issuance of collapsible breathing masks months ago had kept them safe . . . so far.

That night he had been forced again to make an example of a member of the tribe who had faltered and placed them in jeopardy. He had forced everyone to watch as he'd placed the woman on her knees, head over a log and had one of the strongest men in the tribe strike her neck with an axe, removing her head. He'd hated to do it because of the effect it had on the other women in the tribe. For the next day or so they had become less malleable. But things would eventually settle back down. It had served its purpose, keeping everyone on their toes.

He was at a complete loss as to what direction to go in from here. He knew they couldn't be more than two hours from New York City. The once great metropolis had taken a direct hit, followed up by a series of secondary hits once the other psychotic leaders of third world powers decided to pile in. When all communication was lost, he could only speculate as to who had done what to whom and why. Did it really matter now anyway? He knew the only thing he had to worry about was where the hell the bomb shelter was. And keeping everyone healthy, of course. That's what gave him his power.

That had never been an easy job even before the bombs. As he'd had told Suzy's grandmother, he wasn't a real doctor. Not like the doctors of his grandparents' era. The general public, like so many other issues, were completely unaware that the profession of physician no longer existed. Those that wanted to be *doctors*, simply studied to become what used to be called physician assistants. That was the doctor of today. It wasn't that the government had tried to hide it, although they had done so quite successfully, it was the fact that no one had paid attention. Their own lives were so all-consuming that few had the energy or inclination to pay attention, allowing the government to slowly strip them of most of their rights, fostering a new reality that few took the time to call into question. *Don't worry, the government will handle it, the government will solve everything, the government will take care of us.*

It also allowed interesting gentlemen like himself to slip into the ranks of the revered medical profession. Men with questionable ethics. It wasn't that he was such a bad guy. He just believed in different things. Like the fact that he was destined for greatness. He'd known that from the time he had discovered that a wide engaging smile could charm even the hardest bitten parent or superior.

His wandering mind thought about Avery and his many talents. Was there any wire, tool, or inanimate object that guy couldn't put to good use? It almost made up for his volatility when it came to dealing with flesh and blood. Before too long, Doc's eyelids drooped and he found himself nodding off to sleep.

Suzy concentrated, straining for sounds, hearing only the distant clatter that meant morning departure was not far off. She tested the silence by softly clearing her throat. Doc remained quiet so she finally relaxed for a few minutes to say her daily prayer to her grandmother to come find her. She swallowed a soft sob, gulping it down her throat as her little-girl perceptions wondered why it was taking so long. Her undeveloped brain warred with her treasured fantasy of rescue. No matter how many times she told the girls who fed her and attempted to comfort her that she would be rescued, they only shook their big heads that sat on emaciated rag-covered bodies with huge sad eyes and looked away. All were silent, not wanting to hurt the little girl with the truth of her reality. A few even envied the special treatment the five-year-old received.

Poor Suzy, not an ounce of fat remained on her bones. She refused to eat and often found herself in the arms of some of the men from the tribe as Doc directed her to be force-fed. It was the only thing that kept her alive; that and the delusion of rescue by her beloved grandmother. In the last few months, the reality of her captivity and the circumstances in which she lived had served to erase any trace of the happy, joyful child, along with most of the memories of her five years. She no longer remembered her mama and papa, her sister Jennifer, Seth, or even where she was from. The only probable reason she was still alive was her agonized screams for her grandmother to rescue her and take her to the magic bomb shelter when she was first captured. After she screamed and cried herself out, Doc was able to get enough monosyllabic answers out of her to convince him that the sanctuary was real.

Suzy shuddered as she felt Doc place a heavy hand on her thin shoulder. She began to tremble instantly. He turned her over, glancing down at the hardened crust of last night's gray gruel that decorated her hand-me-down shirt. The infinitesimal spark that was actually Suzy receded from her eyes to take refuge in the primal part of her mind that protects us all from facing horror. The only thing that Doc could see was an empty husk. She instinctively knew he had exhausted all hope of finding a way to reach her and extract even a morsel of information that would guide them further.

"I'm sorry, little one. But maybe it's better this way. My men will leave you alone." Taking her in his arms, he did an uncharacteristic thing. He hugged her and held her close. The spark that was the child Suzy flared, burning bright before receding back to its place of refuge.

From outside the lean-to came shouting. Men converged from everywhere, departure forgotten as everyone waited to hear the news brought by their advance team. The woman caught each other's eyes, glances of terror shared by all, as they wondered what new fate lay before them with the obvious urgency of the news.

Doc laid Suzy back on her broken cot and stood as his men approached. He ran his fingers through his lank, greasy hair and secured it with a band, allowing it to drape down his back like his men, then stepped out to meet them. The stench of the camp's unwashed bodies hit him in waves as the crowd around his lean-to thickened.

"Well, gentlemen, it appears you have some news for me?" He listened intently to the report from the scouts who stayed at least half a day in front of the tribe. Yes, there was a discovery. Not the bomb shelter they were hoping for, but maybe something else that might save them; something that would shelter them from the poisonous winds that were surely bound to catch them eventually in their hot indiscriminate soupy grip.

"Well, for God's sakes, gentlemen. Would one of you kindly get to the point?" From the ranks of the scouts a young man in his mid-twenties stepped up. He held a piece of sun-worn plastic in his hands. A sign, its letters faded, but still readable. The young man's fetid smile split from ear to ear even as he brushed at the flies that swarmed over the open sores on his forehead.

"And there's water too, Doc," he exclaimed as the rest of the tribe hugged and slapped each other on the back. For in his hands lay what they would view as their temporary salvation, little knowing they would be fated to call it home for as long as most of them would survive. He stepped closer to Doc, holding up the sign for all to see. It read simply: The Franklin Mine ca 1910. The zinc and mineral fluorescence capital of the world.

Little did they know they were only ten short miles from the Hive.

# Chapter 2

Lorna pulled hard on the contraption that Seth had fashioned after the converted wagon had given out for the last time. Who knew an eighty-five-pound teenager could feel so heavy? But it was a miracle that she still lived.

Lorna glanced back at the pile of bones in the two-wheeled sled, not even recognizing Jennifer anymore. She stopped counting the times she had fought with Seth over leaving her behind. *When was that?* she wondered as flakes of cold, wet gray ash fell from the ominous gloomy sky. *Was it a month ago? No, I was warm then. Maybe last year . . . I think Suzy was a baby then. Nah, that can't be right. I need Clyde. He can help me. I need to get to Clyde. Then I can pick Suzy up at her school. Yup, can't forget to pick up Suzy.* She shuddered as she thought about Suzy waiting for her at school. "Can't leave my baby doll alone," Lorna muttered as she brushed ineffectively at her blood as it continued to drip from her nose, a constant occurrence these days.

Her finger caught on the rags that adorned her, holding together her own emaciated frame that kept moving forward beyond all reason.

"Ahhhh." She bent over in pain, dropping the bar that enabled her to pull Jen as another paper-thin fingernail ripped off her hand. She fumbled to untangle it from its nest of rags, forcing her unbalanced form to fall to the ground.

"Help meeee . . . Seeeth." Her voice whispered its forlorn plea; a refrain that repeated itself every day in response to any deviation from their long journey.

The easily distracted Lorna no longer saw Seth as an enemy in her delusion. Small comfort to Seth who had the responsibility of keeping them safe and keeping Lorna moving forward to Sussex County, where they now traipsed after skirting the not so greater metro area of New York City in an attempt to avoid the fallout from the bombs.

"Seeeeth." The empty whisper came at him again. He felt too weary to answer. Not that she would respond with anything like a cogent reply anyway. He picked up a stone and lobbed it at her as she lay disoriented on the ground, trying to get back on her feet.

"Get up, old woman." He swallowed his distaste. *The stupid fool. I can't believe she's got me this far.*

Seth had only one concern now: that he would be able to find the big granite rock in the woods. He watched as Lorna crawled on the ground like an animal, grunting and blubbering his name through the blood and snot that ran down her chin.

He wasn't much better off himself as his ear, butchered by Avery, refused to heal, leaking an odorous fluid. He hoped fervently that medical care would be available once they found the sanctuary. Eyeing up Lorna, he wondered how long she would last. They must be somewhere in the vicinity of the sanctuary now.

It was a delicate balancing act with the water. He needed to keep Jen alive if he wanted Lorna to cooperate. And he needed to keep Lorna alive long enough to talk their way into the sanctuary. Such a dilemma. He couldn't really let Lorna live past the moment they gained entrance. He watched her frantic moaning and struggles to stand, blood from her nose now splattered all over the wretched heap that was all that they had left of Jennifer. *Well, they can't blame that on me.*

Seth wondered if he would be able to pull off his plan. He hoped that in the surprise of their sudden appearance, he would be able to distract the people there enough with cries of help for Jennifer for him to give Lorna's neck a discreet snap. She was the only one who could rat him out. Even though she was a burnt-out husk of microbes and radiation sickness, he worried about how responsive she might be after some good medical care. Seth grinned, his heart racing as he contemplated how he would kill Lorna.

Ambling over to her in his own feeble fashion, he gripped her under her arm, the flesh feeling loose and unconnected to her bones.

The smell of urine assailed his nostrils. With a grunt, he strained to bring Lorna to her feet so they could attempt to get up the hill that led to the forest perched at the edge of what looked like a deserted neighborhood of tiny ranch houses and a few split levels.

He heard the squeak and rendering tear of metal as he glimpsed a child's swing set tumble to the ground behind a modest home that had collapsed on itself. This was Lily Pond Road.

Turning back to Lorna, he just hoped they would have the strength to drag Jennifer up the hill and through the woods.

"For Christ's sake, Lorna. You have to help yourself a little. I can't do it all." Lorna looked at him as if she didn't recognize him. Seth sighed. He could see Lorna was blanking out again and going to be next to useless, just when he needed her the most. How the hell was he going to find the trail to the rock without her directions? She said *to follow the trail* a few months ago when he had pressed her for specifics. *What the hell is that supposed to mean?*

He knew she wanted to get there as much as he did, but he had to be careful. She might be looking to pay him back for losing Suzy. He had yet to come up with a story to explain that debacle. He reached up to feel where his ear should have been, wincing as the throbbing pain kicked up a notch from his clumsy touch. He cleaned the pus and fluid from his shaking hand, his ragged drawers the only place to wipe.

At least he knew they were in the correct place. He scanned the empty tractor trailers that sat around a small ranch house which no longer featured windows or a front door. The dwelling appeared to mock him with its vacant window eyes, daring him to come inside.

Tearing his gaze from the empty house, he renewed his efforts to get Lorna and Jennifer up the hill. He silently assisted Lorna to her feet, placing her hand back on the metal pull bar. He scrambled to the rear of the makeshift wagon and shouted, "Come *on*, Lorna . . . Pull!"

She turned to look at him, a momentary morsel of clarity flowering in her bloodshot eyes. "Seth, are we on Lily Pond Road?"

Seth trod carefully, not knowing how long Lorna's mental state would stay anchored in the present, or what kind of new trouble she would give him. He grimaced as Lorna's face crumpled and she began to wail. She sank to the ground on her knees, dragging Seth down with her. The sled that supported Jennifer slid a few feet down the hill then halted.

"We didn't go back for Suzy. How could I ignore her?" Lorna squinted at Seth. "She's not at school, is she? We left her behind."

Seth could see the wheels of her mind turning in her eyes, trying to connect the events of the last five months. Lorna's eyes widened as she stared blankly at Seth. Her voice hissed venom, slow and painful. "You low life *scumbag*. You actually think I'm going to have my husband save your pathetic ass after what you did?"

Seth drew his shoulders together as he rose off the ground. He bit down hard on his lip, restraining himself from punching her in the face. He'd been through this many times. If he kept his mouth shut, Lorna's moment of clarity would pass. He reached under her arm to yank her up as she struggled against him.

"Take your bloody hands off me, *you insect*."

Seth raised his hand in the air, stopping a mere few inches from her face. Her red splotchy face leaked blood from her snotty nose as she defiantly stood her ground. Just as he decided to go ahead and slap her anyway, he witnessed the light fade from her eyes to be replaced with pliant confusion.

"Seth, what are you doing? We need to get to the school. I promised Suzy we wouldn't be late. Now help me pick up my bags." Seth lowered his fist as Lorna slipped out of his grasp to scrabble after the wagon.

Sighing with relief, Seth helped her retrieve the rickety wagon and they resumed the trek up the hill to the woods amid breathless grunts; the neighborhood homes mocking their progress with their shouts of death and silence.

"Hold on Lorna . . . hold on." They were having trouble with the wagon. The ruts on the floor of the woods refused to give way as they pulled the wagon behind them, forcing their meager strength to dissipate rapidly. Lorna struggled, flailing ineffectively, creating another obstacle for Seth to deal with.

"Seeeth, it won't . . . it won't."

"It won't what? For Christ sakes, Lorna, you think I can't see?" He stopped to scan the trees, denuded of all life: no leaves, no birds, and no squirrels. He rubbed his sore back, feeling his bones flex like rubber and his muscles quake and chatter. As he watched Lorna mutter to herself, he scanned the faint pathway that disappeared into the barren woods.

"Lorna, we need to talk."

She continued to mutter and pull ineffectually at the wagon.

"*Lorna.* I want to talk to you." He stood in front of her, removing her hands from the wagon's iron pull bar. When she showed some vague sign she was listening, he pointed into the woods. "We can't go any further with the wagon. We need to leave it here while we go look for the boulder." She immediately shook her head and muttered louder. He grabbed her by the hand and dragged her away from the wagon. Lorna's pathetic wail turned to a shriek as Seth pulled her away and deeper into the woods, the two of them stumbling along like drunken barflies.

As luck would have it, they quickly came to the granite boulder. Seth dropped Lorna's hand to wrap his arms around the almost mythical stone, tears of relief coursing from his red-rimmed eyes.

"Oh my blessed Lord, it's here. It's here. I'm saved!" He slapped the boulder with the palm of his hand. Turning with his back resting against the boulder, he found Lorna standing motionless, just staring at him. His happy grin clearly confused her.

"So, Lorna, what do we do next?" He sounded like a puppy that had just been promised a thick juicy steak. "Where's the shelter?" He swiveled his head around, looking high and low around the boulder. "Where's the door?" He glanced back at Lorna and noticed her blank expression, unnaturally quiet. He could see her start to weave and ran to catch her.

"Oh no ya don't. Not when we finally got here." Wrapping her thin arm around his neck, he dragged her around the enormous boulder to search from another angle. He stopped in surprise to see the rise of a hill behind the boulder.

"Well, what do we have here?" Before he could do any further investigation, he heard the rustle of dried bushes. Turning from the hill they confronted the sickly sight of an emaciated feral fox. Dried blood soaked her once fluffy henna fur that decorated her ears. Her eyes flashed wildly, clearly out of her mind with hunger and disease. A low growl deep in the throat of the fox snapped Lorna out of her trance.

As the fox crept closer, froth at its mouth dripped to the ground. It crouched low and tense, ready to attack when Lorna decided to join the growls with her choking and guttural scream. Seth leaned into the hillside, forcing Lorna to shield him as he cowered behind her. The fox sprang to Lorna, clamping its teeth down on her flailing hand.

# Chapter 3

As Kenya and Kane shuffled into Netty's kitchen followed by the rest of the inseparable group—Chloe, Scotty, Echo, and Barney—Caesar poked his head into the room. Chloe gave him a quick pat on the head as Scotty ran for the ubiquitous tiger's water dish. All hungry voices waiting for dinner stopped as Kane lowered Kenya with her big belly into a chair that had been specially made for her. Netty and Abby came rushing over. Abby knelt at Kenya's chair, her arms around the distressed teen, while Netty stood stoically, an unreadable expression in her eyes.

"Oh, you poor sweet child. How in the world did you get to the fields today? I thought we agreed you would stay off your feet? What if something happened? You need to stick close to us."

Kenya rolled her eyes at Abby, her voice impatient. "I'm about going *crazy* here, chickey. This baby doesn't wanta come. And I feel healthy as all get out. I can't just sit around all day. *I'm gunna go nuts.* I want to be with my friends if this damn baby is going to give me such a hard time. Have you figured out *something* to get it out of me yet?" Kenya swiveled her head around to see Netty watching her. She glanced down to see the winged woman quietly wringing her hands.

"What the *f'ing* Lord is the matter with me? Netty, I know you know something. *Why hasn't my baby come?*" A slow rise of hysteria sounded in her voice.

Johno detached himself from his seat at the table next to Crystal, who reached out to drag him back. "Johnny, you know you ain't gunna be able to do anything. Why do ya even bother?"

Johno gave her a gentle quiet motion with his hands and knelt down in front of the anguished teen. He took her hand in his, calmly stroking in a methodic fashion. "Shhhh. There you go, little Miss Kenya. Now we have all been through this before. Do you think anything has changed since yesterday?" Kenya looked into his impassive eyes, finding a calm reassurance. She took a breath, ready to expel all the pent up emotion from the inconvenience of lugging her big belly around all day. The steady pressure of his stroking soothed her. All that came out of her mouth was a whimper.

"But, I . . ." She sniffed.

"Shhhh, I know. We all know, young lady." He continued to stroke her arm, not taking his eyes off her face. "Why don't I have Miss Salina fix up some of that special tea you like?" Kenya's mouth opened, then glumly closed again. She hung her head and whispered, "I don't know how much more I can take, Johno. I want to have a normal life."

Kane's hand found its way to the back of her neck. Her head fell to the side as she enjoyed the sensation of his work-worn fingers kneading her muscles. She managed to fit in a quick grateful smile, never one not to reward her admirers. Turning, she gave her attention back to Johno, whom she could tell was deadly serious, her histrionics clearly wearing down even the most patient man in the Hive.

"You will take exactly as much as it *takes*. This baby is the most important thing in the Hive. Apart from the animals," he added quickly. "It doesn't help the situation when we spend so much of our time beating up Wil and Netty because you haven't had the baby yet."

Kenya rolled her eyes. "I wasn't gunna say anything."

Johno hung his head as the rest of the crowd broke out in laughter because they all knew Kenya would do just that. She did it every day and would probably do it again tomorrow. The ritual was common place, but becoming tiresome.

Salina slid a cup of tea toward the teen, agitation on her face. "Johno, don't be so rough on her. She's just a baby herself."

"I ain't no baby, Miss Salina. Me and my baby can take darn good care of ourselves. And as soon as we get outa this place, Chloe and me are taking the baby and going back to *Sarasota*." Kenya's eyes broadcast the belligerence of youth as she followed Salina's figure back to a seat next to Clyde, her arm slipping around his with easy familiarity. "And Kane's coming too, aren't you, chickey?" She gave him a beguiling smile as Captain Cobby's voice rang out from his position at the head of a table next to the adoring Karen.

"My son isn't going *anywhere*, let alone back to Sarasota. Can somebody talk some sense into this girl? It's been six months, more or less. We know from Echo and Baby that the Earth is full of poisons now."

At the mention of their names, Echo and Baby tottered over to Cobby and stroked and prodded his face, their long leathery fingers soft and loving. He reached out to give the two minions quick hugs.

So much had changed in the six months since their hasty flight during the onset of Armageddon. The minions had begun to express themselves to many of the survivors, to their delight. It was considered an honor if Baby or Echo chose to single you out for attention.

As Johno tried to calm Kenya out of her daily crying jag over the fact she was *still* carrying her unborn child in her belly five months after her due date, Netty backed away from the crowd to search for Wil. Joining the animals by the fireplace, she lowered herself to the floor, exchanging a tense glance with Wil, burdened with meaning.

She quickly smiled as Bonnie welcomed her to join Chance and the dogs who were in their usual frolicking abandon, hoping the exuberant young lady hadn't noticed their exchange.

She pulled a fully grown Barney onto her lap, the happy dog not taking his eyes off Echo, who was working her way over to the fireplace after greeting her favorite people with Baby. Netty scanned the room, noticing the handsome vitality in the crowd.

No longer did the women sport wrinkles or gray hair. No chubby waistlines or ponderous energy levels due to the drain of obesity or chemical-laced food of a progressive population. No diabetes, asthma, allergies or headaches; just buoyant perfect health that they all attributed to the unusual food they ate.

And with perfect health came animal attraction to the other sex. Why not? They were living and working in close quarters. The adults looked younger than they had in ten years. It was only natural and helped pass the time. Many of the new couples had long discarded the secret nature of their budding romances and moved into quarters they could share together, announcing carefully to all that they were a couple.

Netty took in the happy black and white faces of Gloria and Billy, the trucker who no longer toted an inhaler everywhere. Gloria danced her days away, her work a joy, her diabetes gone with the emergence of a strikingly beautiful and youthful figure. And now she had the love of a man who thought she walked on water. What more could she ask for? Even her cache of mice was breeding up a storm, having been relegated to the growing fields to live their lives naturally.

The lean and surly Crystal with her momma pig, Tulip, could be found perpetually nagging at Johno. He, who had fast become a voice of reason in the early days of the frantic adjustments they all were forced to make. Who else could have turned the opinionated and critical Crystal into a quiet and simpering woman in love? Netty acquiesced to the adage that opposites really did attract.

The kids had paired up early. Scotty had Chloe, and Kenya had Kane, although since she had not delivered the baby, Netty could sense Kane's patience wearing thin. She had not failed to notice the tentative knowing smiles Emma and Kane tossed to each other when they thought no one was in the area. With a sigh, she prayed Kane would continue to support Kenya until she adjusted to her new reality, but knowing of the angry demeanor of Johno's man, Elias, after having been discarded by Emma, she thought Bonnie's sister was walking a thin line. It had only been five months since she'd cut him out of her life and he still appeared unwilling to accept the fact. Could be that they had some trouble brewing with the kids.

Ginger Mae had blossomed beyond all anticipation. The scars on her face had completely disappeared. Her bleached hair grew in, disclosing the blonde was really a brunette. When she'd decided to crop the blond ends of her hair, she was adorned with an elegant short pixie that left her closely resembling the old Hollywood movie star, Audrey Hepburn. She had also developed quite a deep bond with the cats and elephants. Netty guessed her favorite must be the matriarch, Tobi. But then the great gray goliath was *everyone's* favorite, wasn't she? Tobi's sensitive nature and remarkable intuitiveness to all that was animal and human made her a great comfort and distraction.

Netty glanced over to Ginger Mae to see her holding court with her remarkable daughter, Daisy, at her side. Dezi was horsing around with Bonnie, who had slipped over to join the hilarity coming from their table.

What surprising buddies they had turned out to be; bonding tightly with the responsibility of caring for the little piglet, Chance, who would have perished without their loving care. Who knew the irrepressible and cocky smart alec would develop into such a reliable caretaker of a piglet?

Chance was the only one of the litter that was allowed to come into the kitchen. He followed Bonnie around as if she were his mother. And if you tried to separate Chance from Dezi, the piglet made such a squalling that no one could bear it. Caesar was none too fond of the noisy piglet himself. So trying to tether him in the corridor with the big tiger had not been a solution. Besides, Chance clearly preferred the company of Echo, Baby and the dogs at dinner time.

"Yikes, let go of my arm, Dezi." Bonnie choked on her laughter as Dezi got her in a headlock.

"Are you going to sweep the floors in the men's dorm like you promised?"

"I don't remember saying that." Bonnie reached under his arms to try to tickle her way to a release.

"You don't remember the deal we made for my spice loaf in exchange for the chore? Babe, I'm gunna have to spank you. Maybe it will help you remember."

Turning the tables on her, Dezi reached down to tickle *her*, getting a shriek for his efforts. Daisy reached over to join the melee.

Netty turned her attention back to Wil, who was watching the elephant keepers arm wrestle at their table. Abby scurried around them, her arms stacked with plates as she attempted to finish setting the tables for dinner. Her tail accidentally brushed one of the wrestlers, causing him to lose his concentration and inadvertently bump a dish to the floor with a clatter. The entire room broke out with laughter and claps. Kimir stood on his chair to watch the unlucky victim of Salina's anger at the broken plate cringe under her admonishing glare.

"Gentlemen, if you insist on behaving like boys, I will have to send you to bed without dinner. One more broken plate and I will . . . I'll . . . hmmm." Her unlined face lit up. "I will make you wash the ladies' laundry for a week." The men booed and hissed at the offending keeper who had broken the plate.

"Wil," Netty whispered to get his attention away from the good-natured brawl that was sure to develop between the keepers and Salina. She heard a shriek as one of them picked Salina up off her feet and swung her around, depositing her on the counter near the sink.

Wil turned his attention back to Netty, the smile in his eyes disappearing as he sobered at the fright in her expression.

"Don't worry so much, Netty. It's going to be okay."

"I don't know how you can say that." Exasperation spat her hisses out like a gun shot. "We need to have a plan, an explanation that will keep them all calm."

Wil reached for her hands. Looking straight into her eyes he asked, "Why don't we just give them the truth?"

She recoiled at the suggestion, jerking her hands from his to worry over her flaxen hair that had tangled in her wing. "You know we can't do that. How do you tell that to Kenya? The poor girl is frightened and upset enough as it is. Some women might consider killing themselves when they hear news like that. You don't understand, Wil. We need to do this in small doses." Her voice became more than a whisper, drawing the attention of Baby by the fireplace. As he joined them, his aura pierced their mind.

"Sister, Brother, change is coming." From afar, Echo called to Barney, her aura lapping over Baby's. Barney ran to Echo who wrapped her arms around her furry love.

Scotty looked up at Netty and Wil, as if he had also heard Baby's pronouncement. From the corner of the room, Peter sat alone, watching and saying nothing as the innocent survivors, oblivious in their pleasure with one another and the good health they enjoyed, happily played on.

**You can read more by going to Amazon or Barnes and Noble and clicking on Evil Among Us, Species Intervention #6609 Book 5**

# Author's Page

J. K. Accinni was born and raised in Sussex County before moving to Randolph, New Jersey, where she lived with her husband, five dogs and eight rabbits, all rescued, and currently resides in Sarasota, Florida. Mrs. Accinni's passion for wildlife conservation has led her all over the world, including three trips to Africa, where ten years ago she and her husband fell in love with a baby elephant named Wendi, who had been rescued by a wildlife group. That baby is the inspiration for the character Tobi, the elephant featured in *Hive*.

The character of Caesar is inspired by a real life iconic tiger from the Big Cat Habitat and Gulf Coast Sanctuary in Sarasota. A portion of the proceeds from her third book, *Armageddon Cometh*, will be donated to the sanctuary in support of the enormous expense required to house and feed the displaced wildlife in their care. Mrs. Accinni invites her readers to visit bigcathabitat.org to view the astounding facility and plan a visit with your family.

Mrs. Accinni also invites you to visit her webpage at www.SpeciesIntervention.com, where information on the Big Cat Habitat and Gulf Coast Sanctuary can also be viewed. Readers are encouraged to comment about the book or your own creature experiences.

www.ingramcontent.com/pod-product-compliance
Lightning Source LLC
Chambersburg PA
CBHW071330250626